P9-DGS-998

BY BARRY LYGA

Houghton Mifflin Company
Boston 2006

Dedicated to Ally, of course.
You were right.

www.houghtonmifflinbooks.com

The text of this book is set in Legacy Serif.

Library of Congress Cataloging-in-Publication Data
Lyga, Barry.
The astonishing adventures of Fanboy & Goth Girl / by Barry Lyga.
p. cm.
Summary: A fifteen-year-old "geek" who keeps a list of the high school jocks and others who torment him, and pours his energy into creating a great graphic novel, encounters Kyra, Goth Girl, who helps change his outlook on almost everything, including himself.
ISBN 0-618-72392-7 (hardcover)
[1. Self-perception—Fiction. 2. Cartoons and comics—Fiction. 3. Geeks (computer enthusiasts)—Fiction. 4. Interpersonal relations—Fiction. 5. High schools—Fiction. 6. Schools—Fiction.] I. Title: Astonishing adventures of Fanboy and Goth Girl. II. Title.
PZ7.L97967Ast 2006
[Fic]—dc22
2005033259

ISBN-13: 978-0-618-72392-8

Manufactured in the United States of America
QUM 10 9 8 7 6 5 4 3 2 1

There are three things in this world that I want more than anything.
I'll tell you the first two, but I'll never tell you the third.

CHAPTER ONE

I WANT TO *NOT* RIDE THE BUS to school every day, but that would be a waste of a really big want—it'll take care of itself eventually. Until then, I put up with it, like today.

So what do I want? I want a copy of *Giant-Size X-Men* #1 in Mint condition.

I would settle for Near Mint, I guess, which would definitely be cheaper, but I'd really like to be able to say that my copy is pretty much perfect. On eBay, a Mint copy starts at at least eight hundred bucks, which is way more than I can afford, but maybe once I get my driver's license, I can get a job after school and put together the money. Sounds crazy, I know—some ancient comic book from the 1970s. But it's important.

I also want a new computer. Multiprocessor, maxed-out memory slots, wireless everything . . . When my parents got divorced, my mom got custody of me, and I got custody of the old Pentium clone that used to sit in the den at our old house. Thanks to the very best in Microsoft/Intel engineering, it crashes every time you exhale too hard in its general vicinity. It's tough to accomplish the kinds of things I want to accomplish with that going on. I want Flash animation! Video editing! Heck, I just want to be able to use Photoshop or Illustrator for ten minutes without rebooting.

Thinking about a pristine *Giant-Size X-Men* #1 and a humming new computer usually gets me through the bus ride to school. Today's an exception. Today, I don't need to spin fantasies because a living, breathing fantasy has just gotten on board: Dina Jurgens, who manages to make climbing the steps to the bus look like something that crazy parents' groups boycott.

It's a good day when a goddess gets on the school bus with you. In my two years suffering as this particular school bus stutters over potholes and gravel, winding its way through the back roads of Brookdale, Dina has only ridden a handful of times.

She's a senior, two years older than I am, but she looks like she could have stepped off a runway somewhere: blond hair, bright green eyes, soft and puffy lips, and a body that's pure torture. There are plenty of hotties at South Brook High, but Dina's a cut above and beyond. Of all the things I hate about South Brook, the fact that she's graduating in a few months is at the top of the list. How am I supposed to go through junior and senior years without catching glimpses of her in the hall?

Dina checks out the seating situation, scanning the back seats, which are packed. The bus driver—a wheezing, leather-faced troll appropriately named Mr. Dull—closes the door and hits the gas, jerking Dina forward a little. She flips her hair out of her eyes, then rolls them at Mr. Dull's temerity. She heads for the first empty seat, which happens to be, well, next to me.

I try to play it cool, but let's be honest—that's tough to do in the presence of a goddess. I go with my first instinct, which is to try to dip my hand into my pocket for the safety totem I keep there. I always feel calmer when I touch it.

But it's awkward getting a hand into your pocket when

you're sitting down, doubly so when there's someone right next to you. My elbow brushes her side, and she looks at me like I planned it. "Hey!"

"Sorry," I mumble. I feel like I should explain that I wasn't *trying* to touch her, but she's already looking away.

"What happened, Dina?" Sounds like Kayla Meyer. A junior, one who hasn't gotten a car yet. One who apparently ranks as Worthy on the Dina Jurgens Scale because her older brother is Steve Meyer, who I *think* dated Dina's older sister or something like that. I don't know. I don't really pay attention to stuff like that.

"My car wouldn't start this morning."

"Bummer."

"Yeah, I told my dad that it *has* to be ready by the weekend because . . ."

I tune it out and keep my head down so that no one will bother me. But being so close to Dina rattles me. I keep wanting to turn and stare, but even *I* know that that's not cool. So I settle for cutting my eyes left as often as I can. I get flashes of skirt and leg and the shadow of what could be a breast, but I'm not sure and I don't want to risk looking for longer than, like, a tenth of a second. So it's sort of like dumping the pieces of a puzzle out on the floor, looking at them, and then trying to put it all together in your head. With your eyes closed. So close! So far!

It goes like that for a little while, the bus jerking and bouncing along, making Dina's anatomy do very interesting things that she's apparently unaware of (and of which I'm woefully underaware, given those quick glances). Dina talks with Kayla, the Usual Idiots yell and chatter, and Mr. Dull's beloved country station blares out of the radio.

At some point, I realize that I probably look like an idiot, my head bent down, doing nothing (apparently), staring down at my feet. I pretend to look for something in my backpack, but there's just school stuff and comic books in there. And God knows I don't want to pull out a comic book while Dina's sitting next to me! I wish I had something—*anything*—else to read, something that didn't scream "Geek!" at the top of its lungs and jump around in nerdly war paint. Like . . . I don't know . . . *Hot Rod*?

When we screech to a tooth-grinding halt at the school, a sudden brilliant stroke hits me. Dina is sitting next to me. On the aisle. She'll get up to leave and I'll get up behind her. Behind her. From here to the exit, I'll be right behind her, with an unobstructed view of The Back of Dina Jurgens. Not as splendid a sight as The Front, but not bad in its own right. Sweet.

So Dina gets up and I grab my backpack (watching her legs as I do so—wow), then get up and move to get behind her—

And Mark Broderick pushes me back. "Move it."

He doesn't even look at me as he does it. He's a big senior with short bleached hair and a face like old hamburger. He dresses like Eminem, if Eminem weighed twenty pounds too much and couldn't keep the sweat stains from spreading out under his armpits. This is the weirdest part—he smells like boiling leather. I've never been able to figure that part out.

Up until now, the only contact I've ever had with him was smelling that unique aroma as he walked past me on the bus. But right now I watch him as he struts up to the door behind Dina. A flood of bigger, meaner, and/or tougher kids fills the aisle, and I'm not about to step into that flood, so I just stand here and wait and watch Mark's back and the buzzcut that clutches his scalp.

Now that I'm standing, it's easy to slip my hand into my pocket. As usual, I feel immediate calm when I touch the bullet that I keep there. I started carrying it about a year ago.

Everything's OK; I've added Mark to The List.

The List

The List is getting pretty long these days. It's a compilation of everyone who's ever pissed me off for no reason whatsoever. All of those Jock Jerks and Clique-its who treat me like dirt just because they can. Someday, when I've left this stupid little hick town with its stupid little hick people, the ones on The List are the ones I'll be sure to remember more than anyone else. I'm not sure how, but I'll remember them. Sometimes I can almost sympathize with those guys who go nuts and shoot up their schools, but no one on The List is worth dying or going to jail for. The best revenge is living well, my dad told me once. So I'd be happy to show up at my tenth reunion in a stretch limo, or with a supermodel on my arm, or with a TV crew filming one of many documentaries about me or something. Just waltz in and make a show of ignoring them all, unless I get the chance to nail someone with just the right comment at just the right time. The difference between *them* and *me* being that I would have a reason for doing it. A stupid fantasy? Maybe. But reliable.

The List started in sixth grade. I was in the school spelling bee. I was the first one to go and I stepped up to the microphone. I had no idea how high it had been turned up or how loud it would be, so I spoke in a loud, clear voice. When I said, "Massachusetts," it came out "MASS" and filled the entire auditorium, like some huge, heavy thundercloud of sound as I realized what was happening, and I managed to quiet down for the rest, but the enormity of my own massive, booming voice and the look of shock on the faces in front of me freaked me out—my voice cracked and shot up like a girl's for "achusetts," and I was so rattled that I didn't even spell it right and I washed out in the first round.

That day I got in the lunch line and Pete Vesentine and Ronnie Warshaw started pushing me and imitating the crack in my voice: "Get out of *line!* Get out of *line!*"

"No, no, like this," Ronnie said, and then said, "MASSa*chu*setts," managing to break on every syllable and throwing in a limp wrist for added comedy.

I was smaller than them and there were two of them and no one was going to help me, but I didn't want to get out of line and go to the back. My mother always told me to ignore bullies, so that's what I tried to do: I just sort of squared my shoulders and got back in line.

"Hey!" Pete this time. "Hey, no butting! You can't butt in line."

"I didn't butt," I said (probably too earnestly). "I was here already."

"You can't butt," Pete said again, and Ronnie backed him up and they pushed me out again, only this time I lost my grip on my lunch money and a quarter fell onto the floor.

I was just about to pick it up when Ronnie stepped on it.

I looked up at him. "Come on, Ronnie," I said, trying to sound calm and reasonable. "Let me have my quarter."

"Let me have my *quar*ter. Let me have my *quar*ter." More falsettos and limp wrists from Pete and Ronnie.

"Come on."

Ronnie shoved with his foot and lifted it off the floor at the last minute. My quarter went skimming down the hall. I chased after it, followed by their laughter. When I reclaimed it and turned around, the line had moved. Ronnie and Pete were giggling to each other, almost at the door that led into the cafeteria. No way they'd let me back in line.

As I took up my new position at the end of the line, I decided to start The List.

CHAPTER TWO

RONNIE AND PETE ARE STILL AROUND. Along with their Cro-Magnon buddies (read: the JJ, the Jock Jerks, the population of the football, soccer, lacrosse, and basketball teams), they dogged me through the rest of middle school. But fortunately high school deposited them in the sort of idiot classes they belong in—basic math, lots of "Tech Ed.," and, my favorite, "Reading" (can you believe they have to have a class called that?)—while I was placed in the "Fast-Track" for gifted and talented students. I almost never see them, except for gym class, where they're pretty easy to avoid.

But they're still on The List. No one gets removed from The List. That's sort of the point.

I give myself a moment to let the sensation of touching the bullet calm me. I found it one night, left neglected and lonely on the workshop bench in the basement at home. The step-fascist must have dropped it behind something and forgot about it. It just sat there on the bare workbench, glinting in a shadowy pocket near a box of screws. I stood there for a long time, having trouble catching my breath. I waited for some-one—Mom, the step-fascist—to show up and say something.

Nothing.

So I grabbed the bullet in a fist closed so tight it went white, and I've had it ever since. My lucky totem; my safety blanket.

Relaxed now, I head into school, where Mark Broderick is swallowed up by the throngs of students (but his name is now indelibly imprinted on The List) and Dina Jurgens goes off into whatever world is inhabited by Senior Goddesses, and I go off to homeroom.

But before I get there, I see Cal by the lockers. He's my only real friend at school, the only one I bother to hang out with outside of school. (Or, the only one who bothers to hang out with *me* might be more accurate.) He's also one of ten black kids at South Brook, and the fact that I know there are exactly ten black kids at my school should tell you something right there.

He's taller than I am and bigger and just generally cooler. Plays football and lacrosse. Wrestles. Unlike the rest of the JJ, though, he's smart and he doesn't treat me like dirt. He loves comic books, too. That's actually how we met—back in eighth grade, he saw me reading *League of Extraordinary Gentlemen* and stopped at my desk. "When did that one come out? I've been waiting for it."

I couldn't believe it—here was a guy who had girls swooning over him, more friends than I could count, and the weird sort of cachet you get by being a fun, friendly black kid in a white school . . . and he was into comic books?

At first I thought it was yet another ruse by some ill-intentioned idiot designed to lead me into a trap for the amusement of others. Like the time a few years ago when I gave a passionate report on collectible card games as a metaphor for cultural change in a social studies class. Todd Bellanger told me afterward that he had some rare Magic: The Gathering cards in his locker. I couldn't believe it. Well, actually, I couldn't believe he had them and I also couldn't believe that Todd was even bothering to talk to me, since he usually was one of my tormentors. But maybe we'd found a common ground.

So I went to his locker, and instead of Magic cards he shoved a bunch of pictures of naked men into my hands, then shouted, "No, I don't want your gay porn!" really loud, so that everyone in the hallway turned and saw me with the pictures and laughed and laughed . . .

So I was suspicious of Cal immediately, especially since I knew little about him—recent transfer, played football, hung out with a lot of jocks. I'd been burned before.

"Yeah, well, this is the issue after the one with the Wright Brothers," I said.

Cal blinked, obviously confused. "What? I must have missed more than one. When did the Wright Brothers show up? I didn't know they were in the story."

They weren't. He had passed my test, and so I cautiously entered into a conversation with him, which eventually evolved into the only friendship I have at South Brook.

"Hey, Cal!" I close in. "I found this website last night that lays out the whole Xorn-is-Magneto thing from Morrison's run on *New X-Men*. This guy, it's unreal. He's got scanned-in panels and pages and he annotated them all and there's a timeline and—"

"Yeah, that's cool," Cal says, but it doesn't sound like he thinks it's cool. He looks around quickly. I've seen this behavior before.

"But I didn't tell you all of it." I'm rushing, trying to get it in. "There's also links to a whole site that shows all the other times

Magneto disguised himself, and a thing about *House of M*—"

"Uh-huh." Cal gives me a quick grin, then walks away. Down the hall, I see Mike Lorenz and Jason Benatovech waving at him. Football players.

Well, that's life being Cal's friend. When the jocks call, he goes. On the mean streets of hick rural high schools, you have to keep up your popularity and your cool factor if you want to survive as a black kid. And being seen with me—especially talking comic books—is the best way to see your cool stock plummet.

Cal doesn't even really know he's doing it. I can tell because he never refers to it, never acts as if he's done anything wrong. It's just survival. Just high school crap. It doesn't bother me. Not anymore. Not really.

CHAPTER THREE

For some reason (it's not important), South Brook High School has been taken hostage. Mike Lorenz, Jason Benatovech, Pete Vesentine, and Ronnie Warshaw are all dead with bullets in their heads. Todd Bellanger has been shot, too, but he's not dead, just writhing in pain and crying. I note with some satisfaction that Mark Broderick is also among the deceased.

I'm hiding in the computer lab, and that's when I realize that everyone is being herded toward the gym. Cal is with them, and he looks angry and scared all at once. I realize that with a single distraction Cal would be able to disarm one of the bad guys and probably rescue everybody (even the ones who don't deserve it).

From the computer lab, I'm able to hack into the bell system, which is all automated. I can kick off the distraction and save everyone.

And that's when my arm explodes.

I look around. My fantasy of the school invasion has to be put on hold. (It's a good fantasy, and I add more details each time I relive it.) What the hell just happened to—

Again. Pain. Erupting in my right shoulder. I rock to one side with the force of the blow and bite my lip to keep from crying out.

I'm in gym class, or, as the idiots who teach it insist on calling it, "Physical Education." "Education," as if they're teaching us something other than the utterly useless skills of volleyball, flag football, and pushups.

And my personal favorite (I'm being sarcastic), dodge ball. What genius invented this game? What unrelentingly stupid jackass decided that it was a good idea to take a cluster of people with widely varying body types, strength levels, and skill sets (to say nothing of ever-shifting moralities and ethics), and then encourage them to *hit each other* with a ball?

I always try to get out early and easily—a glancing shot off my leg or shoulder. So I was standing in the Dead Zone of the game, whiling away "Physical Education" in my fantasy world, when the pain hit me.

And again.

I look over. The only other person in the dodge ball Dead Zone with me is Mitchell Frampton, a big stupid junior with shaggy blond hair that hangs over his eyes. He's grinning a dumb grin, his lower lip dried and cracked as he chews on it, and then he hits me again, in the *exact same spot*. My shoulder feels like it could just detonate, dropping my arm to the floor.

"Pussy," he says. "Pussy. Whatcha gonna do? Pussy." And wham! Again. Same spot. Uncannily in the same damn spot. My vision goes red for a moment with pain.

Why is he doing this? I don't even *know* him. I've never even *talked* to him before. I look around quickly. No one's watching. On the gym floor, everyone's busy being physically educated by firing rubber balls around, what fun. The two gym teachers (sorry, *physical educators*) are standing off in a corner, talking and gesturing to each other, totally useless, not even watching the

Ow! Again!

Not even watching what's going on. I want to yell, but no one would hear me unless I screamed bloody murder at the top of my lungs and then I'd just be another wimp, another wuss, another

Again!

tattletale. I'd be the crybaby, the momma's boy, the pussy, the weakling, the

Again!

victim. Let's see, what else have I been called over the glorious years? How about—

Again!

"Please stop," I say to him.

"Make me." Again. Again. Same spot, over and over. It's as if a Mitchell Frampton's fist-size part of my arm has become a mass of raw meat and screaming nerve endings. "Make me."

I can't. He knows I can't. I'm a computer geek, a comic book geek, a study geek. Even in the Fast-Track classes, I'm apart. To complete the stereotype-made-flesh that is me, I'm also half a head shorter than most guys my age, and while I'm not a ninety-eight-pound skeletal weakling, my body is, in some ways, like one of those armature dolls, all straight, uninterrupted lines, uncut by any sort of evident muscle tone. I've got my South Brook High gym T-shirt on, and that's it as far as armor goes.

"Just ignore them," my mother used to tell me, when I was a kid, when I was younger, when the other kids would tease and make fun. "Why do you care what they think? Just ignore them and they'll go away."

They didn't go away, though. She was wrong about that.

And the more I told her about them, the less she wanted to hear, and even when I was a kid, I could tell that she didn't want to hear about it. She had other things to worry about. She had to leave my dad and run off with her boyfriend, and for some reason she decided to add to the complications by dragging me along, too. Dragging me along, then ignoring me when I told her the other kids were making fun of me, were tormenting me, and what great advice: "Ignore them." So I did, even though they didn't go away, and pretty soon there was nothing to say, nothing to do, because how are you supposed to suddenly stand up to them after years of silence and nothing? Besides, I *can't* get in trouble. I just can't. I have one thing going for me: my brains. My ticket out. And college means transcripts, so unlike the rest of these idiots, my permanent record actually means something.

When I was a kid (when my parents were still married), I was terrified of our basement. My dad had an old winter coat that he left hanging on a hook down there to use if he suddenly needed to go out the basement door for some reason. One time I went downstairs to get something, looked into the darkened basement . . . and saw a shaggy form with arms—*arms,* no doubt about it—lumbering there, leaning against the wall, and I ran like hell, ran up the stairs so fast that when I tripped I fell *up* the stairs into the foyer, slamming my knee into the metal strip that sealed the bottom of the front door, my knee exploding with a pain so sudden and sharp that I thought my leg had been sheared off.

Ten stitches in my knee. Blood everywhere. My first experience with unreasoning, unrelenting pain. I didn't know it at the time, but it was a preview of the rest of my life. Pain for no reason. Pain in different varieties. It was just Dad's coat, of course. Morphed by bad light and a particular angle and a kid with a wild imagination into something out of an old Steve Niles comic. Morphed into pain I didn't even deserve.

So I guess I'm used to it. I just wish my bullet weren't in my gym bag along with my clothes; I need it. But I stand there and stare straight ahead while Mitchell Frampton giggles and keeps hitting that *same damn spot.* And I realize that someone else *does* see. Someone sitting up on the bleachers at the far side of the gym. Someone dressed in black, with black hair, the face just a white blur. Watching.

Good. At least someone sees.

CHAPTER FOUR

But overall it's still a good day. Dina is on the bus for the ride home, and I scored A's on an English essay and a chem test, so all's not too bad. I contrive to get on the bus after Dina, so I do get a moment or two of Watching the Goddess Walk Away, not a bad sight at all.

I finish my trig homework on the bus and read most of the chapter of *Catch-22* that I needed to do, too. Figure an hour at home, tops. Then I can spend the rest of the night on the computer, working on my secret project. Yeah, it's tough to get things accomplished in between crashes and system freezes, but it's worth it—this is going to be my ticket out of Brookdale and away from everyone in it. It's the—

The bus stops to drop Dina off—I watch her smooth, tan legs swish by in the aisle and memorize them.

At home, Mom's half reclining on the sofa in the "family" room. (We're not a family—why pretend?) The step-fascist is home early—oh, joy—standing at the refrigerator. I flip a mental coin. Heads, he's getting a beer. Tails, a beer.

A second later, I hear the click-hiss of a Bud can opening.

He looks at me with that weird combination of contempt and puzzlement. He can't understand a kid who doesn't want to play football or shoot a bow and arrow or drop out of high school like he did. It's been about five years since I stopped even with a polite "Hi" when I see him. He's one case where Mom's advice to "just ignore" seems to work. He sees me, grunts, and goes into the "family" room with Mom, where the TV is offering up a show about remodeling speedboats or something. Yawn. The step-fascist is, I swear, sitting on the edge of his seat.

Mom pretends to be engrossed; she sighs and just lies there, rubbing her hands on her big, stupid, pregnant stomach. When she first told me that she was pregnant, I thought I'd puke. She and the step-fascist called me into the "family" room and tried to make it all a big deal, and Mom's face glowed with something like hope, as if she thought that this would be the special elixir that would make me "come around" to her way of thinking, the element that would make the step-fascist and me get along, and make us a family for real.

"You're going to have a little brother or sister," she said. "Isn't that great?"

"*Half* brother or sister," I pointed out, which, for some reason, earned me a glare and a command to get out of her face for a while.

A week or so later, I e-mailed Planned Parenthood and had them send a bunch of brochures about abortion to our address. *That* didn't go over very well.

I grab some lunchmeat from the fridge and make a sandwich. Before I can leave, Mom says, "The baby kicked today. Want to feel?"

Oh, God. Could there be anything—I mean *anything*—in this world more vile and disgusting than feeling the spawn of the step-fascist kicking up a storm in there? The very idea conjures unstoppable images and thoughts that would have made

Oedipus put out his eyes *and* put a bullet in his head.

"Not particularly." It comes out a little nastier than I intended and I feel bad for a second when Mom's face falls, but when I see the step-fascist shaking his Cro-Magnon-like head, I figure I'm better off.

With my five-star dinner of sandwich, pretzels, and Coke, I head downstairs to my bedroom; I fought like hell to have my room downstairs, away from theirs. The step-fascist pissed and moaned about having to put up walls down in the basement, about losing space from his precious workshop (where he does such important things as banging his thumb with a hammer and listening to right-wing radio), but I got my way in the end.

Homework and dinner done by five. New record. I hear them tramping around upstairs, in particular, one heavy set of feet going back and forth to the fridge. When I close my eyes, I can see the beer can and hear the click-hiss over and over. I had never even seen a beer can in person until Mom moved us in with the step-fascist.

I log on to the computer. It whirrs and clicks and clacks like an old man, and I think of a new computer again and sigh. It'll do for now.

An Instant Message pops up: *send addy?*

It's Cal. It's *always* Cal on IM. No one else IMs me. I don't even bother looking at the window anymore–I just zero in on the text: *send addy?*

Since he ditched me at the lockers this morning, I hadn't had a chance to talk to him the rest of the day. *What are you talking about?* I type. I hate that Internet shorthand crap, all that "u" and "gr8!" and junk like that. What's wrong with spelling and grammar?

Addy from a.m. comes the reply.

Address from this morning? What does he—?

Right: the Grant Morrison stuff. The X-Men websites I told him about. I hunt my Favorites list for the URLs and shoot them over to him. I bite my lip and cross my fingers and pray that I don't lose my dial-up connection or outright crash.

In a few minutes, my ancient hard drive grinds out a few megahertz and I get another message: *^5! gm rocks & his run's cool r u ok?*

I send his high-five back to him and then we're off, "talking" about the site and Grant Morrison's genius, and I'm so happy and distracted that I let myself forget about the punches and the baby and the step-fascist. For a little while, at least.

CHAPTER FIVE

IN THE MORNING, I HEAD FOR THE SHOWER first thing. There's one down here that the step-fascist uses to clean up when he's done working on one of the junkers he claims he's going to make street-legal someday, but I pretty much commandeered it a few years back. It was a sort of silent war—I started using it in the morning so that I didn't have to go upstairs to use the main bathroom. At first no one noticed. (Why should they? The world is Mom and the step-fascist and that's it, right?) By the time they did, it had been a month or more and I had a wash-cloth and shampoo in there, and possession's nine-tenths of the law. One night I heard Mom say, "He's not hurting any-thing and you never really use it anyway," followed by some sort of monosyllabic grunt of accession. Victory was mine. I had taken over another corner of the basement. Let there be march-ing in the streets and dancing girls for my pleasure.

It's cool in the basement, but not *too* cool, so I usually head to the shower with my towel wrapped around my waist and that's it. Imagine my surprise when I find Mom standing there by the washing machine.

"Mom!"

"What!" She jumps as much as a pregnant lady can, and for a second there I'm worried that she might miscarry or go into labor or do something else disgusting. But she just spins around. "What?" she says again. "Don't use that tone with me. I can be down here. You don't own the basement."

"I was just surprised, that's all."

"Surprised that I'm doing laundry?"

Actually, yes. But that's beside the point. I don't really care one way or the other, so I shrug and make a beeline for my Conquered Territory, the First Shower.

"Wait. Donnie, stop." Oh. God. *Donnie.* Like I'm ten years old. Like I'm a little kid. I run through the possibilities and figure that I'm probably due for the "It's Time for All of Us to Think About How to Get Along, for the Baby's Sake" speech. It's one of Mom's favorites, mainly because it requires absolutely no decisiveness on her part. She just runs down the list of everything I've done recently that annoys her and sums up by telling me that she's disappointed that I have this "attitude" and maybe there are ways I can think of to work on that, hmm? Sure, Mom. Just dump all the work on me. No problem.

She pokes my right shoulder and I want to scream, want to bellow in agony. "What's that? What is it, Donnie?"

I hiss in a breath through clenched teeth, my arm suddenly numb with fire where Mitchell Frampton pummeled it yesterday.

"What is this? What happened to you?"

I look at what she's looking at, a massive bruise that discolors my arm from the point of the shoulder muscle up to the clavicle. At the center it's a deep purple that's almost black, lightening to a sickly jaundiced yellow at the edges.

I don't know what to say. Or, actually, I know *exactly* what to say, and that's the problem. *What happened to me, Mom? I fol-*

lowed your advice, that's what happened. I followed it for years and it's just that for once someone decided to go beyond name-calling and sniggering and flipping me off and sticking porn in my hands and the occasional shove or push, so someone finally left a mark that even you can't avoid seeing.

But there's no point in saying that. I'm fifteen now. What would she do? Call the school? Call Frampton's parents? My word against his, and even if they believed me, so what? He gets suspended for a few days and comes back worse than ever.

Well, there *was* that person I saw, that person in black up on the bleachers. But I don't even know who he was, and how would I find him anyway? It's too late to fix it now. I've made it this far. From age nine to here, six miserable years in this crappy little town with its crappy little people and their crappy little tortures. It's April. After this school year ends, I've got two more, then it's college and I'm gone, gone, gone, like the song says.

And I guess there's one other reason not to tell her. I guess there's always the chance that she wouldn't do anything about it. She'd get exasperated and tell me that she can't believe I just stood there and let him hit me, that I didn't say something to anyone, I didn't make it stop and take care of myself—how *could* you, Donnie . . . ?

"I don't know what happened," I tell her, still looking at the bruise. Usually I'm a much better liar. Usually I can come up with stuff on the spot, like the Great Ecuadorian Tortoise Blight. But she caught me off-guard. I never thought about a bruise forming, even though my shoulder hurt and throbbed all night. And I never really expected to see something like concern in her eyes.

"I really don't know," I tell her. It's a bad lie, but it's the one

I'm stuck with, so I have to work with it. "It wasn't there when I got home from school last night." A story pops into my head, complete and fully formed, as they often do: Blame the step-fascist. Tell her he hit me.

No. Too many details to come up with. Too many places to trip up.

"You don't know? Are you sure? Are you lying to me?"

"Why would I lie about something like this?" Oh, the liar's best friend. Because, seriously, why *would* someone lie about something like this? I throw her a bone: "Maybe I bumped it against my nightstand when I was asleep."

As my dad would say, she's not buying it, but there's nothing else on the shelves. I get released from Interrogation and head for the prison showers.

The Panty Algorithm

The bus is, sadly, uneventful, Dina Jurgens's dad having evidently taken care of her car troubles.

In English, though, I get my semi-regular Glimpse of the Panties. Mrs. Hanscomb has our desks arranged in a U formation "so as to foster dialogue between students and discourage the class from becoming a simple lecture." Lisa Carter sits across the U from me, and on days when she wears a skirt she either A) forgets or B) doesn't care. She is no Dina Jurgens, no Senior Goddess, but she has nice legs and it's easy for me to look while pretending to be looking at my notes. To amuse myself, I keep track of the style and color of her panties, jotting down notes in a shorthand code I invented for the purpose. I might just try to work out some sort of database that tracks and predicts her underwear choices. I doubt there's an algorithm for this sort of thing, but it might be interesting to try it.

Lisa seems nice enough. She's a "school friend." We're nice to each other in school and she's never done anything particularly rotten to me, but we would never have any reason to talk outside of school. I feel sort of guilty and sleazy for looking up her skirt, but I do it anyway.

Once I almost told Cal about my visual explorations of Lisa Carter's inner thighs and the all-important Panty Algorithm experiment. He's in Hanscomb's English class, too (off to one side, bad angle for panty-viewing). But I never did because he would think it's pathetic and sad (which it is—at least I'm honest). Cal doesn't need to sneak peeks. When he's not talking to me or hanging out with the Jock Jerks, he's surrounded by freshman and sophomore girls—sometimes even juniors. He flashes that broad, easy grin, tosses out some faux street slang, and gets oohs and coos in response. "When I black it up, they love it," he told me once, and since it was just the two of us, it was OK to talk like intelligent human beings, and we pondered the social implications and origins of such behavior, finally deciding that it's just that South Brook girls are interested in anything that isn't the same old boring white bread.

If they knew that Cal was a secret comic book geek, would they ooh and coo so much?

No, there's no Carter Examinations for Cal. He's seen the real thing up close and personal, he let slip once, then looked embarrassed. While around the JJ, Cal has to play the Conquering Stud Muffin, but with me he's discreet and prefers not to discuss sex, which I find respectful, in a way.

And me? Shocking though it may be, I'm a virgin (no, it's true), but—God bless the Internet, cable TV, and convenience store clerks who don't ask for ID—I've seen enough to know that I want to see more.

A part of me wonders if Lisa knows. If she's some kind of exhibitionist. Is there a particular brand of kink that involves flashing the town geek?

A ball of cold lead forms in my throat and then drops down into my gut. Worse yet, is there a game that calls for getting the town geek hot and bothered with flashes of the Promised Land, then letting a bunch of Neanderthals in letter jackets pound the living crap out of him? That sounds more likely than anything else.

I shiver just once before regaining control of myself. My hand automatically goes into my pocket, where the bullet waits with its almost narcotic touch.

Mrs. Hanscomb is droning on and on about Poe, about opium, about alcohol, about *MEL-an-choly,* and Lisa Carter coughs, shifts in her seat, lets her legs open just a little bit more. More than ever before.

I look, but I'm not happy about it.

CHAPTER SIX

On the way to gym class, Cal catches up to me. There are no jocks around, so he's safe to pull out a comic he found on eBay. It got to his house yesterday.

"How much?" I ask, looking at it. It's an old *Swamp Thing* comic, flimsy and stapled. I've got the collected editions, nice bound softcovers that contain multiple issues, and I think my dad has the originals, like this one, in his collection.

"A bunch," he says, sighing. "Too much. Fifty bucks. But I couldn't resist. I love that Alan Moore stuff."

"Dude, you can get the trade paperback for, like, fifteen bucks, and it's got all four parts, not just this one." I want to wave it in his face, but I'm mindful that he just laid down five Hamiltons for this sucker.

"Yeah, yeah, I know." He shrugs as if to say, *Whaddayawantfromme?* Cal's a serious collector, a total nut for first editions and Mint conditions. Me, I just like the stories. With one exception, I don't care if they're printed on toilet paper and bound with bubblegum.

"But this is how it first came out," he goes on. "This is how people like your dad first saw it and read it. Not all at once in some big collected edition with an introduction and stuff. They saw it one at a time, each month, waiting each month for the next installment. This is like . . ." He takes it back from me, opening it carefully, not wanting to crinkle the paper at the spine where the staples hold the whole thing together. "This is like an historical document."

"No, it's not." Cal is great. Cal's smart. This is Cal at his best, when we're talking. Even when I disagree with him. I can't believe he wastes so much of his time on the football field and all of that nonsense. "It's not an historical document," I tell him. "It's just a comic book. It's the story that matters."

"Yeah?" He grins the grin of someone who knows me *way* too well. "What about *Giant-Size X-Men* #1? In Mint condition?"

He's got me there. "Come on, Cal. That's different. You know it. You know—"

"Look." He holds the comic open for me. At the end of the story there's a page of tight, small text. "Letters page," he says with a note of triumph. "Back then, they used to publish letters in the back of each issue. From readers. And the editors and writers would answer them."

"So? Like I've never read an old comic before. I know that."

"So, they don't reprint the letters pages when they do the collected editions. All of that stuff is just gone, man. But when you go back and read them, you get to see how people reacted *when the comic came out*. You get to see what the fans were thinking while the story was developing. You get insight from the editor about what was going on. It's a window into the creative process."

His eyes are shining as he says this, and it's a damn shame that, over Cal's shoulder, I see Vesentine and a few other guys heading toward us. My heart's actually racing. This is the kind of conversation I love to have. And Cal loves it, too. But any second now, he's going to have to put that comic book into his locker and, like a Durlan or a Skrull, he'll change.

"Yeah, it's a window," I tell him, and start to turn away.

"Hey. Where are you going?"

"Gym," I remind him, then cut down the hall before I bear witness once again to the transformation of Cool Cal, Comic Book Guy and Friend into Distant Cal, He of the Unfortunate Friendships and Letter Jacket.

It's the first time, I realize, *I've* ever turned away from *him*. Preemptive. Half of a really good friend, I guess, is better than no friend at all.

CHAPTER SEVEN

GYM CLASS. HOSTAGES. There's a duct access hatch in the weight room. I dodge a hail of bullets . . . A dozen or more jock idiots are cut down right away . . .

The ball glances off my hip, which is fine. I don't mind being the first out. Just head for the Dead Zone and hope the game lasts awhile. The longer the game lasts, the longer I can spend taking advantage of the free time. The hostage scenario is fine, but pointless—I need to spend more time thinking about *Schemata,* working on that.

Mitchell Frampton lumbers over. I can't believe this is an accident. He must have done this on purpose. He leers at me as he comes close. His bottom lip is still cracked. I look away from him, pretending to watch the game.

"Hey," he says.

Just ignore him. That's all I need to do: ignore him.

"Hey."

"What?" Watching the game. As if I care. Scanning the gym. Mr. Burger and Mr. Kaltenbach in a corner, laughing, occasionally watching the ball as it darts from one player to another, paying no mind to the losers in the Dead Zone.

"Look at me when I talk. What're ya, rude?"

So I turn to look at him and just then he punches me in the

shoulder. My head jerks with shock and it's whiplash and my eyes widen in the sudden pain and I don't say anything.

He giggles. "Just wanted to see the look on yer face." And again. Same spot. Pounding me. Punching. My fingers itch and curl. I want to gouge his eyes out. I want to bite into his throat. I want to rake furrows into his stupid, doughy face.

You'll get in trouble.

Just ignore him.

I want to grab that bottom lip and rip it in half, right down the center where it's split already, let it gush, tear his face in two, right down to the bone.

Instead, I just stand there. I go away into my own little world. But before I do, I see someone up on the bleachers again, a black blur with a white blur stuck into it, as if a solid black figure has been mashed in the face with a thumb dipped in white paint.

In the locker room, I find a spot with as few people as possible and change as quickly as possible. We're supposed to take showers, but I didn't work up a sweat, so I'll be skipping that specific ritual of humiliation, thank you very much.

A guy next to me sees the massive bruise on my arm. "God, what a wuss! You got bruised from playing *dodge ball?*"

I look at him, and I realize that I don't know him. I don't even recognize him from walking through the halls or assemblies. I couldn't tell you what grade he's in or what classes he takes. So why does he even bother? Why does he even bother being mean to me?

CHAPTER EIGHT

HOMEWORK IS "THE PIT AND THE PENDULUM," ten trigonometry problems, a chapter of bio, and an essay on William Jennings Bryan. I've read the Poe before, the trig's a cakewalk, and the bio goes down on the bus. At least I'm done with gym for the week. And maybe next week they'll finally have the sod put down on the field outside so we won't be playing dodge ball anymore. If we are, I'll have to take the unprecedented step of trying to stay in the game. Just long enough that I won't be alone with Frampton in the Dead Zone. He wouldn't hit me while other people are standing right there, would he?

Then again, who ever thought he'd hit me at all? A teacher could look over and see at any moment, but he just doesn't care. Or doesn't think. One or the other or both. Who knows how Cro-Magnon brains work? And really, given that it's gym class, I guess it isn't that much of a risk for him. After all, Mr. Burger's the one who, last year, yelled at me when I dropped a fly ball during baseball. Bad enough I can't play the damn game to begin with, but now I have to get noise from the teachers, too? So regardless of what's really happening, what would Burger choose to see–some big lug punching that useless wuss. "Eh, fine. It'll toughen the little pussy up."

I can see that.

Mom's not home when the bus drops me off. I make a sandwich and steal some of the step-fascist's potato chips. He's picky about his potato chips—he only likes the ruffle-cut kind, so I'm not supposed to eat them, but I swipe some whenever I can. I take a Coke to go with it all and head down to my room.

The step-fascist himself is toiling over one of his many hunting rifles, which is disassembled on the workbench. I can smell gun oil and Budweiser. Alcohol and firearms. Good combination. He doesn't even grunt an acknowledgment of my presence, which is fine—I don't want to have to break out my Human-to-Monosyllable Dictionary. I make sure to lock my bedroom door.

So, William Jennings Bryan. Come on, people, give me a challenge. Cross of gold. Populism. Blah, blah, blah. I knock out ten pages on early-twentieth-century American politics, then scale back to six because Mr. Bachman doesn't appreciate my in-depth analyses, nor does he necessarily have the ability to understand them. (I happened to see his lesson plans once—they'd been downloaded from some website. Only the best and brightest at South Brook High.)

I IM Cal, but he reminds me that he's got lacrosse practice. *Talk l8r* he tells me, then signs off.

I spend a little time on the Web, checking the prices of a new Mac and eBay's latest on *Giant-Size X-Men*. Apple's offering a free printer with the computer, which is great. Now only if they'd offer a free *computer* with the computer. Ten different people are offering the comic on eBay, each auction at different stages, all but one out of my reach. That last one is only a day old, though, so the price will skyrocket later. I put in a bid anyway, just in case. With millions of people bidding on millions of things all over the world, all day long, there's gotta be a chance that someone will screw up and overlook a particular auction, right?

Then, the big event: I check on the details of the comic book convention that will be held next weekend. It's an hour away, down in the heart of the city, but it's the only convention anywhere near Brookdale (defining "near" to mean "any distance that does not require a plane, train, or bus"). It's the first year for this particular convention. I've been following it online, from website to website, message board to message board as the organizers talked and chatted about their plans, beginning with the germ of an idea last winter, now grown into something that is *almost* a convention. Something that, soon, will *be* a convention. Comic book retailers from around the country. Representatives from publishers big and small. Freebies. Guys who publish their own stuff, hawking their wares. Artists and writers and editors—people who are just names in a credit box or on a website or in a *Wizard* article. They'll be here. Just an hour away.

But that's not why I care. What I care about is Bendis. Bendis will be there.

I check the website every day, sometimes twice a day. His name is still at the top of the list on the page titled "Guests!"

GUESTS!

Meet an array of astonishing artists, writers, and other creators! Including:

Brian Michael Bendis: Writer of *New Avengers, House of M, Ultimate Spider-Man, Powers,* and many, many more! Multiple Eisner Award winner!

There's more, but I don't care. Bendis.

There's a little blurb at the bottom of the "Guests!" page that says, "All guests presence are tentative." (I didn't write that. I'm just quoting bad grammar.) "Convention not responsible for travel delays, etc. All guests subject to change."

So I check. Every day. To make sure. Certain that there'll be a message on the site one day that says, "We regret to inform you that Brian Michael Bendis will be unable to attend . . ." Because that's how things usually work out for me. But so far, so good.

My daily Bendis-panic quelled, I scrounge around for the pages of *Schemata* that I printed out the other day. Pages 1–10 are in a stack on my desk. Pages 15–21 are in the printer. I find page 23 under my bed. Don't know how it got there.

I could just print out the missing pages, but I made some notes on them before, so I go on the hunt. Upstairs in the family room, Mom—who managed to come home silently while I was absorbed with the Web—and the step-fascist are sitting up, watching something on TV. There's a sheaf of papers on the coffee table. My pages. I remember now: I looked them over while watching TV up here the other day.

The step-fascist's superhearing picks up the thunderous roar of my stocking feet on shag, and he offers up a look of annoyance. I play my part and ignore it completely as I lean in to take the papers.

"You're in the way," Mom complains.

I grab the papers, which are, I see too late, under a plate, a plate that makes an almost musical clatter-clang when I pull the papers out like a magician with a tablecloth.

"Shhh!"

Yeah, yeah. I riffle through the sheaf quickly to make sure I have everything I need. There are food crumbs and a coffee stain on one page, and I can swear I smell beer. But that could just be the ever-present *eau d' Bud.*

"Do you have to stand there making that noise? We're trying to watch a movie."

I want to give Mom and her stupid pregnant stomach a glare, but there's no point. I back out of the room and head downstairs.

The pages are pretty gross. For all I know, the step-fascist had his feet on them. As I walk through the basement back to my room, I forget about the beer smell when a new one hits me: gun oil.

I look around. No one. Nothing. I'm alone in the basement. The lights are out, the only illumination coming from my bedroom door, partly open, spilling out a wedge of light for me to follow. The furnace, the water heater, the big workbench—they're blocky, shadowy *things* in the dark. It's like the basement in the old house. Dad's coat.

I stand here in the basement now, even though it's a different basement, even though I'm older. Not to prove to anyone in particular that I can, but just to prove it to myself. I stand here and I breathe in the smell of gun oil, and I realize that no one is moving upstairs, the whole world is still, just me and the dark.

Bravery proven, I duck into my room before the monsters can get me.

CHAPTER NINE

I USED TO SLEEP. Or I tried, at least. I used to lie in bed for hours, the lights out, watching the digits on my clock change ever so slowly. I would play games to make myself not stare at the clock. I would make myself promise not to look for five minutes, to close my eyes and try to sleep for five minutes. After five minutes I would look, only to find that two minutes had passed.

Stories filled and swelled my mind as I tried to sleep. Characters introduced themselves, told me their histories, then went off in search of tales to inhabit, and I always found a good one. Then I would get caught up in perfecting the narrative, developing the story flow, dictating dialogue in my head, and I would be up, and up, and up forever, the minutes running fast when I was writing in my mind, crawling when I closed my eyes.

There's just no point to sleeping. Not if you simply can't fall asleep, anyway. So I stay up instead. Mom will sometimes check to make sure I'm in bed—she performs this maternal duty by looking into the basement to see that there's no light shining underneath my door. I used to put a towel there to block the light, but apparently in a dark basement, you can still see light limning the entire door in the tiny space between the jamb and the door. So now I have a black sheet of plastic that I hang over the door and weight at the floor so that no light can escape.

So I can stay up as late as I want. And I do. I write the stories for real, and sometime between three and four I take down the plastic, climb into bed, and read until my eyelids and my hands drop at the same time.

This is my ritual. This is how I do it. And Mom would never understand, so what she doesn't know won't hurt her.

Tonight, though, I'm not at the computer. I'm just curled up in bed, my fist a tight knot. I can feel the bullet but I can't see it, which is safe. I have to be careful with it. My fingers are pressed close together, completely concealing the bullet. I can take it anywhere. No one can tell. No one knows what I have in my hand.

It's just a bullet. Not a gun. I think of an old saying: "Guns don't kill people. *Bullets* kill people."

Usually, when I'm not carrying it around in my pocket, I keep the bullet hidden in an old hard drive case on my desk. Mom would never look in there for anything, so it's a good hiding place. Stick it in there every night, retrieve it every morning. But right now I keep it clutched in one hand while I flip through the pages of *Schemata,* organizing them with my free hand. The bullet is comforting. Like the baby blanket I threw out a few years ago. Like an old teddy bear.

I page through *Schemata,* revising in my mind as I go along. Soon I'll get up and go to the computer to make corrections, but I'll need both hands for that, and for now I just—

My computer beeps at me. It's the instant message sound.

I dive out of bed, launching myself at the computer. Once everyone's in bed I'm allowed to leave the dial-up connection on, and I forgot to turn down the volume! I hit the "Accept" button before the computer can chime again, then quickly turn the volume all the way down to "Mute" as the message window unfolds onto my screen. I sit in my chair, my own breath suddenly loud, wondering if somehow Mom heard the chime, if she was lurking near the stairs, or if the sound carried through the vents somehow . . .

Nothing.

In my rush, I dropped the bullet. It's lying on the floor. I pick it up and put it next to my keyboard, then check the time. Almost midnight. Must have been a long lacrosse practice—Cal's up pretty late to be IM-ing me.

Then I see the instant message window. Surrounded by a crowd of overlapping windows for other documents, it's a tight fit. It says:

Why do you let him hit you?

CHAPTER TEN

FOR A SECOND—JUST A SECOND—I wonder how he knows. I haven't told Cal about Frampton punching me, though the thought is tempting. In one of my favorite fantasies (slightly below the hostage story line), I tell Cal about the people who've been bugging me and he gets pissed and dishes out some righteous justice, which inspires me as well, and I get my licks in on a variety of jocks, losers, and scumbags.

I close some of the windows on my screen so that I can see the *entire* IM window. The sender's name is wrong. I assumed it was Cal, but the screen name isn't IamaChildMolester (Cal's sick sense of humor at work). It's Promethea387.

Which I should have known without ever even looking at the screen name. Cal would have typed: *y do u let him hit u?*

Instant Message spam. That's all it is. I sink back in my chair, relieved and disappointed at the same time. That carefully constructed, edited, and reedited fantasy in which Cal and I wreak havoc and ass-kicking on the unending hordes of Jock Jerks that roam South Brook High like the buffalo killers of the Plains crumbles into dust. (Though I'll resurrect it someday, I know.)

Promethea387.

Why do you let him hit you?

I can't figure out what kind of spam that would be, though. It's not for Viagra or Nigerian bank accounts or herbal remedies or the kind of sex that doesn't make it onto cable. Spamming for people who are abused? What kind of sense does *that* make? Is it some kind of public service spam, designed to get the attention of women who are being beaten by their husbands? I don't get it.

I check the window thoroughly. It's definitely an IM window, not an ad or a pop-up.

Promethea387.

And why would a spammer use the name of an Alan Moore character from a comic book that isn't being published anymore?

I stare at the window, but it doesn't change. It can't be a coincidence. I flash to Cal's morbid screen name. What if it's one of those sick guys who troll the 'net looking for kids they can seduce and snatch? *Why do you let him hit you?* would be a good opening line, especially for some kid who's being smacked around at home. Get the kid's confidence, offer to help out, reel him in . . .

But it just doesn't *sound* right. It's that Alan Moore reference. Why would someone aiming for little kids use a character from a comic book written for adults? Why not Superman or Batman or something from *Yu-Gi-Oh!* or . . .

It just doesn't make sense.

I look at the bullet, gleaming next to the keyboard. Almost like it's a talisman, I stroke it briefly with the tip of a finger.

There's only one way to find out what's going on. I hit "Reply" and I start to type: *What—*

Online

XianWalker76: *What do you mean?*

Promethea387: *Why do you let him hit you?*

XianWalker76: *I don't know what you're talking about.*

Promethea387: *Bull. Mitchell Frampton. In gym class. He hits you over and over and you just stand there. Why?*

XianWalker: *Who wants to know?*

Promethea387: *Why do you care?*

XianWalker76: *Because I'm not in the habit of discussing things with faceless, anonymous sock puppets who appear from nowhere. Or am I supposed to believe you're actually Promethea?*

Promethea387: *"faceless, anonymous sock puppets." Isn't that saying the same thing three different ways?*

XianWalker76: *Stop dodging the question.*

Promethea387: *Stop dodging mine. I asked first.*

XianWalker76: *That's a mature, reasonable perspective. Are you five?*

Promethea387: *Sorry. I'm "not in the habit of discussing things" like my age with "faceless, anonymous sock puppets" on the internet who could turn out to be chicken hawks. I'm somewhere between ten and a hundred, though.*

XianWalker76: *Ha ha. You started this, and you know who I am already. Pretty pathetic dodge.*

Promethea387: *No more pathetic than your dodging in gym class. Or do you try to get hit?*

XianWalker76: *Well, now I know who you are. Or what you are, at least. Hope you had your fun and you and your jock buddies got your fair share of laughs. I'm signing off.*

Promethea387: *You think I'm a jock? I thought you were smart. And I wouldn't blame you for trying to get hit—gets you out of the game that much sooner. If only you didn't have that other little problem. You know, the big blond idiot with the punching fetish.*

XianWalker76: *Whatever. I'm done. Lose my screen name.*

Promethea387: *Check your e-mail.*

CHAPTER ELEVEN

I BLINK AS I CLOSE OUT the IM window. *Check your e-mail.* My hand has gone slick on the mouse, the onscreen pointer wavering over the "Log Out" button.

I'm pretty sure it's some jock moron from school. Probably got my screen name from something Cal said or did, something he did that inadvertently let slip how to find me online. I was an idiot to think that *no one* saw Frampton punching me. So Vesentine or Warshaw or one of those jackasses decided to mess with my head. Bunch of muscle-head freaks, sitting up at night, laughing their remaining brains out, trying to get me to say something sad or pathetic or incriminating online, something they can e-mail to everyone they know, something they can post on the web.

The more I think about it . . . The pointer vibrates. I let go of the mouse and snatch up the bullet, rubbing its cool, smooth surface between my palms until it warms. They probably even set up the whole thing to begin with. Why else would Frampton just appear and decide to start hitting me? Why do it twice?

Check your e-mail.

Yeah, right. It's probably more gay porn.

Check your e-mail.

In the comics, Promethea was a sort of physical and metaphysical avatar for the nature of ideas themselves. She was the incarnation of imagination, and her purpose, if I remember right, was to bring about the end of the comic book universe she inhabited. Sort of a metatextual commentary on the self-destructive cycle of superhero comics or something like that. I don't remember exactly. Cal would know.

"She." That's the thing. Promethea's a female character. Why would a bunch of jocks decide to use her to trip me up? Lull me into a false sense of complacency? Maybe they just saw the name on one of Cal's comics or something . . . ?

The bullet's warm now, a tight knot of brass in the center of my hands, which have now gone white with tension. I'm going to log out. I'm going to disconnect and go back to *Schemata*.

I hold the bullet in one hand, grab the mouse with the other, and click "Check My E-mail" before I lose my nerve.

In there among the usual spam is a message from Promethea387, with a little paper clip next to it. An attachment.

I open the e-mail, thinking, "Virus, trojan horse, worm, spyware," but it's just a message that says, "See?" and a JPEG.

The JPEG is a crappy lo-res image, slightly blurry and small, but unmistakable. It's me in gym class, my face frozen in an expression of surprise and pain as Mitchell Frampton's fist slams into my shoulder. The extreme foreground is a blur of bodies playing dodge ball.

I stare at it for long seconds. The angle . . . No one playing dodge ball could take a picture. And the angle . . . It's so *wrong*. It's just off somehow. I don't–

And I think of a black blur with a white blur stuck into it, a face like a thumb dipped in white paint.

I bring up the instant message program and pound out a message to Promethea387: *Who are you . . . and why do you sit up in the bleachers during gym?*

The pointer vibrates again, then I hit "Send" before I can change my mind. The bullet grows hot, mashed between my hands as I rock back and forth like a toddler who needs to go to the bathroom, waiting. My message is thrown out into cyberspace. Is Promethea even online anymore?

I'm chewing my bottom lip and thinking that I'm too late when the IM comes back: *Nice to meet you. Check your e-mail again.*

My e-mail has another message from Promethea387, this one with multiple JPEGs attached, all of them in that same crummy format, all of them still eminently readable: Frampton punching me again. Frampton's arm pulled back. Mr. Burger and Mr. Kaltenbach in a corner, ignoring the gym as they laugh at something on Mr. Burger's clipboard.

I'm absorbing all of this when the IM program pops up a window again.

Sometimes don't you just wish someone would break into school and kill all of them?

CHAPTER TWELVE

*D*ON'T YOU JUST WISH SOMEONE ***would break into school and kill all of them?*** It echoes in my head all night and all day. Because when you come right down to it, I guess that's what I *have* been wishing. Never in such stark terms, though, and never out loud like that . . . if an instant message counts as "out loud." I figure it does, in some way.

If Promethea387 hadn't brought that question up, I probably would have signed off last night and never given another thought to my mystery IMer. Instead, I'm going to *meet* this person after school today. I'm not even really sure why. Maybe it's sleep deprivation—I slept a couple of hours last night, finally logging off the computer at four-thirty a.m., waking up when I heard Mom and the step-fascist tromping around upstairs at six or so. Even for me, that's not much sleep.

This morning, though, I got through first-period biology and second-period social studies with no problem. My secret weapon in these situations? Mom's stash of Excedrin Migraine, gone unused during her pregnancy. The stuff's loaded with caffeine, strictly verboten for the gravid among us. Headaches are caused by the expansion of blood vessels, which causes pain because they get too big for their allotted space and get squeezed. Caffeine, being a diuretic, causes the blood vessels to constrict. That's the magic of Excedrin Migraine.

Wash a handful of those suckers down with a Coke, and all's right with the world no matter how tired you are.

I'm glad I know things like that. Sometimes being the smart kid is fun. Other times, it's not.

For example, there was dirt in my locker this morning. Someone had obviously poured it in through the ventilation slots at the top, which must have taken them a while—the slots open *down,* which means that you'd have to force the dirt up into the slots a little bit at a time and let it drop inside. Someone had patience, though, and managed to get a good bit in there. I didn't even realize it until just now after third period; as I stooped to get my English books from the bottom of the locker, I saw the dirt and figured it out. Who was around my locker this morning, who had been out of place, waiting to see my reaction? At least I disappointed them.

I touch the bullet briefly.

Cal claps me on the shoulder as I head to English. "Hey, man, I finally did it!"

"Did what?" Cal's presence spikes a thought: Whoever put the dirt in my locker has to be involved in an afterschool activity so that they could have done it last night after I left. Which narrows my suspects to half the athletes in school and the band, but I just don't seem to inspire hatred in the band.

"Finally beat you on a paper," he says, and whips out a sheaf of stapled papers with the title "Who Watches the Watchman?: Emerson's Transparent Eyeball and the American Transcendentalists." Mrs. Hanscomb has written "98%" and some generic complimentary teacher-talk on the cover.

"You just couldn't resist an Alan Moore reference in your title, could you?"

He points to one of her comments. "She thinks I'm referencing Juvenal's *Satires*."

"How did you get your paper back so early?"

"She's giving them back in class today. I ran into her this morning and she gave it to me." He grins and waves it in my face again. "It took me almost the whole year, but I *finally* beat you in this class. No *way* you get higher than a ninety-eight. Doesn't happen."

"Congratulations."

"That's all you have to say? That's it?"

I probably should have more to say, especially considering all the good-natured ribbing I give Cal on a regular basis about my grades and his, but I'm humming from the caffeine buzz and my brain is still processing last night's IM and e-mail chat-fest.

In English, Mrs. Hanscomb hands me my paper as soon as I walk into the room. The bell hasn't rung yet and everyone's still settling into their seats, including Lisa Carter, wearing, today, a pair of nicely tight blue jeans that are pleasing to the eye but do absolutely nothing to help the ongoing Panty Algorithm investigation. Cal is joking and laughing behind me, reading Mrs. Hanscomb's comments on his paper just loud enough for me to hear them, exulting in his triumph.

I look at my paper and I can't help it. I explode with laughter and collapse onto the floor.

"What?" Cal looks around. "What? Don't. Don't tell me."

So I don't. I just lie there laughing, and hold the paper up for him.

"Ninety-nine? Ninety-nine? No *way!* I can't believe this!"

The bell rings and Mrs. Hanscomb tells Cal to take his seat. Glancing my way, she says, "You, too," and I pick myself up and walk to my desk, aware of the eyes on me. I couldn't help it, though. I just had to laugh.

"The American body paradox," Mrs. Hanscomb says, hoisting herself to sit on her desk and crossing her legs. "Who can tell me about this?"

"Beats me," Cal says. "I only got a ninety-eight on my paper. Ask him." And he hooks a thumb in my direction.

The class laughs, and maybe it's just the caffeine, but I laugh along with them.

"I mean, his hobby is tearing the erasers off his pencils," Cal goes on.

Mrs. Hanscomb allows herself a grin. "OK, Calvin, that's enough."

"When he gets a perfect paper, his grade point average goes *down*."

And now the laughter takes on a slightly dark tinge, a bad flavor, as if dipped in a solution containing the slightest percentage of vinegar. Mrs. Hanscomb tells Cal it's enough again, and he flashes me a grin before tucking his paper away in a folder, but now I'm conspicuous and the laughter's echoing in my head. I slip my hand into my pocket and stroke the tips of my fingers against the bullet. I feel calm almost immediately.

It's not good to remind them that I exist. Not good at all. I can't afford to let myself feel good, to let my guard down, to think for a single moment that I belong.

Because I don't.

CHAPTER THIRTEEN

AT THE END OF THE DAY, I skip the bus. I've managed to sweep most of the dirt out of my locker onto the floor, where it's scattered by the constant march of feet up and down the hall. Cal catches me on his way to the buses: "Hey, man, you coming to the game tonight?"

The game? I think about it for a second—I seem to remember something about a lacrosse game being mentioned on the morning announcements. Despite his intellect, Cal suffers from the misapprehension that I secretly harbor some measure of concern about the school's sports teams.

"No," I tell him.

"Come on! You *never* come."

Which really tells you all you need to know right there.

"You should see us. If we win, we go on to the county playoffs."

I can't imagine anything in this world I care about less. "Sorry," I tell him, shrugging my shoulders as if that action somehow absolves me of any responsibility for the decision.

He just rolls his eyes with an expression that says, "There you go again." Not that I've given him any cause to think so, but he seems to believe that my dislike of the Jock Jerks is passive, as if I just can't be bothered to go to sporting events. But I *actively* don't care about them. I mean, I *work* at not caring about those morons!

He tosses a salute my way as he heads down the hall. I wave weakly. Have fun, lacrosse boy.

I go outside, skirt the bus line, and go around the building before anyone can notice me. There's an elementary school, the imaginatively named South Brook Elementary School, nearby. You cross an access road and go down a hill, and there it is.

And there I go, my backpack bumping against my shoulder blades as I stutter-walk down the incline. I hope I'm right about this. If not, I'll be calling Mom for a ride and she'll be pissed that I missed the bus.

I spot someone on the playground behind the elementary school, a small figure dressed in black sitting on one of the swings. For a moment I kick into paranoid mode: This could all still be a trap. It would be an easy setup. Lure me out here with some e-mails and Instant Messages, then pound the crap out of me. I should turn around and huff my way back up the hill. I might still be able to catch the bus.

But there's no one else around, and the figure in black is just sitting there all alone, barely moving on the swing.

I walk up to her. She's wearing long sleeves even though it's hot out, some kind of black shirt with buttons up the side instead of the front, opened at the top to show her neck and part of that well between the neck and shoulder on her left side. The shirt's untucked, flapping over black jeans, which lead to black socks and black shoes. Her hair is black—either dyed or just naturally made out of semihardened ink. It's like something that swallows light, thick and endlessly dark and chopped short on top and in back, hanging long and low in front. She's looking down at her shoes, which trace lazy arcs in the sand as she drifts on the swing.

"So," I say. "Promethea, huh?" Brilliant introduction. I should have had something better planned.

She looks up at me, not bothering to push her hair away from her eyes or her forehead. Her face is so pale . . . It's so pale that I can't even think of something to compare it to. Chalk? Kabuki makeup? Liquid Paper? Her eyes are brown stamps on it, her nose a bump that sparkles with a red stone through one side. Her mouth twists in a sneer; her lower lip is pierced at the corner, and the ring somehow makes the sneer broader. Now that she's raised her head, I can see that she's wearing a necklace with a reversed smiley face on it: a black circle with yellow lines making up the face, like a photo negative.

"Yeah. Promethea. Got a problem with it, fanboy?"

Her voice is exactly as I expected it from her online messages: low, sardonic, defensive. Sort of like what I would sound like if I were a girl, I guess.

"No. But now that I see you, I figured you for more of a *Sandman* type." Take that.

"Oh, please, fanboy. Spare me your crap."

"You mean you *don't* like Gaiman?"

She rolls her eyes and pulls a pack of cigarettes from somewhere under her shirt, probably tucked into her waistband. As she lights up, I take her in—she's almost painfully thin, like her whole body's an afterthought.

"I like him fine. All the cool screen names were taken, so I went with Promethea. Is that all right? Do I pass your test, or do I have to name the founding members of the Legion of Super-Jackoffs?"

"Hey, you asked *me* here. You IM'd *me*."

She stands up, tilts her head back, and blows smoke straight up into the sky. She's almost my height, but some of that is the shoes, which, I notice, have thick, chunky heels.

"Yeah, yeah. I know."

"You got here pretty fast. I left right after the last bell. How'd you beat me here?"

"I blew off last period."

"Oh." I've never skipped a class in my life. I don't even know how you'd do it. Doesn't someone notice you're missing and report you? I want to ask her, but I feel like that would be unsophisticated somehow.

"So, why?" she asks, sucking on the cigarette again, gazing at me. She's pretending to be bored, but her eyes give her away. She's hungry for something—something new. Something different.

"Why what?"

"You know. You never answered me. Why do you let him hit you?"

We stand there, staring at each other. My blood is pounding in my temples and I can feel the beginnings of a massive headache. It's not just the smell of the cigarette—once caffeine washes out of your system, your constricted blood vessels bounce back. Caffeine withdrawal. Just like any drug, it bites you in the ass at some point.

"You're right," I tell her, not sure why. "Sometimes I *do* wish someone would break into the school and kill all of them."

She grins. "Yeah. I figured that."

Goth Girl

Her name is Kyra. We walk the elementary school grounds together, alone.

"I'm just so tired of that gym class shit," she says. "That's just so over for me. Like I need that kind of noise, you know? So I swiped one of my sister's doctor's notes and took it into school. Her name's Katherine, and the note just says 'K. Sellers' on it, so the school nurse thinks it's about me."

"What did it say?"

She shrugs and flicks her cigarette butt out into the grass. I bite my lip. I want to pick it up so that some little elementary school kid won't eat it or something, but she's just walking along and I have to keep up.

"Something about depression and shit like that. My sister's a freakin' pharmacy on spiked heels ever since she lost the kid."

"Lost the kid?"

"Yeah. Dumb bitch couldn't even remember when to take the stupid pill, you know? She washed outta nursing school because of the morning sickness and then she had a, y'know, like a miscarriage, and now she just sits there all the time, watching TV and eating Cheetos and ballooning up like she's preggers all over again. But whatever. It got me out of gym."

"Don't . . . don't your parents—"

"My dad? As long as no one burns the house down, he doesn't care what the hell goes on."

"Oh. Oh. My parents are divorced, too."

She stops for a moment and I almost walk into her. She sweeps that long, annoying hank of jet black hair out of her eyes. "I never said my parents were divorced, fanboy."

"Stop calling me 'fanboy,' OK?"

"Why? You read superheroes, right? You and your buddy, the superstar jock? Are you two queer on each other or something? Not that I care."

"No! And I don't just read superheroes," I tell her.

"Uh-huh. OK."

"You read comic books, too," I remind her.

"Not superhero shit."

"Oh, please!" For a second I forget that I'm on the verge of having an honest-to-God new friend. Her hypocrisy just bugs the hell out of me. She's been rambling and talking because let's face it, I don't know how to talk to people, but I *do* know about comic books. "*Sandman* started out as a superhero comic! The first volume had the friggin' Justice League in it and Batman shows up at the funeral at the end of the series! You Vertigo people are so damn pretentious. You can't—"

"I don't *just* read Vertigo, fanboy. You ever hear of Sara Varon? Adrian Tomine? Chynna Clugston-Major?"

"Yes."

"You ever *read* their stuff?"

I'm silent.

"That's what I figured."

I want to tell her about *Schemata*. I just want to tell her all about it, but I can't. I'm too afraid. I haven't told *anyone* about it. Not even Cal. No one.

"Your idea of 'mature comics' is Brian Michael Bendis," she goes on, snorting his name. "Just because he drops the F-bomb every other word in *Powers*—"

"It's a good comic," I interrupt. "And he also did the *Jinx* stuff, which wasn't superheroes at all, and it was good stuff."

She grins at me. She has a way of grinning—it's not every time she grins, but sometimes—where the little silver ring in the corner of her mouth somehow tilts up and makes her seem happy and almost, *almost,* beautiful. She magically produces the pack of cigarettes from under her shirt. "You're fun." She holds out the pack. "Smoke?"

"No, thanks."

"Goody two-shoes." She lights up and makes the pack disappear.

"Nothing goody two-shoes about it," I tell her, defensive. "I just have an allergic reaction to lung cancer. Gives me tumors."

She blinks, then laughs, loud and long and sustained. "Oh, damn! That's good. That's *good.*"

We've made a circuit of the elementary school by now, back to the swing set. She sits on a swing and gestures for me to sit next to her, which I do.

"I was sitting up there on the bleachers, like I always do," she says, kicking off and swinging out. I follow suit, a half-second out of sync with her. "And I saw it. He just started hitting you. I couldn't believe it. And no one saw. No one noticed. It was like watching a movie or something. Like there was a screen there and everyone was just ignoring what was showing. Over and over. Hitting you." She reaches out, across the space and the half-second between us, and taps my shoulder. The bruise still hurts, but I force myself not to flinch. Bad enough she's seen it already. Bad enough she knows what a wimp I am.

"And I just watched," she goes on. "You just stood there. Like a . . ." She gives me a second to run through my mental roster of the words I've heard used in this context.

"Like an Indian warrior," she says finally. My jaw drops and I lose the rhythm of the swing, jittering to a stop as my feet drag in the dirt. She keeps swinging, ignoring me.

"Maybe that's the wrong way to put it. But you were, like, almost *noble,* you know? You didn't shout or scream or cry or anything. You just stood there and took it. You never let him know it hurt you."

I watch her swing, my throat jammed painfully with a lump that won't go away. A part of me wants to burst into tears and throw my arms around her. But I guess that wouldn't be noble or Indian warrior-like.

She drifts to a stop next to me. "So when he did it the next day . . ." She fumbles around under her shirt again, this time on the buttoned side. I catch a glimpse of smooth hip, slightly darker than her face, which must be powdered, I guess. She produces a flip phone and slaps it open so that it points at me. "I pulled out my phone and took some pictures."

"Why?"

We watch each other over the phone for a second. Her cigarette hangs from the corner of her mouth. She snaps the phone shut and tucks it away, then taps her cigarette's ash off and sucks in more smoke. "I don't know. I really don't. Like I said: noble. Indian warrior. All that shit. I figured . . . I figured I'd take a picture of it. Keep it to prove to myself that not everyone at that place"—she gestures vaguely in the direction of the high school—"is a Neanderthal."

"Most of them, though . . ." I let it hang.

"Yeah. Someone could walk through the halls with a machine gun and kill ninety-nine percent of the people in that place and I wouldn't care."

For some reason, 99 percent makes me think of my English paper, tucked away in my backpack. "That many? Really?"

She shrugs. "Why not?"

I've never thought of *that* many. I don't even *know* most of the people at South Brook. I try to keep my head down and stay out of trouble. There's a small group of them I'd like to see disappear—the ones on The List—but that's it. There are about two thousand people at the school, if you include the teachers. Killing 99 percent of them would leave . . . Jesus, only twenty. I can think of a dozen teachers *alone* I wouldn't want dead.

"Just sounds like a high percentage to me," I tell her. Even in the bloodiest, most brutal iteration of my hostage fantasy, most of the school survives. Most of the casualties fall into a specific range of athletes in the sophomore class. I barely know any juniors, seniors, or freshmen. Nothing against them.

"Who cares? Wipe 'em all out. Screw 'em. Assholes."

Without even realizing that I'm doing it, I pull the bullet out of my pocket, toss it in the air, and catch it. I guess I'm trying to be cool and blasé, but I almost fumble the bullet when it hits my palm.

"Damn!" She whistles and looks in my hand. "You always carry ammo with you?"

"Not usually. My stepfather has guns all over the house. I grabbed this one a while back."

"Why?"

"No reason."

She arches an eyebrow. "Oh?"

I shrug. I'm not going to tell her how I've clutched it for hours like a security blanket. How I slip my hand into my pocket to caress it during the day whenever I feel nervous or threatened. How it calms me every time, like a balm or a cup of hot tea.

Instead, I jump the bullet from hand to hand for a few passes, watching it glitter in the sunlight, watching her eyes brighten as they follow it. Then I drop it into my pocket and check my watch. "You said last night that you'd get me home."

"Bored with me already?" But she grins when she says it, and I find myself grinning back.

"I've met my quota for Neil Gaiman goth girls today. Sorry."

"That's all right. I just needed to befriend a superhero geek for my volunteer credits."

She leads me back up the hill to the high school. Everyone's gone now and the place is quiet, except for the lacrosse team, running back and forth on the field, shouting at each other. Kyra and I roll our eyes at each other in shared disgust and disdain.

There's a beat-up compact car in the parking lot. Kyra motions for me to get in as she unlocks it.

"You have a *car*?" I had assumed she was a sophomore like me, maybe even a freshman.

"Nah, it's my sister's."

"She lets you borrow it?"

"You weren't listening before, were you? Cheetos. TV. Ballooning. Et cetera."

"Right."

She guns the engine and takes off. "You have your license?"

"Learner's permit," I tell her, surprised by my lack of shame. I should feel like a loser, confessing my age like that to her, but I don't seem to care.

"Yeah, me, too." She takes a corner way too fast, skidding into the oncoming lane. Fortunately, no one is coming in that direction.

"Are you nuts?" I scream. "You can't drive alone, then! It's illegal!"

"So's bringing a bullet to school," she points out, tapping the brake perfunctorily as she glides through a stop sign.

"That's different." I watch the streets for pedestrians and cops. So far, so good.

"How is it different? We're both breaking the law. You think a judge cares? Hell, you're probably worse than me; they'd Zero Tolerance your ass outta school, but I'd probably get a slap on the wrist."

"It's a *bullet,* not a *gun*. I'm not gonna *kill* anyone with just a bullet. You could kill someone because you don't know how to drive!"

"Sure." She tugs the wheel, rounds a corner with a screech of tires. "Big whoop. You think that's gonna make a difference to *them?*" I'm not sure who *they* are: parents, cops, judges, teachers? She accelerates and my heart pounds. I'm terrified, but I don't want to admit it. "What makes you think this is any worse that toting ammo in your pocket?"

I'm struggling with this one—the speed, the car, and she's kinda, a little bit right, in some sense. "Because some things are just *wrong,* that's all. And you don't have to explain them all the time. Some things are right and some things are wrong."

"You've been reading too many comic books."

"No, you haven't been reading *enough* comic books."

She grins that magical ring-tilting grin and slows down. "Will you feel better if I obey posted speed limits and road signs?"

I manage a shrug and an aloof gaze out the passenger-side window. "Whatever makes you happy."

She giggles but drives under the speed limit until she drops me off at home. I go around to her side to thank her for the lift, then stand awkwardly by the car, not sure what I should do next.

She saves me: "Later, fanboy," she says, and peels away in a squeal of tires and a plume of exhaust.

CHAPTER FOURTEEN

I DO MY DAILY BENDIS-CHECK (all's still on track) and then mess around with *Schemata* for a while. The house was empty when I got home, so no need to explain why I was late or why someone was dropping me off. I was all ready to explain how I'd missed the bus and this girl offered to drive me home, but no need for the lie.

It's stupid, but I keep thinking about her. She's foulmouthed, annoying, and opinionated, but except for the foulmouthed bit, a lot of people probably think the same about me, so no big deal. She's no Senior Goddess. She isn't even Lisa Carter. She's a typical goth girl Gaiman freak, but she talked to me at least, she hung out with me. She teased me, but not in a mean way or anything.

She called me noble.

I wonder what the deal is with her sister? And her mother. She said her parents weren't divorced, so does her mother live with her and just not get involved?

As if on cue, I hear the front door open and the step-fascist sighs as he comes in. I'm up in the family room by now, channel-surfing, and I figure it's time to get out of Dodge. I turn off the TV and brush past him in the kitchen on my way to the stairs and my dungeon.

"Hey," he says. "You know where your mother is?"

I freeze at the top of the stairs. I want nothing more than to let rip with that classic retort—"It wasn't my turn to watch her." But honestly, I'm a little afraid of the guy. He's bigger than I am, he drinks a lot, and he owns guns. He's like Mitchell Frampton in fast-forward.

So I jam my hand into my pocket and touch the bullet.

"No. I don't know where she is."

I hear him open the pantry, then the rustle of a potato chip bag. A *nearly empty* potato chip bag. Whoops. Busted. If eyesight were gravity, I'd be crushed right about now by the g-force of his glare at my back.

So, slink down the stairs or hang around up here and pretend I'm innocent?

He solves it for me: "Hey."

Time to take the medicine. Yeah, yeah, I ate your lousy chips. Deal with it. That's what I *want* to say. What I *plan* to say. But I know I'll wimp out. I'll just listen to him give me hell and then I'll go downstairs and—

"You forget something?"

I turn around. He's pointing into the family room. I can make out the coffee table and the pages of *Schemata* that I left there.

"Oh. Yeah." I fetch the pages. When I pass him, he tilts the chips bag up into his upturned mouth, pouring the crumbs in, then shrugs, mashes the bag into a ball, and tosses it into the trash. I clutch the pages in one hand and slip the other back into my pocket to touch the talisman, the bullet, as I head down to my room.

Later, I'm lying awake at night (or, actually, early Saturday morning), rolling the bullet between two fingers, thinking about how boring the weekend's going to be. It would be great to see Kyra again. Not for any particular reason. Just because it's good to talk to someone else about comic books. It's good to have someone else to talk to, period.

Someone who calls me "fanboy," yes, but also calls me an Indian warrior.

Next thing I know, she's *here,* she's right in my room. It's out of nowhere. I don't know how she got here. Her hair is blond, though, and she has it tied back, but otherwise she's the same. Her blouse is a little bigger, though, because it's hanging off her shoulder, which is tan, for some reason, and she gives me that grin, the one that makes the ring in her lip move, and it's not Kyra. How could I think it was Kyra? It's Dina Jurgens. In my house. In my *bedroom.* I'm looking right at her, staring, really, watching her straight on, not out of the corner of my eye, not a furtive, stolen glance. I'm *studying* her, *memorizing* her. For the first time, I don't have to look away, and, God, she's more beautiful than I thought, more perfect than I ever imagined. She's curves and arcs, flesh poetry written in sines and cosines and the special geometries reserved for the circumference of a thigh, the radius of a breast, the perimeter of a mouth, curving just right. She's coming closer, getting onto the bed, walking across it on her knees, toward me.

I wake up just before she touches me. Typical.

I lie in bed for a moment, staring up at the ceiling. The lights are on. Did I fall asleep? Or was it some sort of waking dream? And why do I always wake up just before the good parts? Is it because I have no experience for my brain to access to mimic that?

The bullet fell out of my hand during the dream; it glints from the floor next to my backpack. I reach out to pick it up and notice my English paper sticking out of my bag. Mrs. Hanscomb's large "99%" gets a smile from me . . . until I remember Kyra saying that she'd like to see 99 percent of the school dead.

She can't possibly be serious, can she? She must have just been engaging in hyperbole. That's all.

My IM program chirps for my attention. Since it's a weekend night, I don't have to bother with the plastic over the door and turning down the volume; Mom doesn't mind me staying up on the weekends. I slip into my chair and drop the bullet next to the keyboard.

Promethea387: *How's it going?*

XianWalker76: *Fine. How are you?*

Promethea387: *How's your shoulder?*

I pump my arm a couple of times. Not sure why, but that's what tough guys in movies do when people ask them how their arms are. The spot where Frampton used me as a piñata for two days straight is less purple now, more yellow. Tender to the touch, but not painful.

XianWalker76: *It feels OK. Just bruised.*

Promethea387: *What are you doing tomorrow?*

I shrug, which is stupid because she can't see me. What's the right answer to that? Say "nothing" and I'm a loser. Make something up and I miss out on whatever she's getting at. Whoever thought I'd have this problem?

My IM bings again, which is annoying. *Give me a second,* I start to type, but then I see why it chirped: It's from another user.

IamaChildMolester: *hey man guess what*

Oh, crap. The window with my conversation with Kyra glares at me like a collection of angry relatives, her last question particularly annoyed. Cal's window is a pesky kid cousin, tugging at my leg and whining, "See what I did? See what I did?"

XianWalker76: *Cal, can we talk later?*

IamaChildMolester: *r u ok?*

XianWalker76: *I'm fine. Just in the middle of some stuff.*

IamaChildMolester: *ur mom? stepdad?*

XianWalker76: *No, seriously, everything's fine.*

IamaChildMolester: *we 1 the game 2nite. wanted to tell u. just got back from the party @ ves's.*

XianWalker76: *That's great, Cal. I'll call you tomorrow.*

IamaChildMolester: *going to the counties!!!! :)*

XianWalker76: *Terrific. Talk tomorrow, OK?*

IamaChildMolester: *r u ok? really?*

XianWalker76: *Yep. :)*

IamaChildMolester: *ok. c-ya*

XianWalker76: *Nothing I can't put off. Why?*

Promethea387: *What took you so long?*

XianWalker76: *Sorry. Slow connection, I guess? So what's up tomorrow?*

Promethea387: *Figured we could hang some more.*

XianWalker76: *I'll call you tomorrow.*

Promethea387: *You don't have my phone number.*

XianWalker76: *Sorry. Hit the wrong key. I meant to say, "I'll have to check with my mother. She's pretty bitchy about people coming over."*

Promethea387: *Who said anything about coming over? I'll pick you up and we'll drive around. I even promise to obey stop signs.*

XianWalker76: *Terrific. Talk tomorrow, OK?*

Promethea387: *Yeah, that's what I'm saying.*

XianWalker76: *Give me your phone number?*

Promethea387: *Why? I know where you live. I'll stop by at noon. Later.*

I shut down the last window and breathe a sigh of relief. That was stupid. Why didn't I just tell Cal I was talking to someone else? Why didn't I just ask Kyra to hold on for a second?

As usual, I skim through the chat logs quickly to make sure I didn't say anything too stupid. It also helps to refresh my memory in case I made up some sort of little helper lie. I wince at the glitches where I cut-and-pasted to save time. "ves's." That would be Vesentine's house.

Noon. She'll pick me up at noon. What *is* this? Is she my girlfriend or something? She *did* call me noble.

I pick up the bullet and toss it up and down a few times. I don't understand the world at all.

CHAPTER FIFTEEN

LATER THAT MORNING, after an uncharacteristic five hours of sleep, I tell Mom that I'm going out for a little while.

"Where are you going? I can't drive you today. I have to go–"

"Don't worry about it." I can finesse this–she's busy, so she's not paying 100 percent attention to me. She's sitting at the kitchen table, some sort of catalog of baby stuff open before her. The pages are dog-eared and plastered with Post-its. Outside, the step-fascist is making loud, unnatural sounds with a chainsaw and the pile of wood behind the shed. Every few seconds, the saw makes a noise that sounds almost like a human yelp: "Weee-ow!"

"Don't worry about it?" She turns away from the catalog. "Where are you going?"

I actually don't know. "Around. Just hanging around."

"With who? Cal?"

"No."

"Then with *who?*"

"Jeez, Mom, a friend, OK? What's the big deal?" Finesse is not an option, apparently.

Mom gnaws on her bottom lip. "A friend?"

"Yeah."

"Who?"

"Her name's—"

"Her?"

"Can I finish? Her name's Kyra."

"Kyra. How did you meet her?"

That's one story that wouldn't go over well. Anything that starts with "I met her on the Internet" is just a bad idea. "She goes to school with me."

"How come you've never mentioned her before?"

"Mom! Do I have to tell you *everything*?" Oh, crap. That was the *wrong* thing to say. Mom's eyes narrow.

"What else aren't you telling me?"

"Nothing, Mom. I just met her a few days ago, that's all."

"Is she coming over *here?*" Mom has some sort of bizarre, paranoid reaction to people coming to our house. She doesn't even like it when my grandparents come over. She likes it to be her, the step-fascist, and, I guess, me. I think it's because back in our old neighborhood people used to stop by uninvited all the time, knocking at the front door, showing up on the porch, faces pressed to the kitchen door. I liked it—it was fun, having people show up all the time. But Mom hated it. She said she felt like she was living in a fishbowl, like she had no privacy. "I couldn't even come home from the supermarket," I heard her tell the step-fascist once, "without the phone ringing with ten people asking what I bought and what I was fixing for dinner."

So, part of my job as son is to quell her terror. "No, Mom. She's just picking me up."

"She drives? She's older than you?"

Oh, for God's sake, why do I keep screwing this up with the truth? "Yeah, she's a year older and she has her license. We're going to the comic book store over in Canterstown. I *never* get to go there and it's a lot better than Space Bazaar." There.

"She's a year older than you . . ."

"Yes."

"And she's a new friend?"

"Yes, Mom."

Mom smiles. "That's great, honey. That's really great. See, I *told* you you'd make new friends here."

It must be nice to be able to ignore reality the way my mother does; we've lived in Brookdale for six years, ever since the divorce, when she moved me away from my school and my friends. Ever since then, every time I've asked to have a friend from my old neighborhood come over or spend a weekend, she's gone into her paranoia mode and told me, "You'll make new friends here." Six years, and I've made exactly two friends and she thinks that's a good track record. Unreal.

I've got an hour before Kyra gets here. I don't know if this is a date or what. I don't know anything. But best foot forward and all that. I shower, mess around with some of Mom's mousse until I get my hair looking sort of like something that might one time have been on TV, spritz a bunch of cologne all over. I check myself in the mirror: Shave or not? Clean-cut look or rough stubble guy? And does the stubble really look rough and cool, or is it just sloppy? Can I do a goatee or not?

Better safe than sorry: I shave. Very carefully, so as not to nick myself.

Clothes. I look at the clock. Twenty minutes to go. Casual or what? Goth Girl won't care about neatness, right? It's warm out, so I go with olive green shorts, a yellow T-shirt, and a red golf shirt over top. Layers make me look less skinny.

By five of noon, I'm heading out the door. Mom shouts,

"When are you coming back?"

Beats the hell out of me. "Eight!" I shout back, and go outside before she can say anything.

I wait at the end of the driveway, checking my watch every few seconds. By noon, I'm still waiting.

By five after, I'm still waiting.

And by ten after.

This is all a joke, isn't it? Just another stupid joke. String along the geek who has no friends . . . Man, I blew off talking to *Cal* to talk to her last night! Cal . . . I was supposed to call him. I should go back inside and call him.

I look up the street, searching for her car. This would be a pretty elaborate joke, wouldn't it? The instant messages, the pictures, the meeting at the elementary school? Am I worth such preparation and planning?

Quarter after noon. I should call Cal. But maybe she got lost. Maybe she forgot how to get here.

I hear a car up the street and look, but it's not hers. Almost twenty after. Man, I'm a chump.

The car stops almost directly in front of me and the passenger door thunk!s as it unlocks. Kyra looks at me from the driver's seat, an eyebrow arched. She's done something to her hair so that it's spiked and standing straight up, but at least now I can see her eyes. For a second, I'm frozen; she looks different and the car isn't a compact—it's like a little four-by-four.

The passenger window whirrs down. "You coming or not?" And she gives me the magic grin.

I climb in. "Sorry. I didn't recognize the car." My heart beats a little quicker as I close the door and we take off. "Whose car is this?"

"My sister's."

"You said that car yesterday was your sister's."

"This is her *other* car."

"Your sister has *two* cars?"

"The idiot who knocked her up left it behind when he ran like hell. It was sitting in our driveway for, like, six months, so finally my sister said the hell with it and started using it."

She's wearing black again, but this time short sleeves that reveal slim, pale arms down to wrists that are bound in wide leather bands studded with metal pyramids. Her blouse is loose, buttoned up to the throat, where she still wears her weird reverse smiley face. As she brakes at a stop sign, I check her feet, which are in glossy black boots that come up to her calf. She has on baggy black shorts, and between the end of the shorts and the top of the boots there's a good six inches of dead-white leg.

She's wearing black lipstick, and I wonder what it would be like to kiss black lipstick, to have a coal smudge on your face.

"Where are we going?"

She shrugs. "Where do you want to go?"

I almost say "Comi-Corps," which is the store in Canterstown.

"Doesn't matter."

"That's what I like to hear." And she hits the gas. Hard.

CHAPTER SIXTEEN

A PART OF ME WANTS TO KNOW how I ended up on a beautiful spring Saturday, lying on a grassy hill under the sun with a girl who seems to like talking to me, with nothing to worry about and no one else around for miles.

Part of me wants to know. The rest of me really doesn't care.

We drove around Brookdale for a while, which is an exercise in extraordinary patience because there's nothing to see. It was also an exercise in boredom because Kyra, good to her word, was focusing very intently on driving. She had a cigarette tucked between her lips but had forgotten to light it—that's how hard she was concentrating. Every time I started to speak, she'd shush me with a "hsst!" that seemed somehow, oddly, maternal.

"This *sucks,*" she said at a stoplight. "We have to *go* somewhere. Where do you want to *go?*"

I couldn't think of any place that didn't sound unbefitting for a noble Indian warrior. Comi-Corps would have been cool—it's the best comic book store for miles around and I almost never get to go there. Better yet would have been Space Bazaar. To walk in there with a girl . . . I'd be a hero for months.

But I didn't want those losers drooling all over Kyra. Even though she wasn't really all that sexy, she was kind of pretty in the face and she was my friend and the guys at Space Bazaar would have been real jerks to her.

She drove around for a while longer, then set her jaw as if making a decision. Soon we were on the outskirts of Brookdale, where Route 54 stretches for miles and miles, south to Finn's Crossing and north to Canterstown. There's nothing but empty farmland on Route 54, except for a housing development that went in a couple of years ago, a lonely cluster of cloned houses squatting on the side of the road.

Kyra pulled into the development and guided the car past quiet houses that may as well have been from a ghost town. At the end of the development the road terminated in a circle of five houses, beyond which loomed trees and tall grass.

"C'mon," she said, finally lighting the cigarette after she killed the engine.

Technically, it was trespassing. We walked right through someone's yard, sneaked behind their house, then headed into the woods. Just when I was starting to worry about getting lost, the woods opened up into a broad clearing. I could see fallow farmland in the distance. The ground sloped down to a chain-link fence, which ran in a rough oblong around a weedy, muddy flat, then sloped back up on all sides of the oblong. It was like the ground made a bowl here.

Kyra sat down on the slope, then lay flat on her back, a black line on the green grass. I sat down next to her and listened to the wind in the leaves, the rustle of grass, a croaking that could have been a frog or just wind in a hollow log. Kyra blew plumes of smoke into the sky.

We said nothing for the longest time.

I guess that part of me that wants to know is persistent. I

know how I got here. But sitting here now, in the quiet, needing to say nothing, feeling no need to speak, just watching her black lips surrender white-gray clouds, it really doesn't matter.

CHAPTER SEVENTEEN

"YOU LIKE THIS PLACE?" she asks after a while.

She's been lying there with her eyes closed, so I've been watching her fearlessly. At the sound of her voice, I avert my eyes as if caught doing something, even though she's still not looking.

"It's nice."

"Nice?" She opens one eye and blows smoke through her nostrils, snorting aurally *and* visually. "Nice? That's it?"

"I'm not big on nature stuff. It's pretty."

She laughs. "It's a testament to stupidity is what it is." She flicks the cigarette butt down the slope in the general direction of the fenced-in swamp. "It used to be beautiful here. There was a pond down there." She points to the fence. "Then they built the houses back there, and the idiots who bought the houses decided that they didn't want the pond because they were all afraid of mosquitoes breeding in it. So they drained it and figured they'd build a playground instead."

"And?"

"And look." With a hand, she sweeps the entire vista. "No one could be bothered. They drained it, the imaginary mosquito problem went away, and they couldn't be bothered to do anything else. So what could have been a little bit of unspoiled nature in the middle of more stupid cookie-cutter houses, they made a dumb-ass swamp and fenced it in so the dumb-ass kids they all bred won't accidentally fall in." She looks at me seriously. "People are stupid. People suck. Period."

"Yeah. I know."

"That's what I like about you."

I shiver even though it's warm. What's going on here? *That's what I like about you*. What am I supposed to do? Does she want to be my girlfriend? That's impossible. The silence hangs in the air, heavy and impossible to ignore, so I say the first thing that comes to my mind:

"There's a comic book convention next weekend. You want to go?"

"Are you asking me on a *date,* fanboy?"

Back to fanboy, then. In which case, no, I'm *not* asking her on a date.

"Just wondering if you wanted to go, that's all."

"Anyone there I care about?"

I should have checked that. I *will* check that. I tell her so, then add, "Bendis will be there. I know *you* don't care, but that's a pretty big deal, whether you like his stuff or not."

"Whatever." Dismissive hand wave.

"Oh, come on! Come on! You have to admit it–it's a big deal. He's, he's an Eisner winner and stuff. Come on."

"OK, OK, it's a big deal, fanboy."

Hey, the Goth Girl likes to condescend! For some reason it doesn't really bother me. It's actually sort of cool. I like arguing.

"It's a bigger deal than if *Neil Gaiman* came," I say, stressing his name like a lovesick girl. I throw in some batting of the eyelashes for effect.

"Oh, please, it *so* is not."

"Yes, it is."

"No way. Bendis is this little superhero writer, and Gaiman, Gaiman's a best-selling *novelist.* A *novelist,* OK? People other than emotionally stunted adolescents read his stuff."

"Then why do *you* read it?" I ask.

She giggles. She actually *giggles.* I thought that would piss her off.

"He just reads a bunch of history books and comes up with bogus crap to tie it all together."

"Like your guy is any better."

"We're not *talking* about my guy." I'm going to check. I really am. I'm going to check the website and look to see if someone from Top Shelf or Fantagraphics or whatever is going to be there, and then I'll see if she wants to go, not because it would be a date but just because it would be cool to have someone go with Cal and me. Someone *else.*

But in the meantime, I start to gear up: She wants to talk about Neil Gaiman? Fine. I can do that. Where are the Greek gods in *American Gods,* I'll ask her. Wouldn't it make sense that Hercules would be around? What about Santa Claus? What about a god of democracy? Racism? He didn't think about it at all.

"What would you normally be doing?"

I open my mouth to let the Gaiman stuff come out, but instead I nearly choke. "Huh?"

She sits up, pulling her knees up to her chest and hugging them tight. "What would you normally be doing on a Saturday?" Her eyes are luminous and somehow huge set against the pale nothing of her face. "If you weren't hanging out with me?"

"I . . ." What *would* I be doing? Talking to Cal, if he didn't have a game. Reading, maybe. That's . . . That's it. God, my life *sucks!* "Probably nothing," I admit. Man, it kills me how I keep forgetting to lie to her! What the hell is wrong with me? "Probably hang out with Cal. But he would have a game or practice today, so I'd probably, you know, watch TV. Read something." Work on *Schemata*. But I don't tell her that. It's not a lie; it's an omission.

"You don't have any other friends?"

I don't know if she means "other friends" than Cal or "other friends" than her. But it doesn't matter. There's a tone in her voice—it takes a second to recognize it, but I pick it out. Concern. Sincerity.

"I've got . . . There are some guys from my old neighborhood. From Lake Eliot, near Finn's Crossing?" She nods. "It's a stupid name. There's no lake there. But that's where my dad lives and that's where I grew up until my mom moved us here. There are some guys there and I see them in the summer when I live with my dad, but it's . . ." God, this is tough to talk about. I think I've always compartmentalized my dad and my mom: When I'm with one, I try not to think of the other. Two different worlds. Can't breathe both kinds of atmosphere at once; you have to go through an airlock first. "It's like 'out of sight, out of mind,' you know? They don't call me and I don't call them, but when I visit my dad, I see them. Sometimes. Less and less. I mean, it's tough, only seeing them once a month and then over the summer."

She's staring at me. She's been staring at me the whole time, perfectly still. With horror, I realize that my left eye is starting to water. I'm going to cry. I'm going to cry while the only girl who's ever said a word to me outside of school watches.

I cough, clear my throat, then rub both eyes. I don't know what I'm trying to pull, but all of these shenanigans have got *both* eyes watering now, but at least it's like I've got allergies or something.

"You OK?" she asks.

"Yeah. Something in my throat." I clear it a couple more times for effect. I need to change the topic. No way am I going to start bawling in front of her. That's just *not* going to happen.

"How do you use your sister's cars without your parents finding out?"

She sighs as if disappointed and stretches, yawning, throwing her head back, flinging her arms up into the air and arching her back. I can't help it—I steal a lingering image with my eyes: graceful neck, slim waist, baggy black shirt fluttering in the breeze like a dark cloud, hiding everything. She shakes herself, conjures her cigarettes, and lights up.

"I told you," she says, blowing a stream of smoke my way, "my mother's out of the picture."

"No, you didn't. You told me your parents weren't divorced."

"They're not. My mother's dead. The Big C. Lung cancer."

Oh. Oh. What do I say here? What do you say? I don't know anyone whose parents are dead. I don't know anyone like this. What do you say?

"Yeah, good ol' adenocarcinoma," she says sarcastically. "It's the up-and-coming thing in lung cancer these days. I mean, it used to be that squamous cell lung cancer was the big one, but these days, if you want to get lung cancer in the U.S., you go with adenocarcinoma. That's the one all the cool kids are getting."

Oh my God. Yesterday. Yesterday, when she offered me a cigarette—

"It's all these little cube- and column-shaped cells," she goes on, not looking at me now, adding clouds of smoke to the ones in the sky, "and they just cluster and grow in your lungs, around the edges mostly. It spreads fast and they usually can't even operate."

—she offered me a cigarette yesterday and I said, "I have an allergic reaction to lung cancer. Gives me tumors." Oh my God, how could I have done that? I'm slime. I'm such a piece of slime.

"You—" I can't get the words out. I have to apologize. I didn't understand. I didn't know. I have to tell her all of this, but I'm trying to do it all at once. "You, your cigarettes—"

She misunderstands. She snorts and turns to me. "Oh, yeah, here I am smoking, isn't it ironic, whatever, get off my back."

"That's not what I was going to say."

"My mom wasn't even the smoker. I mean, if you want to talk about irony, there it is for you. My *dad* was a friggin' three-pack-a-day man. You know how I know? When I was a kid, I used to empty the ashtrays and I would count the butts. I didn't even know why. I just did it to occupy my mind while I was emptying the ashtrays. It was like a game. Like a game." Her voice catches and she drags harder on the cigarette, then exhales an aggressive fog bank of nicotine and tar and tobacco. "But Mom never smoked. How's that for irony? Dad's healthy as a horse, can run a mile. Mom croaked. Women are more likely to get lung cancer. Did you know that?"

I shake my head. I want to tell her to stop smoking because I've just learned that women are more likely to get lung cancer.

"So Mom dies and Dad decides to stop smoking, which is a real bitch, let me tell you, because a lot of places card you these days, so it's tough for me to find my smokes."

"What about . . ." God, where do I go from here? She's huffing and puffing on her cigarette, rocking back and forth a little bit. "What about your sister? Does she–"

"Look, let's just . . ." She's inhaled that cigarette down to the butt in record time. She stares at it like she's seeing it for the first time, then flicks it away. She draws in a deep breath. "Let's drop it. I don't want to talk about it."

"That's fine. We don't have to talk about anything you don't want to talk about."

"Oh, please. That kind of–that kind of shit sounds like the crap my therapist says."

Therapist. Right. Now what do I say? I don't know anyone who goes to a therapist. Or at least, I didn't until just now. Mom wanted me to see a child therapist when the divorce happened, but I wouldn't go.

"Therapist, huh?" Oh, that was smooth. I'm as subtle as a fart.

"Yeah. I have to go once a week."

Time to play the empathy card, I guess. "My mom wanted me to go to one a while back. But I didn't."

"Yeah, well . . ." She lies back in the grass again. "I don't have a choice."

"There's always a choice." I'm Mr. Empowerment.

"No. The court makes me go."

The–? What?

"Court? Why?" Mistake. As soon as I say it, I realize it's a mistake. I've gone over the line, crossed the Rubicon, left Dagobah too early.

She sits up, tucking her knees up toward her chest again, resting her cheek on them so that she can look at me. Her eyes aren't brown, I notice—they're hazel. Glimmering sienna-gold. What? What am I saying? I don't know. It's like messed-up poetry, like e. e. cummings. She's so pale. It can't just be powder, can it? It's like there's something missing from her skin, like she's an albino. She grins the magic grin. That ring in her lip . . . God, suddenly I want to kiss it. I want to brush my lips against it. Black-smudged lips.

"It's OK," she says. "You can ask. I don't mind." She fiddles with the leather bands around her wrists and slips them off, then holds both hands out to me, palms up, so that I can see the crisscrossing pattern on each wrist. The scar tissue is white, a dead white, almost a match for the hue of her skin. If she hadn't shoved it in my face and if it weren't for the fact that the scars are raised from her otherwise flawless flesh, I wouldn't even have noticed them.

"Oh." My shyness and my curiosity fix bayonets and go to war—I want to pretend I never said or saw anything, but I also want to touch her wrists. They're like a topographical map: raised ridges representing mountain ranges built through trauma and age. What would they feel like under my fingertips? I think of the scar tissue on my knee, memento of my mad dash up the stairs when Dad's old coat goosed my imagination; it's senseless, a dead zone on my body where I can feel nothing.

Could I feel her pulse through her scars, or are they too thick? Would it be like reading the pulse of someone who's dead?

"I'm sorry," I say. It's what adults say all the time when they're actually not apologizing. When someone dies or is injured. When something bad happens. They say it so easily then, when there's nothing really at stake for them. I say it to her, meaning it the same way, but somehow when it comes out, I'm apologizing for asking the question, apologizing for looking, apologizing for not having been there, even though I only just met her.

"It doesn't matter." She straps the bands on, covering up the scars, as if they never were.

CHAPTER EIGHTEEN

SILENCE. SILENCE FOR A *LONG* TIME. It bothers me until I decide that it's not a big deal, that someone doesn't always have to be talking. And then the silence just becomes relaxing, and we're just two people lying on the grass together, watching the sun as it starts to dip beneath the horizon.

"It's like I said before," she says at last. "People suck. Period. They're stupid and clueless and when you tell them that they're stupid and clueless, they just get pissed off because they know it's the truth and they can't be bothered to change it. I mean, it's like Mrs. Sawyer, in history. Do you have her?"

"Last year."

"You had her as a freshman?"

I shrug. I skipped most of the usual freshman classes and went straight into sophomore-level classes.

"Anyway, she's so stupid that she doesn't even *know* she's stupid. Someone made up some story about turtles or something and she believed it—"

"The Great Ecuadorian Tortoise Blight of 1928?"

"Don't interrupt me. But, yeah. The tortoise thing. Someone made it up and she believed it, and even when she found out it was a lie, she still goes around telling people about it, telling people how she got fooled! I mean, how stupid is that? It's like *advertising* that you're a moron."

"I made that up."

She sits upright and leans over me. I smell grass and tobacco and something sweet. Perfume? Her eyes dance and the ring in her lip jiggles as she grins. "You made it up? Really? You're not shitting me?"

"No. It was me."

The Great Ecuadorian Tortoise Blight of 1928

In U.S. History last year, Mrs. Sawyer asked us for "the single cause of the Great Depression," the question asked to a room of silence and gazes suddenly cast down onto notebooks. I can't speak for anyone else, but I didn't raise my hand simply because there *was* no "single cause" of the Great Depression. We'd just read a chapter that pretty much spelled that out.

After a few moments of painful silence, I tried to clarify the issue: "Mrs. Sawyer, there really wasn't a *single*—"

"I want," she said, cutting me off, "the *single cause,* the *one thing* that caused the Great Depression."

I couldn't believe it. I was dumbstruck by the stupidity *and* the temerity. I don't know why I did what I did next, but somehow all of the contempt and creativity bubbling in my head boiled over in that moment and I found myself raising my hand. When Mrs. Sawyer called on me, I said, "The sea turtles."

If possible, the room grew even more silent. A roomful of sophomores, plus Cal and a couple of stray juniors, looked at me, wondering, *What the hell is he up to?*

"The *sea* turtles?" Mrs. Sawyer asked, narrowing her eyes.

"Specifically, large sea turtles. The ones that live off the Galápagos Islands." I don't know where it was coming from. I was making it up on the spot. Some leftover, random data from a Travel Channel special, maybe. I don't know. "They died. That caused the Great Depression."

I think that if a student had laughed, Mrs. Sawyer probably would have either laughed, too, and then went on, or would have thrown me out of class. But no one moved. No one spoke. No one breathed. So she just looked at me. Maybe she thought I'd run out of steam.

Not a chance. "It's famous," I went on. "In 1928, there was a massive kill off the Galápagos Islands. Hundreds of thousands of sea turtles died."

"And this caused the Great Depression how?"

"The British imported a *lot* of sea turtles back then," I went on. I had it all linked up now. It all made sense. I could do this. "They made turtle soup and they used the skin to make leather—belts, shoes, boots, stuff like that." She was nodding a little bit. Why not—that part was plausible. "When the turtles died off, the British stopped importing, but it had a ripple effect on their economy. It messed up their trade policy. No one in South America would trade with *them* because they'd wrecked the Ecuadorian economy. So the British were losing money and trading partners. They had to stabilize their economy, so they did it the quickest way possible: They stopped payment on their World War I debts to the United States."

Mrs. Sawyer's eyebrows arched.

"When they did that, the ripple effect hit *here*. The U.S. was suddenly losing a big chunk of expected revenue. The government started to work out a new payment plan with England, but word had already filtered to Wall Street, where investors got nervous. Within a year, the stock market crashed, which caused the run on the banks, which led to the Depression."

Still, silence. No one said a word. A single giggle would have ruined it.

"Really?" she asked.

"Yes."

"And where did you learn this?" She hefted the history text.

"I saw it on the History Channel," I told her.

Silence. A lie like this works for one reason: because people think, *Why the hell would he lie about something like this?*

"He's right," Cal said suddenly. "I saw that show, too."

I blinked. Someone I didn't know—a junior, someone on a sports team with Cal—raised his hand. "Yeah, I saw that one. It was a couple months ago. They did a whole thing on the turtles."

Maybe half a dozen heads nodded in unison. I couldn't believe it. I had to put the cap on it.

"It was the Great Ecuadorian Tortoise Blight of 1928," I told her. "The single cause of the Great Depression."

Mrs. Sawyer's eyes widened, and, much to my surprise, I could tell that she actually *believed* me. It was the crowning achievement of my high school career, and it came in my freshman year.

CHAPTER NINETEEN

"*You* made that up." Kyra laughs. "Oh, man! That's *awesome.* You're my hero!"

Her hero. God, I'm glad it's getting dark out, so that she can't see the look on my face. Mainly because I'm not sure *what* the look on my face is.

"I overheard her saying to someone later that she felt bad that she didn't know about the turtles." I laugh, too, remembering. "Eventually, she figured out the truth. I figured she'd be pissed at me, but instead she said it was very creative—no kidding!—and asked me to write it up for her. I didn't know she was telling people about it."

"See, that's what I meant before. People who are so stupid that they don't mind telling you that they're stupid."

"Not everyone's like that." I can't believe I've met someone who hates people more than I do.

She sits there for a minute, quiet. She lights up a cigarette, the flame bright in the darkness. Then she looks at me. "No, not everyone."

I can't read her in the dark. She's all highlights—the lip ring, the stud in her nose, the sharp relief of her eyebrows against her colorless skin. It's too dark.

Too dark.

I look at my watch. It's eight-thirty.

"Got a hot date?" she asks, gesturing at my watch.

"No. I, uh . . ." I don't want to tell her that I told Mom I'd be home at eight. It's not like I'm a little kid. What's the big deal?

"Do you have to get home?"

"I told my mom eight . . ." There I go again, not lying.

"Want to leave? Are you gonna get in trouble?"

I can't imagine why. It's not like I'm out at two in the morning carjacking people. It's not even completely dark out yet, and I'm just sitting here, not hurting anyone.

"We can hang a little while longer."

She sighs. "Good."

I sit and watch her while she gazes at the muddy park-that-never-was. I consider working up the courage to put my arm around her, maybe kiss her on the cheek, but who am I kidding?

CHAPTER TWENTY

A LITTLE WHILE LATER, we climb back into the car and head out onto Route 54. We need the headlights now, and the road is busy with mall traffic. Never did kiss her, of course, but that's OK.

A minivan buzzes past us. I catch a glimpse of the rear bumper, and the sticker there.

"I hate that."

"What?" Kyra asks.

I didn't realize I'd said it out loud.

"Come on, you can tell me."

"No, no, it's nothing."

"It's something. You've got your arms crossed over your chest and you're looking all pissed. Was it the minivan? I hate those things, too."

"Just let it rest."

"Nah. I don't let things rest. Get real. What was it?"

"You'll think it's stupid."

She hums a bit to herself as we drive. "Probably. But tell me anyway."

I sink down in my seat a little bit. Arms still crossed. I'm aware of how childishly defensive I must look, but I can't seem to help it. "It's stupid. It was the bumper sticker."

"Bumper sticker?" I wait, but no laughter is forthcoming.

"Yeah, the bumper sticker. It was one of those ones that says 'My kid can beat up—'"

"'—your honor student,'" she finishes. "Yeah, I've seen 'em. They're stupid. Why do you let it get to you? Just because you're an honor student? Hate to break it you, but their kid probably *can* beat you up."

"That's not it." And then, even though I don't intend to, I let it go. All of it. How for years I watched cars with bumper stickers shouting the praises of idiot football players and jackass soccer players, the same people who have made my life miserable since I was old enough to understand the word *miserable* (which was younger than you'd think). Seeing them and their ilk feted and toasted everywhere—on TV, in school, in books, in conversations, at picnics. It's like no one else in the world matters. Then, one day, someone decides to throw a little attention and a little validation in the direction of people like me, people who have one thing going for them in this world—their brains.

"I mean," I tell her, "we live in a country that hates smart people. There's this absolutely virulent strain of anti-intellectualism that runs through America like a—"

"Absolutely what of what?"

"Never mind. It's just that it did my heart good the first time I saw one of those bumper stickers that says, 'My child is an honor student at South Brook High.' It was like the antidote to all of the sports bumper stickers. No one gives you high-fives or cheers for being smart, but at least it was something.

"But of *course* we couldn't let the brainy kids feel good about themselves for five minutes, right? We couldn't let the smart kids have something as small and insignificant as a bumper sticker. So all those Jock Jerks and their parents had to go out and get those new bumper stickers. Just putting the uppity brains back in their place. 'It doesn't matter how smart you are. We can still beat you up.'" And yeah, I remember the way I felt when I saw one of those "beat up" stickers. It was like, "Why do people I don't even know hate me? Just for being smart? What sin is that?"

I sit up straight in my seat, memory fading to the present as Kyra guns the engine. "What are you doing?"

She doesn't answer, but there's a grim set to her lips, and she's leaning forward as if her slim frame's weight could somehow urge the car faster. She's almost brutally intent, her lips curled into a snarl, her eyes straining.

"What are you *doing?*" We're zipping by the other cars on the road; the engine growls and the road noise jumps. She dodges from one lane to another, then back again after passing an SUV, and I realize what she's doing.

"No! Kyra! Don't!" We're closing on the minivan with the "My kid can beat up your honor student" bumper sticker. "Don't ram her!"

"Chill out, girly girl. We've got air bags."

"Christ! Kyra! There could be little kids in that–"

"So what? They'll just grow up into more Jock Jerks. A new generation. Who cares? Anyone who would put a dumb-ass bumper sticker like that on their car needs to be yanked outta the gene pool."

"Is it worth totaling your car?" I'm desperate–it's not her car, after all, but maybe her sister won't appreciate the damage, if she notices between bouts of depression-induced Cheetos eating.

Her fingers loosen a little bit on the steering wheel, but

she's still got the gas pedal jammed against the floor. "Maybe. Maybe not. I don't know. I thought you wanted people like this dead. Thought we agreed on stuff like that."

The List scrolls through my mind. Death and/or dismemberment keeps my spirits up some nights, true, but at the end of the day I just want these people to go away and leave me alone. Preferably after acknowledging that they treated me like dirt and shouldn't have. But for all I know, the minivan people up ahead never even spit in my general direction. They're clueless, but that's not a capital offense.

"Dead is a pretty long way to go, Kyra. Come on. You don't really want to kill people, do you?"

She chews on her bottom lip for a second, then grins. Ring tilt. "I got it."

"Got what?"

She tightens her grip on the wheel again and the car lurches into another lane. The engine growls louder, which I didn't think was possible. The minivan starts to come into view alongside us.

"What are you doing?" Has she seen too many cop shows? You can't try to knock a minivan off the road with a car this small!

"Gonna get in front of them. Hit the brakes. Let them nail us."

"Are you insane?" I spin around to look at her, but she's intent on the road.

"Like I said—we have air bags. Don't worry about it. It'll mess up her car, and her insurance will have to pay for it since *she* hit *us*."

"Kyra!" I don't know what scares me more—that she's going

to do this, or that she's thought it out so well.

"What?" she asks, annoyed, turning to me at last.

"You can't just do this!"

"I can do whatever . . . ah, shit!"

"What?" I look over my shoulder, out the window. The minivan has dropped behind us, slowing, its turn signal blinking.

"Shit!" Kyra yells again, then slams on the brakes and yanks the wheel, sending us careening into the other lane. My stomach doesn't get the memo and stays six to ten feet behind us as we skid over the tarmac. The minivan's nowhere in sight, already turned off. "Damn it! Lost 'em!"

"Thank God," I moan as Kyra settles back into the flow of traffic. Horns blare all around us, as if we somehow couldn't be aware of the automotive acrobatics we just performed, but Kyra just rolls down her window and blithely flips off all and sundry.

"I can't believe you were going to do that."

Kyra chuckles as she lights up a cigarette. She leaves the window down and holds the cigarette outside when not dragging on it. "You know what your problem is? You have no guts."

"No kidding."

"You agreed with that pretty fast." Plume of smoke out the window.

"I was joking. Didn't you call me a noble Indian or something?"

"Yeah, I'm having trouble reconciling your apparent fearlessness and gutlessness."

"There's a difference between fearless and stupid. You know that, right?"

She shrugs. "If you say so." She arches an eyebrow at me, favors me with a ring-tilt grin, and goes back to her cigarette.

I check my seat belt, just to be sure.

CHAPTER TWENTY-ONE

GET THIS: MOM'S PISSED.

My watch and the dashboard clock on Kyra's sister's ex-boyfriend's car agree that it's no more than five past nine, but when I walk through the front door, Mom starts screaming at me before she even comes into view from the "family" room. I almost jump out of my skin. Thank God Kyra just dropped me off and didn't actually come in—this would be mortifying.

"Where have you been?" Mom demands, rolling into the foyer from the kitchen threshold, her pregnant belly suddenly aggressive, like a tank or something. "You said eight o'clock and I want to know where you've been!"

I just stand there, shocked into silence. She's glaring at me, her eyes flashing, her jaw set. She's really, *really* pissed off! I can't believe it. I didn't *do* anything. I mean, imagine if she knew what Kyra almost did!

"I was—I was out." I should have *let* Kyra ram that minivan. Then Mom would be sorry. She'd be picking me up at the hospital. She'd be sorry.

"I *know* that. Where *were* you? You were supposed to be home at eight. You're an hour late."

I half expect her to break into some sort of rap. Eight, late, don't hesi*tate*. Something.

"We lost track of time," I lie, which is the easy way out.

"Oh, *did* you? You lost track of time, huh? Why? What were you doing that you lost track of time?"

And then she shouts–actually *shouts,* her face all red, her neck straining–so loud that I know they can hear her up the block: "ANSWER ME!"

But I've got nothing. I wasn't doing *anything.* "Mom, we weren't doing anything. We were just hanging out."

"Hanging out? For nine hours? Hanging out?"

What the hell has gotten into her? "Mom, I'm sorry I'm late, but"–*I didn't think you even heard me when I said eight, and I was lying anyway*–"I mean, I just forgot to look at my watch, is all."

"Because you were with your little friend, right? Doing what? Where?"

Oh, God. I see it now. "Mom, we weren't . . . We really . . . We didn't *do* anything." God, how the hell do I tell my mother I didn't have sex?

"Oh? What do you mean by that?"

"I mean whatever you *think* I mean. God, Mom!" I'm not. I am *not* going to tell my pregnant mother that I didn't have sex. I mean, what the hell? What *is* this? Not everyone's a freakin' animal like she is. Not everyone can't control themselves.

"This is how it's going to be now?" she asks. "This is what you've decided? It's not bad enough that you lock yourself in your room all the time and don't talk to anyone, but now you're going to do *this* to me, too?"

What?

"This is the example you're going to set for your little sister?"

"It's not going to be my sister!" It's out before I even realize it. "It's going to be my *half* sister, OK?" Will you get it straight?

I want to go on. Will you get it straight that it's *half* because Dad had *nothing* to do with this, and it drives me nuts when she calls it my sister.

I made a mistake before. I thought she was mad. But she wasn't. *Now* she's mad. Her eyes bug out. "I am so TIRED of that! This is not about YOU! This baby is coming whether you want it or not, so GET USED TO IT!"

I don't want it! I don't! I grit my teeth instead and stare at her.

"You are going to have to GET USED TO IT! Your father and I are NOT getting back together. And I don't care HOW unhappy you are, it is NOT going to change a thing!"

She's gonna shout herself into a miscarriage, and for a minute I'm terrified. I'm absolutely terrified that something's going to rupture or break or explode or whatever, and there's going to be blood on the floor and 911 and I'm going to get blamed for killing my half sister before she's even born.

"Now WHAT WERE YOU DOING ALL DAY?"

I realize that I'm shaking. I'm afraid to open my mouth, afraid to speak, so we just stare at each other.

"Go to your room," she says finally, calming down.

"What?"

"I said 'Go to your room.' You're grounded."

"For what?"

"Go!" I start to head for the stairs, but then she stops me. "But first go get your stuff from the family room. You left more of your pages lying all over the place."

So suddenly I'm one of the trolls in *The Three Billy Goats Gruff,* banished to the dark, dank spot under the bridge, all because I came home an hour late the *one time* I bothered to go out at all. The one time I spent the day with a friend, my mother—the same woman who is constantly telling me to make friends—punishes me for doing exactly what she's been hounding me to do for years.

There are a million—a *billion*—things to say, but none of them wants to come out. I just stand there in mute, stupid rage and disbelief. How can I argue with someone who has so completely abandoned even the *pretense* of consistency and logic? Do pregnancy hormones cause brain damage? And is it contagious—because that could explain the step-fascist.

Under her watchful, angry eyes, I go upstairs and find some pages from *Schemata* in the family room, partly hidden under a newspaper. The step-fascist is watching TV—professional wrestling. Two guys dressed like bad superheroes pretend to pound the crap out of each other while the crowd roars approval. He doesn't look at me and I don't look at him as I gather my papers and head out. Then downstairs, into the dungeon.

But the dungeon's OK. I don't mind the dungeon. Grounding me is sort of like telling a pedophile he has to hang around a nursery school. I've got the phone and my computer in my room: What else do I need?

I pop open the hard drive case and there's the bullet, a little brassy star. I somehow forgot to take it with me today. Funny how I didn't really miss it when I was with Kyra.

I lie on my bed and smooth out the *Schemata* pages before me, looking for bad continuity and goofy balloon placement. The whole time, I roll the bullet between my palms. Such a small thing. A little bit of metal and some powder. That's all it is. That's all it takes.

After a while, I hear footsteps overhead—bedtime. The steps don't stop where they should, though—they continue to the staircase, then come down.

Crap. I tuck the bullet into my pocket. I don't need this.

A moment later, there's a knock at my door. I consider pretending to be asleep, but my light's on and she's seen that, I'm sure.

"Come in."

Mom waddles in. She gives a little sigh as she glances around the room, taking in the chaotic piles of books and paper, and I can see her decision to say nothing about the mess as it flits across her face.

"I need to talk to you," she says.

Tell me you're leaving him, I think. *Tell me you guys are getting a divorce. You know how to do it. You practiced with Dad.*

She pulls over my computer chair and lowers herself into it. "I'm sorry I yelled at you. I lost my temper. Hormones . . ." She smiles, but I'm not buying.

"I didn't do anything," I tell her.

"I was your age once. I know what . . . I know the feelings that you can get. I'm not so old that I don't remember."

Oh, thank God for the self-control that descends from nowhere and enables me to keep myself from staring pointedly at her belly and saying, "Obviously." And did she actually say, "I was your age once"? Is there a script somewhere for parents? Can I just read it instead of listening to it?

"I know that you have all of these feelings inside and that you want to—"

"Mom!" I can't take it. "Mom, I swear to *God* that I didn't do anything. We just hung out and talked. I *swear.* OK?"

She shakes her head. "This is the first girlfriend you've ever had—"

"Jeez, Mom! She's not my girlfriend! She's just a friend!"

Now she cocks her head. "Is there something you want to tell me? I mean, you've never seemed interested in girls, and I want you to know that you can tell me *anything*. I might get angry, but I won't *stay* angry, and I'll always—"

"I'm not gay!" I can't believe this! "I'm not gay and I didn't do anything tonight. We just lost track of time. God, Mom, have I ever done anything stupid before? Have I ever screwed up? Have I ever lied?" No fair with that last one—I lie all the time, but she doesn't know that. And it's not like I lie about important stuff.

She watches me. I feel desperate and stupid. I wish my dad were here. He would understand. He would laugh and say, "Miggy, don't worry about it." That's what he called Mom—Miggy. Some nickname from college. I miss hearing it.

"You know you can tell me anything, right?" she asks, as if the fate of the world hangs in the balance.

I try to match her gravity. "Yes, Mom."

"And you promise me you'll always be careful?"

"I promise to stop having unprotected sex with Haitian immigrants and intravenous drug users," I tell her, just as serious.

In spite of herself, she laughs, then "Oofs" as she levers herself out of the chair.

"How long am I grounded?"

"You're not grounded. I shouldn't have done that."

Like it makes a difference. I spend most of my time in my room anyway.

"Don't stay up too late."

"It's the weekend."

"I know it's the weekend. But you need your sleep."

Hmm. I watch her leave, closing the door behind her, then listen to her on the steps. Does she know I haven't been sleeping? What trail could I be leaving?

Nah, I'm covered.

Once I hear her shut the bedroom door upstairs, I give them an hour or so to fall asleep, then I commandeer the telephone to log on. An e-mail from Cal, which reminds me that I was supposed to call him today and forgot. I type one-handed, the bullet back between my fingers. I send some IMs out into cyberspace, but Cal's not online right now.

Quick Bendis check, and all's right with the world: Comic book creator extraordinaire Brian Michael Bendis is still slated to appear at the comic book convention one week from today. I chew on my bottom lip, fiddling with the bullet. *Schemata.* I need to have more of it ready by then. One week. Less, really, because the show starts Saturday morning. Six days.

And six nights, fortunately.

After a while, the IM screen pops up with a new message. I accept.

Promethea387: *Today was great, wasn't it?*

Despite the shouting match and almost getting grounded? I toss the bullet up in the air and catch it.

XianWalker76: *Yes. It was.*

CHAPTER TWENTY-TWO

DINA JURGENS CRAWLS TO ME. I don't know why she's crawling, but that's OK. She stops before me, kneeling, gazing up at me. I put a hand on her head, feeling the softness of her blond hair. It's warm, so warm. She smiles at me.

"You're my hero," she says, only it isn't her voice—it's Kyra's. "You're a noble Indian warrior."

I stare at my fingers, intertwined in her hair. They don't look like mine. They're strong and rough. Calloused. Veiny. Almost muscular, but that's impossible because there are no muscles in the fingers, just tendons. But these are strong hands. Kirby hands, all out of proportion and drastic. Gripping Dina while she talks in Kyra's voice, and I suddenly have an insight. I realize something very important and very fundamental about *Powers,* which is Bendis's best comic book series. I've never seen anyone mention this on a message board or in a review. It's so important, so central to the conceit of the entire series that I can't believe no one's ever realized it before. When I tell him this, he'll recognize a kindred spirit right away. He'll—

I wake up, my bedroom still lit, the bullet clutched in one sweaty, tight, very ordinary hand. I'm breathing fast and I'm alone, of course, with Dina nowhere to be seen.

I can't remember the essential thing about *Powers,* the thing that seemed so important in my dream. It's lost along with whatever else I had or almost had while asleep.

I check the convention website. I'm not sure if any of the guests are ones that Kyra would want to meet, but I copy the list anyway, deleting anyone who works for DC or Marvel or Image, then e-mail her the edited roster. I hope she wants to come. Not like a date or anything. It would just be good to have her there, with me and with Cal. It's weird: I haven't told Cal about Kyra yet. He doesn't know that she likes comics or that she likes hanging out with me, or anything like that. Why is that? Am I afraid that she'll be like every other girl I've ever known and be more interested in Cal than in me?

Nah. I don't see that. Not that I'm anything to write home about, but she seems to like me for who I am, as unlikely as that may be. Her contempt for the Jock Jerks matches my own, maybe even surpasses it, and I don't think that Cal's ability to quote chapter and verse from the works of Moore and Gaiman will necessarily give Kyra cause to cut him any slack.

But she's got the list now. So we'll see. No hard drive tonight; I go back to sleep, one fist jammed under my pillow, the bullet tight within.

CHAPTER TWENTY-THREE

IN THE MORNING, MOM YELLS for me to answer the phone as I step out of the shower. The step-fascist is puttering around his workshop, accomplishing nothing that I can tell, and for a moment I panic that he's looking for a missing bullet. But he just putters.

Back in my bedroom, I close the door, drop my towel, and grab the phone.

"Got it, Mom. Hey, Cal."

I hear Mom hang up, then: "Wrong, fanboy."

"Kyra! Hey!" I figured it would be Cal—he's the only one who ever calls (except for Dad, but Mom's voice always gets icy when *he* calls, and she always says, "It's your *father,*" as if she can't believe he has the gall). I suddenly realize that I'm naked, which shouldn't bother me since it's the phone, but for some reason it does.

"How's it hanging?" Kyra asks, and now I think I'm blushing. It's just an expression, but jeez!

"Hold on a sec," I tell her, then grab my robe and put it on. "OK, I'm back."

"So, what's up?"

"Nothing. Hey, how did you get my number?"

"Phone book. You know, it's one of those books *without* pictures?"

"Hilarious."

"So what are we doing today?"

I think back to last night and Mom yelling, then the conversation that followed. Not sure which was worse. "Well . . ."

"Did you get in trouble last night?"

"No, not really.

"You're lying."

"Yeah, I am." Why is it so easy to tell the truth to her? More important, why is it so tough to lie?

"I'm sorry." She sounds sincere, too. "Look, we'll take it easy on your mom, OK?"

I almost say, "Good," because I really need to work on *Schemata,* in preparation for Bendis this weekend. But on the other hand, it would be great to see Kyra again. "Did you get my e-mail?"

"Yeah."

Emptiness on the line between us. Is this it? Do I make this an official date by asking her to go with me? And why am I even *thinking* this way? This is *Kyra*. Kyra, who smokes and curses and drives too fast (and illegally). I don't want to date her. Even when she shows up in my dreams, she's wearing Dina's body.

She's still waiting. Waiting for me to ask her to go to the convention with me? Waiting for what? She's just sarcastic enough to laugh if I do.

I settle on neutral ground: "Think you might go?"

She lets out a heavy sigh, a *really* heavy sigh that almost has weight over the phone. I can't tell if she's disappointed or sad. But then I realize that she was probably just exhaling cigarette smoke. "Don't know. Not many people there for me to see."

I'm not going to beg her. I've got Cal to hang out with, and that'll be more fun anyway. We read most of the same comics, after all. And besides, once I meet Bendis, I don't know how things are going to go. I might have to ditch Cal to talk with Bendis.

"You still planning on going?" she asks, almost a little too casually.

"Yeah. I have to show Bendis—" And I stop, horrified with myself because I almost said it.

"Show Bendis?" In my mind's eye, I can see her suddenly leaning forward, wherever she is. Maybe in her bedroom, sitting on the floor with her back against her bed. She's got low lighting and posters of Morpheus and Death on her walls. Everything's black and gray. "Show Bendis what?"

"Nothing," I mumble, glancing guiltily at my desk and the pages of *Schemata* there. The computer screen shows page 24, where Courteney walks through a forest of screaming children.

"Show him what? Come on, tell me. What are you gonna show him? Come on."

"Nothing, OK? Jeez."

"You're lying. I can tell. I can tell when you're lying. Come on, what's the big deal? Just tell me. Did you draw something? I didn't know you were an artist. What did you draw? Spider-Man? Please tell me it's not Spider-Man."

"I didn't draw anything." Another lie, the evidence all around me in my room.

"Yes, you did. I knew it. I knew you wanted to be a comic book artist. I could just tell. You want to draw Spider-Man, right? Or Daredevil. Or Batman."

"Bendis doesn't write Batman." Change the subject.

"Whatever. You're Mr. Superhero, aren't you? You want to draw—"

"It's not about superheroes!" I yell into the phone, then freeze, wondering if anyone heard me, if the step-fascist heard from just beyond the door.

"Calm down, fanboy. Don't blow a gasket, OK?"

"He doesn't just do superheroes," I tell her. "He did crime comics and Eliot Ness stuff and a comic book about Hollywood and—"

"So what's yours, then? Come on, you can tell me. I swear to God I won't laugh. I promise."

I sit down on the bed and reach out for the bullet, still tucked under my pillow. I didn't need it before with Kyra, but now she's got me all worked up.

But I'm going to do it. I think I'm going to tell her. I don't think I can stop myself.

The bullet's a cool point in my fist, fading to body temperature.

Schemata. It's the most important thing—

"I haven't even told Cal," I tell her.

She says nothing. I hear her exhale more smoke.

"OK," I tell her. "OK. I'll tell you some of it. But I can't stay on the phone too long—"

She squeals on the other end. "I'm coming over!"

CHAPTER TWENTY-FOUR

MOM'S "NO ONE IN THE HOUSE" paranoia/psychosis is still intact and in full force, so we decide to head to the mall—talk and eat lunch and kill two birds with one stone. She picks me up in yet another car—a dinged-up little import.

"Do you have your own parking lot somewhere?" Look at me, tossing out one-liners! I feel giddy and ridiculous.

"Rein in the brain, fanboy. It's just a rental. The other one's in the shop."

I hop in. Mom's watching from the door. I make myself wave and smile, while saying to Kyra, "Get us out of here."

I assured Mom that I'll be home by six at the latest, giving myself plenty of time to eat and bum around and do nothing all day before I have to be home. Mom pretended to buy it—again, nothing else on the shelves, right?—and then gave me a handful of change that clangs embarrassingly in my pocket. I'm supposed to call her by five no matter what.

Once out of sight of the house, she's Danger Kyra again. Not quite flooring it, but definitely starting to revert back to the lunatic who first drove me. "Why do you live with your mom and not your dad? Sounds like your mom bugs the shit out of you."

If anyone else asked me, I would either tell them to shut up, or I would shut up myself and just not answer. I always *wanted* to live with Dad. He's less strict, for one thing. And there's no step-fascist there, either. Plus, he's the *good guy*. Mom *cheated* on him.

"She got custody," I tell her. Which sounds so *lame*. Sounds like I'm an object that can be passed around. It's pathetic, really.

"So some judge just tells you where you have to live?" She lights up a cigarette and drags on it aggressively, like she's sucking in anger and courage. "Man, that blows. Some *judge* . . ." She lets loose with a cloud of smoke that substitutes for words.

I don't remember a judge, though. It was eight or nine years ago, so I was still in elementary school. I don't know if they ever went to court. Did they just work it out between the two of them? I never thought about it. One day they just said I would be living with Mom and . . .

God, did my dad even *fight* for me? Did he even *ask* for me?

"You OK over there?" she asks, and I realize I've been staring out the window with my fists clenched.

"Yeah." I clear my throat. "Yeah, I just . . . You know, she *does* drive me crazy, but I see my dad once a month and on vacations, and . . ."

"That must be cool." She's not just saying it. She sounds like she means it, or at least hopes it's true.

"Yeah, he's . . . he's got an Xbox." Ugh. That's so . . . "He's pretty busy, so even when I'm over there . . . He goes on a lot of dates. He's out a lot." Which is Mom's fault. Because she left him. So that's why I spend so much time playing Xbox.

Right?

"Why did we stop?" I ask her.

"Because we're here."

We're in a parking lot. Somehow we got to the mall and I wasn't even paying attention. Thank God.

It's a weird experience, walking through the mall with Kyra. I see other couples holding hands, but we're not. Because we're not a couple. Did I say "other" couples? What am I thinking? That's stupid.

I see kids from school and I ignore them, which is fine because they ignore me, too. Kyra moves through the crowds like she's a pissed-off movie star. She's so small and thin that it would be funny, but I can somehow see her throwing one of those sharp, bony shoulders into someone and knocking them down on pure adrenaline and attitude alone.

In the food court, I use Mom's change to buy a soda to go with my bad Chinese food. I'm trying to hold back some cash—I'm not sure if this is a date or not. Do I pay for Kyra's lunch, too?

Turns out to be a nonissue. She heads off to a pizza place on her own and comes back with a slice of mushroom pizza.

I take a deep breath. I can't believe I'm going to tell her about *Schemata.*

We sit down at a table in the middle of the food court. Part of me is terrified by the openness and sheer *public-ness* (is that a word?) of it all. But no one can hear me over the noise. Kyra chomps on her pizza. "Well? Come on! Tell me!" She's practically vibrating.

"OK, so . . ." I pause. I need a second. I eat some General Tso's and sip my soda.

"Come on, come on!" she says.

"All right already!" I'm going to do it. I really am.

Just then, a girl—a woman—comes into my field of view on

my left side, walking past our table. I just catch a glimpse at first, but it's enough to tell me that she's gorgeous. (It's my guy-dar at work, sensing beautiful women in 360 degrees.) Out of the corner of my eye, I make my first assessment: thigh, leg, breast (it's like a chicken—how weird), all in profile.

I'm at a table with Kyra, so I have to be subtle. I pretend to be looking at something else, but I track the woman with my eyes as she passes the table, goes behind Kyra, and walks off. God! She's gorgeous! She has to be in her twenties at least. College girl. Reddish blond hair, capri pants that are so tight that she has to be wearing a thong or maybe nothing at all . . . God, I love and hate this world all at once.

I sip at my soda. Kyra chuckles. "What's so funny?" I ask.

She purses her lips, then swivels in her chair to watch the college girl walking off. Oh. Busted.

"Hey, not bad," she says, nodding as if appraising a used car. "Not bad at all." She turns back to me and leans over, conspiring. "You like that? Hmm?"

So, do I apologize here? It's not like I'm *dating* Kyra. It's not like she's my girlfriend or anything. Right? I mean, how can she be pissed at me? She has no right.

"Do you like that? I think you do."

"Stop it," I mumble, looking down at my food. She's pissed.

Or not. "Go ahead," she says, and I realize she's not pissed at all. She's *amused*. "Go ahead—try to get it. Go for it. I won't stop you." She leans back in her chair, hands laced behind her head. "I'll wait here for you. You go give it your best shot."

Big sigh on my end. Yeah, this is working out *really* well. "No, that's OK. Thanks anyway."

Her eyes dance. "Why? Because I'm here?"

Nah, because I don't have a shot. Let's be real. But I'll be polite: "Yeah, I guess so."

She sits up straight again and goes for the pizza. "That's very nice of you." I shrug, which I figure is the safest thing to do right now. "Hey, wait."

"What?"

She leans forward, scrutinizing me. "Are you falling in love with me?"

I almost spit out a chunk of spicy chicken. "Don't be ridiculous!"

"Are you sure?"

"Well, yeah! I think I'd know!" Jeez! When did this get so out of hand?

"Because you better not. I'm warning you."

No chance of *that* happening, Goth Girl. "Trust me, I won't."

She eyes me warily, like I'm a wounded ferret that can't be trusted not to make one last lunge. "Good."

That goes double for me. I change the subject: "You want to hear about this or not?" Can't believe I'm *eager* to talk about *Schemata* now! Better than further embarrassing myself.

She smiles at me in a way that says that she knows I'm doing this to change the subject . . . and that she's decided to let me get away with it. Bites into her pizza. "Yeah. Go."

Schemata

It's a word for systems used to define and organize information and experiences.

I don't even know how to explain it. Not entirely. Which I guess is why I had to make it into a graphic novel. If I could sum it up in a couple of sentences, I wouldn't need to spend so much time writing and drawing it.

Yes, writing *and* drawing it. Like Bendis used to. He was an artist and a writer when he started out, before he got so popular for his writing that he stopped drawing.

I wanted to do something big and important. Something enduring and meaningful, like the stuff they make us read in school. People don't always *like* that stuff, but they read it because it's deep and it *matters*. All my life I've read comic books, and they break down into two categories: the ones people take seriously as literature, and the ones that are about superheroes. And you can count the ones that cross into both groups on the fingers of both hands.

But Bendis, you see, Bendis makes even his superhero comics important. He makes Spider-Man seem like a real person with real problems. And he makes the cops in *Powers* so interesting and so authentic that you forget that they live in a world where superheroes exist. It's like these stories *matter,* but no one takes them as seriously as they should because they have people who can fly or shoot lasers out of their eyes or whatever.

I want to bridge that gap. Yeah, for a long time I wanted to draw comics and I'm a decent artist, I guess, but then I started to think about how to do something big. Like I said, something enduring.

So there's *Schemata.* I don't know how long it'll be when it's finished. Craig Thompson's *Blankets* (Kyra read it and loved it) was 600 pages when it was published. *From Hell* was even longer. Jeff Smith did 1,300 pages of *Bone* and Dave Sim spent 30 years of his life on *Cerebus,* but my dad says that Sim lost his mind halfway through, so it wasn't worth it.

I don't know if *Schemata* will get into any of that territory. It's more than a hundred pages right now, and I'm still going. I'll keep going until it's done.

It's not about a superhero. It's about a woman who has a super-power, but she doesn't wear a costume or fight crime or anything like that. Because this is a serious story and I want people to take it seriously.

The main character's name is Courteney Abbott Pierce DelVecchio. She's a teacher in an inner-city school. I did all kinds of research. I even called the city school board and e-mailed the guy who does the education reporting on the Channel 5 news. I asked my dad to drive me downtown once and I took pictures of everything for reference.

So Courteney has a husband and a daughter and a class of really messed-up kids. She also has a super-power: She can take people's fears, dreams, thoughts, and desires, and turn them into three-dimensional images that she can see. So she can literally grab your nightmares and walk through them. She can walk in your shoes. Feel your fears. Live your dreams.

But like I said, she doesn't put on a costume and become Dream Lass or anything. The story is titled *Schemata,* right? And if *you* could do what Courteney can, you wouldn't go out and beat up muggers, would you?

But how *would* it affect your life? What *would* you do?

So Courteney starts using her powers to look into the minds of her students. To try to help them. It's a nightmarish quest, in a way, a journey through the very worst of a child's terrors.

And it only gets worse when she starts to turn her powers on her husband. Because what is *he* thinking?

And it . . .

It . . .

It just gets bigger. And deeper. It's about spirit and fear and emotion and love and *everything.* Everything that matters.

On Saturday, I'm going to show Bendis what I've got so far. I'm going to tell him the story and how he inspired it. And he'll put me in touch with the right people at Marvel. They might want me to publish it as a series of comics first, but I want to do it all at once, as a graphic novel. So I might have to convince them, but that's OK. I'm willing to do that. I'm willing to fight for it.

Online

Promethea387: *Can you get one of your stepfather's guns?*

XianWalker76: *Why?*

Promethea387: *Just wondering.*

XianWalker76: *You planning on shooting someone? :)*

Promethea387: *I didn't ask for bullets, fanboy.*

XianWalker76: *Bullets are easy to get.*

Promethea387: *I would only need one anyway.*

XianWalker76: *What?*

Promethea387: *I've been thinking about your comic book, the one you told me about at lunch. It sounds pretty heavy.*

XianWalker76: *You said you wouldn't make fun of me.*

Promethea387: *I'm not making fun of you. I mean it. It's deep. I wouldn't still be online with you if I thought it was a joke.*

XianWalker76: *You didn't say anything this afternoon. You just took me home.*

Promethea387: *I was thinking. You gave me a lot to think about. And besides, I figured you'd appreciate the time to relive that skanky college chick who walked past us.*

XianWalker76: *Will you let that go?*

Promethea387: *Just explaining things for you, that's all. Can I see it?*

XianWalker76: *See what?*

Promethea387: *The comic book, you dope!*

XianWalker76: *I don't know. I haven't shown it to anyone. And it's a graphic novel, not a comic book.*

Promethea387: *Yeah, I know. You also hadn't told anyone about it until me. Let me see it. You're going to show it to Bendis this weekend, right?*

XianWalker76: *Yes.*

Promethea387: *So, don't you want someone else to look at it first?*

XianWalker76: *I guess that's a good idea.*

Promethea387: *So bring it to school tomorrow. I'll look at it.*

XianWalker76: *I don't want anyone else to see it.*

Promethea387: *Don't be so paranoid. We can look at it in the car after school and I'll drive you home again.*

XianWalker76: *But I need to live to Saturday. :)*

Promethea387: *I hope this thing isn't a comedy.*

CHAPTER TWENTY-FIVE

MONDAY MORNING AT THE BUS STOP, I wait, standing a little bit aside, wondering if maybe Dina will end up on the bus again today, wondering about the comics in my backpack, wondering about the scene on page 10 of *Schemata,* wondering a bunch of things, because I do that, I think of them all at once.

You'd think after so many years at the same bus stop with the same kids that I would have made some friends in the neighborhood. But you'd be wrong. When your mother won't let you invite anyone over to the house, it's tough to make friends. And when people rarely visit your house, when your mother never gets involved with anyone else in the neighborhood, your house–and, by extension, everyone in it–starts to pick up that almost odiferous air of weirdness and *otherness* that marks you for isolation on good days, terrorizing on bad days.

Today's a good day. They leave me alone.

Dina's not on the bus (of course not–long shot, but it happened once, so it could happen again). I keep my backpack clutched tight to me. It has pages from *Schemata* in it, and I don't want anyone to see them.

At school, I shuffle things in my backpack, concealing the

Schemata pages between two folders for classes that I don't have on Monday. They'll be hidden there until later. I almost jump out of my skin when someone taps me on the shoulder from behind.

I spin around, my backpack held up like a shield. But it's Cal, watching me with concern in his eyes.

"Were you at your dad's this weekend?"

"No."

"Because I tried to e-mail you and IM you, but you never got back to me. I figured you must have been out of town."

Safe assumption. In the history of our friendship, I can't imagine a single time when I would have let a communication from Cal go unanswered. Let's face it—it's not like I typically have anything else to do.

But I was out all weekend, and even when I was in I didn't want to interrupt my e-mails and IMs with Kyra. Cal's windows kept popping up, threatening to crash my ancient system. Just the appearance of the windows themselves slowed my IM program down. That one session of dueling IMs on Friday was enough for me. I need that new computer. I need that PowerMac. I really do.

It's not until right now, with Cal standing in front of me, that I realize how extraordinary it was, what I did this weekend. Ignoring his messages. I've never done that, but I didn't even give it a second thought until now.

"I'm sorry. I was having computer problems."

"You need to download a Windows patch. I'll e-mail the link to you."

"Nah, I don't—"

"It's no big deal. Don't worry about it."

"OK."

"Look, I wanted to tell you that we won the game Saturday, but you probably saw the papers."

Not hardly. "Really?" I feign interest.

"Yeah!" His eyes start to dance. "We're going to the playoffs! Can you believe it? I mean, half the team is from the JV side. Most of us just started playing this year. It's unreal."

"Sure is."

"So you *gotta* come to the game, man. I mean, really. Come on. You *never* come, but this is the *playoffs*. You gotta see us play."

Again, he just doesn't get it. It's like he thinks I've been waiting for an invitation and then I'd come to the games. It's more than that. But he's earnest and he's my friend. It won't kill me to do it this once. It's the only friendly thing to do. Don't know why *I'm* in such a good mood. "Yeah, OK. So when is it?"

"One o'clock. Saturday."

I start to smile because he's joking with me, but his face doesn't change at all. Nothing but broad, open excitement there, a big smile, flashing white teeth, eyes lit with joy. He's not joking.

"Saturday? Dude . . ."

"Yeah, at one. Right here on the field—"

"Cal, Saturday's the show."

He stares at me. Slowly, his face turns into something like puzzlement.

"The show," I tell him. I can't believe I have to *remind* him of this. "The comic book show. Bendis . . . ?"

He blinks. He licks his lips. "Hey, look. This . . . Man, this is the *playoffs*, you know?"

No way. I *cannot* believe this is happening. I cannot believe that this stuff is more important—"Cal, you can't do it. We have to go to the show. We've been planning this—"

"It's the *playoffs*."

"—for *months*. *Months*. What are you *doing* to me—"

"I can't let the team down. Come on, we can go to another convention—"

"*Bendis* is at this one. There *is* no other—"

"Dude, you can see him another time. There's—"

"Stop it!" I almost shout it. Some people nearby turn and look at us. They're wondering when the stud athlete will decide his pet geek isn't funny anymore and pound me into the ground. I can't help myself, though. I lower my voice, but my tone is the same. I reach into my pocket for the bullet, the safety totem. "There *is* no other show."

"There will be."

He doesn't get it. I've never showed him *Schemata*. "You don't understand. There'll be other lacrosse games. It's just a game. This is *important*."

He steps away like I hit him, a laughable prospect, but neither of us is smiling. "Do you understand what I'm telling you?" he asks. "This is the *playoffs*."

"Yeah, I get it. I get it because you've only said it a million freaking times in the past ten seconds. God, I should have known." I'm heated up now. "I should have known you wouldn't go through with this. I thought you were my friend, but you're just another jock—" And I stop myself, because this isn't me. It isn't like me to do this. I didn't mean to say any of this.

I look up at Cal. I'll explain it better. More calmly. But he's looking at me with something so huge and so ugly in his eyes

. . . I can't believe it. It's not anger or even sadness. It's . . . I don't know. It's . . .

He backs away from me, shaking his head.

"Cal, wait a sec." But he's turning. He's really leaving!

No, no, no, no, no!

And the bell rings for homeroom, and I can't go after him.

CHAPTER TWENTY-SIX

MONDAY FIRST PERIOD IS MRS. HANSCOMB'S English class. My brain is in a blender. Cal sits and doesn't look anywhere near me. Across the room, Lisa Carter reveals lime green panties that could be a thong, but I don't even spare a second glance or go to my notebook. The Panty Algorithm experiment is suspended until further notice.

I'm sorry, I think fiercely, concentrating, imagining concentric circles of telepathy emanating from my forehead like an old drawing of Professor X. But if Cal's picking up on my vibe, he doesn't show it.

I've gone and lost my best friend in the world.

Mrs. Hanscomb calls on me to answer a question about Poe even though I haven't raised my hand. I hate that. Why do that to me? Why not just announce to the class, "You're all a bunch of idiots, so I'll call on the class brainiac because even though he didn't raise his hand, I know he knows the answer."

I just look at her. Poe. Melancholy. Despair. Drugs and alcohol.

Smart man. I slip my hand into my pocket for the comfort of the bullet.

"He was a genius," I tell her. I don't know if it answers her question or not. "But no one knew that in his lifetime." I think of the pages of *Schemata* in my backpack. I think of melancholy and despair.

She goes on to someone else. Good.

Between first and second period, I try to catch up to Cal, but no good. I see Kyra heading to one of her classes, and she winks at me. Between looking for Cal and the wink, I'm so flustered that I almost commit suicide-by-senior, coming perilously close to colliding with someone ten times my size and garbed in a letter jacket. Kyra's hair is spikier than usual and she's wearing a long-sleeved black sweater even though it's warm. Covering up those wrists. Always covering up those wrists.

Cal is gone by the time I collect myself, and I make it to history just ahead of the bell.

The more I start to think about it (and I *do* think about it, while Mr. Bachman drones on about the Cross of Gold), the more I get pissed off. How many years have we been friends? And he doesn't even let me finish? Doesn't give me the benefit of the doubt? He chooses *them* over me? Over *me?* The only person he can have an intelligent conversation with in this town? The only one at this school he can talk to about race? The only other person who knows that *The Autobiography of Malcolm X* was written by someone other than Malcolm X? The only white person at this school who doesn't say stupid crap in February like "Why isn't there a *White* History Month?"

He's going to give up this comic book convention, this one chance to meet some of our idols, for a stupid *game?* A *game* played with Neanderthals who can barely put together coherent English sentences? And *I'm* the bad guy?

No way. No way.

CHAPTER TWENTY-SEVEN

TERRORISTS HAVE SEIZED SOUTH BROOK HIGH SCHOOL. The usual suspects are dead or dying. I'm in the computer room, tapped into the security system, watching everything. Cal stands up and a terrorist gets a bead on him. All I have to do is activate the bell and the terrorist will be distracted long enough for Cal to escape.

That's all I have to do.

But I don't.

Cal goes down in a hail of–

No.

Cal gets winged, spins around in a spray of his own blood and collapses–

No.

Cal ducks, but hits his head and the terrorist thinks he's dead–

No.

I don't know. Not anymore.

God, Cal hangs out with all of them. All of my tormentors. Pete Vesentine. Ronnie Warshaw. Todd Bellanger. Mike Lorenz. Jason Benatovech. Almost the entire roster of The List.

And Cal knows so many of my secrets. I've *cried* in front of him, when I talked about missing my dad. I've told him almost everything. God, I told him that I liked Dina Jurgens! God, he knows *everything.* I thought it was hell here before–Cal can make it worse. He can make it so much worse. All he has to do is talk.

In gym, I don't even care that we're playing dodge ball again. I welcome the glancing blow that sends me into No Man's Land. And then, just because the world hasn't dumped on me enough, Mitchell Frampton is there with me.

I stare straight ahead, then look up slightly as his first blow pounds my shoulder. Kyra's sitting up in the bleachers, so I stand there, trying to look like an Indian warrior.

CHAPTER TWENTY-EIGHT

I USED TO THINK THAT IF IT EVER GOT BAD–*really* bad–that Cal would be on my side. That he'd choose me.

So, I was wrong.

I don't even bother looking for him for the rest of the day. My shoulder feels like pounded hamburger, but my head feels even worse.

I see Kyra a couple more times, passing her in the hallway. She walks with her books clasped to her chest, like she's hiding something, her arms thin black bands crisscrossed over geometry and history texts. She's wearing black eye makeup and she keeps her lips pressed tightly together, as if daring someone to ask her to talk, but when she sees me, she flashes that magic grin, that tilted lip-piercing, just long enough for me to register it, then she's back to Hard-Core Kyra again as she walks by.

I also see Dina in the hallways, as I usually do on Mondays and Thursdays. She's surrounded by a cluster of lesser Senior Goddesses (demi-goddesses, I guess), brunettes and dirty-blondes and girls desperately trying to be as gorgeous, but it's like Venus and the sun. Only one is the real deal. The other's just a pretender that fools roosters sometimes.

The whole time I'm in the hall, I keep a hand in my pocket, on the bullet. Even in class I try to keep my fingers at least resting on my leg right where the bullet lies.

I can't stop myself from thinking of the Joker. I don't know why. Cal always used to talk about how he liked A. J. Lieberman's version, how he thought it was interesting that Lieberman saw the Joker as an intellectual presence despite his insanity. I preferred Frank Miller's version, the one that embodies insanity almost as an elemental force of nature. We eked three hours out of that topic alone, hanging out at his house, flipping through his collection. I completely lost track of time, that's how happy and engrossed I was.

Won't be happening again. And Kyra isn't the sort who would spend more than ten seconds even *thinking* about the Joker, much less discussing him as if he mattered.

At the end of the day, I grab my books and head straight for the bus. I don't understand how it happened. I still don't get it. How did I make this the worst possible day?

Before I can get on the bus, a car horn blows enough to annoy me into looking up. Kyra pulls up in a big chunky Buick that's got to be at least a hundred years old, battleship gray and designed to fight a war. She's too blasé to wave or anything to get my attention; she just leans back in the seat, staring straight ahead while one of the bus drivers starts flapping his hands at her, yelling at her to get out of the bus lane.

The idea of going through the bus trip is sheer mental torture. I hop into the car. It smells like menthol.

"The rental had to go back," she tells me before I can even ask.

"Don't tell me this is your sister's *other* other car."

"No, dumb-ass. This is Dad's."

She hits the gas and we're gone.

"I had to look around for you. Why were you getting on the bus?"

Is that a note of hurt in her voice? Did she miss me? I hope so. She's my only friend right now.

"I forgot. I had a bad day."

"Yeah? I saw Frampton pounding on you again."

"No, it wasn't that. Cal and I had an argument. I don't think we're friends anymore."

She pulls into the parking lot of a gas station, out of sight of the tanks. "Aw, did you guys have a spat?"

"Shut up."

"Lovers' quarrel?"

"You're not funny."

"You need to loosen up."

"Says the girl in all black."

"Oh, please. See this?" She points to the reverse-image smiley face, which she always wears at her throat. "It's, like, a statement. It's a whole post-Goth thing. No one gets it. This Goth Girl shit is, like, 2001 or something."

"Post-Goth? You're making this up."

She shrugs. "Doesn't matter. You gotta be you, right? Just let everyone else go to hell. They don't matter. *You* matter. *This* matters." She taps my forehead, and I feel like something warm has entered there, then spread until it suffuses my whole body. "Now show me this comic book."

I hesitate, clutching my backpack. I can't do it. It's too much. I've never shown it to anyone before. Not even Cal.

But Cal didn't really care, did he? Lacrosse was more important. He's not the one sitting in a parking lot with me, gazing at me with unreadable hazel eyes that demand compliance. "C'mon. Let me see."

I sigh and open my backpack. I brought ten pages in all, the ones that are most finished. They're not in any particular sequence. Two of them are just Courteney talking to her class, but I like the details I added, like the lesson written in chalk on the board, and the kid in the back row who's prepping a spitball that will be thrown on another page.

I hand the pages over. I feel like I should say something, make some kind of presentation speech.

She clears her throat and settles in, turning in her seat so that she's got her back against the door, her feet up on the seat between us. She's wearing black shorts that are baggy and loose, and I realize that I could probably look up them if I wanted to, which—let's be honest—I *do* want to, even though she's just Kyra, not Dina, not even Lisa Carter. She's got black sandals on, which she kicks off now, revealing black-tipped toes that are almost too close to my leg for comfort. I humor myself—for just a second—that she's trying some kind of coy seduction, but she's not even looking at me. Her face is covered by the papers.

I wait. This is excruciating in its own way, waiting to see what she thinks. Is she going to hate it? Laugh at it? Should I have brought different pages? What do I do while I'm waiting? I can only occupy myself with *not* looking up her shorts for so long.

"Um, on these pages, the—"

"Shh!" she tells me.

Right.

A rustle of paper and she turns a page out so that I can see it. "Spent a lot of time on *this* one."

It's an almost blank page, with Courteney in the upper-left-hand corner, her eyes open in shock as she stares at nothingness.

"There's going to be a computer effect there. I haven't Photoshopped it yet."

"I figured." She lowers the papers to grin at me, magic grin. "De-stress, OK? I'm just messing with you." To drive home the point, she nudges my thigh with her toes, then leaves her foot resting against my leg. It's like five tiny, soft, hot pokers are lying up against me.

I roll down the window a little bit, just to let out some of the menthol smell. Why are her toes so hot?

"This is . . ."

I don't want to whip around like I'm too eager, but I do turn to face her, which somehow puts her feet up *on* my leg, practically in my lap.

"This is kinda cool . . ."

Yes!

". . . I guess . . ."

"What do you mean, you guess?"

She shuffles the pages and starts organizing them in her lap. "It's tough to tell with just these pages. But the art is really good. It's not what I thought it would be. It's a little more cartoony than I figured for a superhero guy."

"It's not a superhero comic."

"I know. I know." She stares down at the pages in her lap. "And your dialogue is pretty good. I mean, I had to remind myself it was a *guy* writing a woman."

"Thanks."

"It's pretty good." She tosses the pages at me and kicks her feet out of my lap, almost catching my chin as I grab for the paper. By the time I've got *Schemata* back in my backpack, she's tucked her feet into her sandals. She lights up a cigarette, then starts the car.

"Where are we going now?" I've begun to accept that I'll never know with her, but I'm willing to just stick along for the ride.

"Taking you home."

"I thought we were gonna hang out again."

"Not anymore." She flicks her eyes left and right, then pulls out into traffic. "Taking you home so you can work on more of that"—she tilts her head generally toward my backpack—"and show me some more tomorrow."

I wonder if it would be going too far to flip down the visor and check my smile in the mirror?

"If you've got something you want, you have to go for it, you know?" she says, talking around the cigarette. "You can't let shit like Frampton or your buddy the jock interfere, see? Screw 'em."

I hadn't even been thinking about Cal until she brought him up.

"Other people are just . . . there." She drags heavily on the cigarette, blows a stream of smoke out the window, then flicks the butt out after it. "If they aren't helping, they're just in the way. Weave around them, knock them over, do whatever you have to, but get past them."

"Which are you?"

"It's like dealing with the teachers and the other idiots who run that place." She's ignoring me. I realize that I should keep an eye on the road for her, just in case. "Beginning of the year, the Spermling called me into his office."

Mr. Sperling is the assistant principal. Some kids call him the Spermling. I don't really think it's funny, but it is a little amusing to hear Kyra say it.

"He's all passive-aggressive and shit, making me wait

outside his office, then calling me in, then making me sit there while he's on the phone pretending to be important. Like he'd be a friggin' assistant principal in the middle of nowhere if he mattered *at all*.

"So he finally decides to admit I'm sitting there and he says to me, 'Your teachers are getting a little bit tired of your acting out. We *all* are.' And I said, 'Tough titty.'"

"You *said* that?"

"Yeah."

"Wow." I roll through the implications of saying "tough titty" to my mom, to the step-fascist, to anyone. "You're hard-core," I tell her.

She rolls her eyes. "Yeah, I'm Batman. So he gets all red-faced and starts playing with this pen on his desk, bending it, tapping it, you know? But I just wasn't going to put up with his shit."

"Did you tell him about your sister?"

"I told him I didn't care if people were pissed about my 'acting out,'" she goes on, ignoring my question. "I mean, he's this creepy little pissant. Who the hell is he to tell me what to do and how to act?"

He's the assistant principal, I want to say . . . but why should that matter?

"He's a gross little perv. He stands in the main lobby every morning when we all come in and you can see him staring at the girls." She looks over at me, and I guess something shows on my face because she indulges me with the magic grin. "Hey, it's cool for *you* to stare at the girls. You're not, like, a hundred and ten years old and married. But I was just sick of him and his shit, so I told him that if he bothered me again,

I was going to tell the police that he molested me."

"You *what?*"

"You should have seen the look on his face!" She rears back, laughing, smoke purling from her nostrils like a dragon. I do a quick road check and it appears that I won't be dying today. "Oh, shit, man, it was *hilarious.* I mean, I think he *has* molested one of the girls before. Or at least thought about it, because he damn near broke the pen in two and his eyes got wide and he started to stutter about 'let's be reasonable' and 'why would you lie like that?' and all of that crap, but, man, he looked *guilty*. And I knew I had him. I just had him. So I got up and left, but before I left I untucked my shirt and I undid a couple of buttons and I sniffled a little bit when I walked past the secretary's desk. Just to make an impression, you know? Just in case.

"Adults are idiots. They think they're in charge and they think they have some kind of authority, but you know what? They're idiots. They're just grown-up kids with more money who listen to shitty music and hate everyone younger than them because they know they've screwed up their lives and they want another shot at it. But all of us, all of us kids think that adults are in charge, too. They've got us messed up, up here." She points to her head. "So they get away with all kinds of crap." She sniffs. "But if you have the balls to tell them to shove it, they crumble. Easy."

I see myself telling Mom to shove it, the step-fascist, Mr. Sperling. Cue amusing animation of them all literally crumbling to pieces like stale cake.

"Your chick gets that," she says, turning into my neighborhood.

I blink, not sure what she means. It isn't until she's dropped me off (with nary a wave goodbye) that I realize she means Courteney. Courteney, who can see the truth of the world. My chick.

My chick gets it.

Tuesday Forever

I sit in my room for a while, staring at the computer, which is almost daring me to turn it on. I'm afraid. I'm on the bed, holding the bullet, watching the dead monitor. If I turn it on, I'm afraid Cal will e-mail me . . .

No. That's not true. I'm afraid he *won't*.

After a while, my stomach starts to complain. I hide the bullet in the hard drive case and go upstairs for a sandwich and Coke. The step-fascist is unpacking grocery bags, unloading what looks suspiciously like ingredients for chili. My stomach lurches. The step-fascist makes truly evil chili. It stinks up the house for days and burns more than swallowing a blowtorch. Its heat is torture, but also its only saving grace—by the time you get to your second spoonful, your mouth is seared beyond the ability to taste any longer.

Mom is chattering about a baby shower. She sounds happy and excited, and I get a weird spike of empathic pleasure for her through my chest. I'm glad she's happy. Good. Someone should be.

But then again, I'm happy, too. A little bit, at least. Kyra likes *Schemata*. I got Little Miss Indy-Alternative-Goth-Gaiman Fan to like my graphic novel. They call that "crossover appeal."

Back downstairs, I eat one-handed, the bullet in the other. Mom calls down, "Good night," too achy and pregnant to bother coming down the stairs, I guess. I tape the plastic sheet up over my door to block out the betraying light, then switch on the computer. My e-mail program automatically launches and starts up the Internet connection, but I kill it. No Internet. Not tonight.

It's me and a hundred pages of *Schemata*. That's all that matters. Colleges will be impressed by an applicant who has published his own graphic novel in high school. I'll get scholarships, which means I'll be able to go out of state. Get away from here. Start new somewhere else. That's what it's all about, really. I don't need Cal. I just need *Schemata*. But I need it done *right,* so that Bendis is blown away by it. So that he flips out when he sees it and calls his publisher on his cell phone.

I lean in close to the monitor, tracing arcs and curves I laid down months ago, cleaning up sketchy, unfinished images, adjusting line weights. I don't have a graphics tablet; I draw everything with the mouse. Back when I started out, I drew everything freehand in pencil, then scanned it into the computer to ink it, but my scanner is so slow that it was excruciating. I taught myself to draw with the mouse, which is so counterintuitive that it's ridiculous, but I figure that drawing itself is a learned skill, right? No one is born with an innate ability to hold a pencil; there's no evolutionary advantage to it. We learn to do it that way. So that means we can learn to do it another way, which is what I taught myself.

I like that line of thinking. I make a note to myself to use it in the story somehow. Maybe Courteney can give a lecture on learned versus natural skills.

The page in front of me starts to blur. I pop some Excedrin for the caffeine. Movies and books extol the virtues of the all-nighter. The hero is always dead tired, but it's always worth it, have you ever noticed that?

I have thick binders filled with original drafts of pages, pencil sketches of characters, ideas, tag lines, bits of dialogue. Once I'm happy with the art, I go through the binders and pick out the dialogue that I intended for each scene, adjusting it as I go to adapt to whatever changes I made on the pages on the fly. This is actually the toughest part: not the writing or the drawing, but the *lettering*. Figuring out where to put the word balloons. Trying not to obscure too much art, or too much of anything important, at least. Making sure that the balloons are placed so that the dialogue flows naturally and leads the reader's eye correctly. Prose writers have it easy: Everything starts in the upper-left-hand corner of the page and goes downhill from there. In a comic book, you start in the upper-left-hand corner, but from there you can go right, down, diagonal, whatever. You can have panel borders, or none. You can have word balloons that are connected, disconnected, broken. You can have characters speak from off-panel, or in voice-over captions. You have to decide if the words are important enough to cover up the artwork that's telling half the story.

Bendis's dialogue is perfect. Every time. He puts more words on a page than most comic book writers, but somehow it all fits. It never seems cramped or overdone or flowery or padded. It's always an *extension* of the artwork. It's the first thing he'll notice in *Schemata,* I'm sure, so mine has to be just as perfect as his.

Sometime around four o'clock, I figure the Internet is safe.

I log on to check the convention website. Bendis is still scheduled for the show. Nothing has changed.

There's an e-mail from Kyra waiting for me. She says that if I'm reading her e-mail, I'm wasting my time and I should get back to work. My muzzy head conjures, again, an image of me kissing those black-lipsticked lips, which I have no desire to do, so I don't know where it came from. I'm tired. I can barely type at this point. I tell her I'm fine, just busy, then shut down the computer.

The thought of taking down my plastic shield makes me even more exhausted. But I can't afford to have Mom decide to wake me up in the morning and find it, so I force myself to stand up. I tear down the plastic, fold it up and tuck it under the desk, then turn out the light and collapse onto my bed. I should be able to get a couple of hours of sleep.

Instead, I lie there, my mind racing even as my body begs for sleep. I see Cal walking away from me, Lisa Carter's legs parting, a glimmer of green winking at me, Kyra winking at me, her arms sheathed in black, Dina reaching out to touch me, Cal walking away, Courteney from *Schemata* moving as if animated by Pixar, Cal walking away, Bendis grinning at me, frozen like the author photo I've seen on his website, grinning, Cal, Lisa, Kyra, Dina, and my alarm goes off, it's time to get up, it's Tuesday, but it's already been Tuesday forever.

CHAPTER TWENTY-NINE

THIS IS WHAT A ZOMBIE FEELS LIKE, I'm sure. My brain is floating somewhere a foot or two above my body and maybe ten inches back, trailing along. I get the ritual shoves and "accidental" kicks on the bus, but I barely feel them. I don't care.

Same thing at school. There's probably a locker somewhere along the hallway dented with an imprint of my body. It's just the odds, given how many times I've been pushed aside into them.

But in two more years I can go to college. Go to college far away, where no one knows me, where I can start over. And in college, everyone is smart, so it'll be OK to be myself and I won't be a freak anymore.

Tuesday . . . I force my mind to function as I stand at my locker, staring with something that, I'm sure, looks like dumb amazement at the books within. I can't remember my Tuesday schedule. I know I don't have gym on Tuesday because my gym bag is at home, *ipso facto*, or should that be *ergo*? I can never remember. God, I'm rambling in my own head. But I'm missing something, I think. Something in my locker. Or my backpack. Something's not there.

Cal's locker is three down from mine. I hear his voice and it takes every muscle in my neck, a Herculean effort of will and strength, not to look over. He's talking to someone, talking about lacrosse, using that faux street patois he affects when he's busy out-cooling the white kids. I know that. I know it's a put on. He told me.

I know his secrets. He knows mine, but I know his.

What I *don't* know is what I have first period. I don't recognize any of my books. Am I really reading *The House of the Seven Gables*? For which class? Or was that last semester and I forgot to turn it in?

Someone sidles up to me, almost silent. "You OK?"

I look over at Kyra. For the first time, I'm looking *down* at her. She must be wearing what-do-you-call-em: not-heels. Not heels. Flat things. Flats.

Her hair is different somehow. It's not slick or spiked or sleepy. Just clean and shiny and pulled back in a ponytail that looks ridiculously jaunty on my black-garbed little muse. And something else.

Lips. Red lips. Red lipstick, not black. I lick my lips before I can stop myself.

"I don't know," I tell her. I think it's been a few hours since she asked the question. "I'm tired."

"No kidding." She pokes my chest, drags her finger up, flipping the collar of my shirt into position. "Get to homeroom, fanboy. You've got a perfect record."

I turn back to my locker. Biology, I think. Yes. Tuesdays and Thursdays. I grab the bio book. God, it's heavy. I look around for Kyra. She's gone. Was she even here?

I turn toward homeroom just in time to see Cal walking off with a pack of List-dwellers. He's doing some MTV/BET hand motions, and they're all eating it up.

I get to homeroom right before the bell. I just want to sleep. What is it I'm missing, anyway?

CHAPTER THIRTY

My dad told me about this study he saw once. This was when *he* was in high school, so we're talking, like, before the Internet, before cable TV, before cell phones. It was a study where they tried to figure out the effects of sleep deprivation, and they showed a film to my dad's class in black-and-white. That's the part of the story that sticks in my head and drives it home to me: The film was in black-and-white. Like a security camera at a convenience store. Now that's primitive.

But in this study they had this guy and they made him stay awake for hours and hours and days and days. With a camera on him the whole time. He sat in this chair and read, and he paced sometimes, and he did everything possible to stay awake while they filmed him.

Now, eventually, the guy started to lose it. He started to hallucinate, seeing things, hearing things. You'd expect that, right?

But here's the weird part: It happened *much* later than anyone expected. They figured the subject would go nuts after a day or two, but he lasted a lot longer than that.

When they went back and checked the tape, here's what they found: *The guy wasn't awake the whole time.* Yeah, there was a camera on him and he *looked* like he was awake, but he was actually taking *micro-naps,* little bouts of sleep that last maybe a second. It's like sleeping during a blink.

I don't know. Maybe that explains how I got through the day. Or maybe it's just an old-fashioned second wind. Whichever, by the time the final bell rings, I'm feeling slightly human again, and some stranger with my handwriting has filled my notebook with some information that is partly legible, and hopefully not on a test in my future.

I duck into the media center for a second and fire up the school website. Every teacher is supposed to post homework assignments each day. I have no idea what my homework is, but fortunately I have this county-mandated cheat sheet. Mrs. Grant, the media specialist, gets my attention and taps her watch, reminding me that I have to get to my bus. I scan the homework list quickly and run for my locker.

I make it to my locker and then out to the bus with time to spare, feeling hugely conspicuous as I gasp for breath. Fortunately, no one's looking.

"Hey!" Someone pokes me in the back and I almost jump over the school.

"Kyra!" I turn to her, ready to yell at her for scaring the hell out of me, but I lose the anger as fast as I gained it. Her hair's still clean and tied back, but her lips are bare. Did the lipstick come off during the day? Did she take it off? Or did I just hallucinate her this morning, pre-micro-naps?

"Wow, I thought you were gonna drop a load in your shorts." She rolls her eyes.

"That's gross."

"You're so easy to offend."

"That's because you're so offensive." Guess my wit caught a nap before.

"Nice one. Nice one." She glances around. She's wearing

black, of course, a blouse that buttons down the center, all puffy and loose like a sack, with sleeves that button tightly at the wrists. High collar. Loose silver belt and then black shorts that hit the knee. Why I care, I couldn't tell you. Actually, I could: It's kind of interesting to see how many different permutations of black there are. This makes me giggle.

"You really *are* tired, aren't you? C'mon, show me the stuff?"

"Stuff?" Show her the stuff? Are we in a movie? Is this the drug sale scene?

"Yeah, the pages. You said you'd bring more today."

"Oh, crap."

She arches an eyebrow at me and cocks her hip. If the hip weren't lost in endless yards of black fabric, it might be sexy. Oh, who am I kidding?

"I left them at home."

"You *what?*"

"I'm an idiot. What do you want? I was tired this morning. I left it all at home. I knew I was missing something today. All I have is a bunch of script pages." I dig into my backpack and wave them at her—nothing more than words, and words do not a graphic novel make.

"Normally I'd be pissed, but your honesty and your willingness to admit you're an idiot has endeared you to me. Come on." She grabs the script pages and tucks them under her arm.

I stand there like a lump as she starts to walk away. What, does *she* have my pages somewhere?

"I said, 'Come on,' fanboy." She comes back and grabs my wrist, pulling me after her. Her fingers are delicate and soft. Weak. But I let her pull me, even though she's pulling me away from my bus, even though people are starting to look now.

"I'm gonna miss my bus."

"You don't need the bus."

"Can I have back my script?"

"No. I'm keeping it so that I can at least read the dialogue and stuff when you keep forgetting pages in the future."

She drags me to the parking lot and a little two-door black coupe. She climbs in on the driver's side and gestures for me to slide in next to her.

Now, I'm dead tired, but I'm not stupid.

"Wait a second. Whose car is *this?*"

"This *was* my mom's. Dad's been saving it for me in the garage. I figured why not use it. It's nicer than my sister's. Now get in so I can drive you home and see the friggin' comic book."

"Graphic novel," I tell her, shutting the door as I settle into the seat. She accelerates and blows out of the parking lot before I can snap my seat belt. Someone shouts and jumps out of the way, and someone else screams. I realize it's me, so I stop.

"I saw Mr. Tollin in the mirror," I tell her. "He was writing down your license plate."

She shrugs. It's almost like saying, "Eh," with her shoulders.

I look at the stereo. There's a CD in the deck. "Your mom listened to Outkast?"

"It's *mine,* dillweed."

Is *dillweed* a promotion from *fanboy*? I'm just frazzled enough to ask. She laughs, and it's a laugh like wind chimes, like ice in a glass, like fireworks.

"Wake up," she says. I wonder why she says it, and I wonder why it's darker, too, until I open my eyes and realize I must have fallen asleep while she drove me home. We're parked outside my house.

"You snore," she tells me, ring tilting like never before.

Oh, Lord. Sleep, a double-edged sword. My brain's back online, just in time for me to fully appreciate my mortal embarrassment. At least I didn't talk in my sleep.

No one' s home. I hesitate a second before I open the door to the house. Mom doesn't like guests . . . But Kyra drove me home. Mom would want me to be polite. You invite people in, right? That's what you do. And it's not like I can stand here at the doorstep and say, "Oops, I forgot, you can't come in. Stay here while I go inside and get the pages, and you can look at them on the porch." Please.

So I let her in and we go downstairs to the basement, which brings an odd light into her eyes for the first time. I explain how I have my room down here, and it's better for privacy, which sounds *really* bad when it comes out of my mouth. I mean *my* privacy, but she thinks I mean something else, and she raises an eyebrow at me.

"I like it quiet," I say, running through a mental checklist before I open my bedroom door: Bed made? Probably. Underwear on the floor? Don't think so. Socks evident to eye or nose? Did laundry Sunday night, so I think I'm safe.

Last: Anything embarrassing on the walls or flat surfaces? Oh, yeah. Only about a million superhero comic books and posters. Too late now.

I open the door and let her in first, then follow, disappointed but resigned to the fact that the universe did not align itself to remove the posters and comics.

She's not bothering with the décor, though. She's staring at my computer. "You did *Schemata* on *that?*"

"Yeah."

"You're kidding me. Where's your tablet?"

"I don't have one."

"So, what, you scan it and ink it onscreen?" She points to my scanner.

"Nah. It's a piece of junk. I draw it with the mouse."

She whistles. "Holy crap. I'm impressed. I mean it." She spies a stack of pages and picks them up. "I can't believe you did this on that old thing." She squints at the computer. "Is that a *modem?* Are you on dial-up?"

I shrug.

"I didn't know. Jeez, no wonder you always took so long to answer my IMs. My dad works for the phone company, so we have free DSL."

"I want your life," I blurt out without thinking. Ah, hell.

She smirks at me; all is forgiven.

"It's just that, you know, this whole thing would go a *lot* faster with a better computer. I get a lot of crashes. I lost six pages one night. That really sucked."

"I bet."

"That's why a new computer is one of my three things. I want to get a Mac," I tell her while she looks through the stack of pages. "I mean, then I could really crank on the pages. I'm using Photoshop 4.0 still. And Illustrator 5. It's just–"

"Three things?" She looks up at me.

"Nothing. Look at those pages. Tell me what you think."

"What three things?" She doesn't care about the pages anymore. "Come on, tell me. I want to know."

"It's nothing! God!"

"Haven't you learned by now that the more you tell me something is nothing, the more I want to know what it is?"

She's grinning. She's amused by the whole thing. Fine, then.

"OK, OK. Look, it's just . . . There are three things I want in this world more than anything else."

"Just three? God, I want, like, a *million* things."

"You didn't listen to me. Not *just* three things—three things more than anything else."

"Oh. Like the top three?"

"Well . . ." I think about it. Not really. I don't know how to explain it. The three things that complete me? That would make life worth living? They both sound pathetic. "Sure. The top three."

She arches an eyebrow in that way she has. "And a new computer is one of them? Really?"

When she says it out loud like that, it does sound sort of pathetic. I mean, a new computer? Kids starving in Indonesia, and I'm jonesing for hardware? "It's not the computer itself. It's what it can mean. It means a better *Schemata*. Less time focusing on keeping the computer running and more time *creating*. Better work. Maybe a cool website to promote it. Maybe do some animation, just to get people's attention. Stuff like that."

She's nodding as I say it. "Yeah, I get that. So, what else?"

"It's stupid. You won't—"

She kicks me in the shin.

"Hey!"

"What did I tell you before? The more you don't tell me . . ."

"Fine. Fine. Jeez." I rub my shin. It didn't really hurt that much, but some part of me notices how she seems almost concerned at evidence of my pain. "I also want a copy of *Giant-Size X-Men* #1. In Mint condition."

She bursts into laughter.

"Yeah, yeah, I know."

"That's *lame!* I'm sorry, fanboy, but even for a superhero geek—"

"I know. Look, I don't usually get into that stuff. I mean, Cal's the one who has this whole obsession with comics-as-historical documents." She looks bored when I bring up Cal. Or *is* it boredom? I don't know. "I just want to read the stories. But my dad's the one who got me into comics. He used to read X-Men and Spider-Man comics to me when I was a kid. And *Giant-Size X-Men* #1 is where it all started. That's where, like, the modern age of Marvel Comics started."

Kyra rolls her eyes. I can tell she's thinking, *Big friggin' deal.*

"It's just that my dad never got that one. And it's really expensive. So Cal says—"

She cuts me off. "Yeah, yeah, he's not the only one who can see the obvious, fanboy. You're completing your dad's collection. Very sweet. Get my insulin, OK?"

It sounds really pathetic when she puts it like that. I shrug my shoulders.

"Oh, come on, I'm sorry. I didn't mean it like that. It actually *is* kinda sweet. It's OK."

I shrug again. "Whatever. Look, just look at the pages, OK?"

"Tell me the third thing."

I freeze.

"Come on. Tell me." She comes close and actually takes my hand. It's like static electricity; I flinch. I've never held hands with a girl before. This isn't even really holding hands, but it's enough.

"Hey." She misinterprets my flinch, tilts my face so that I

have to look at her. “Tell me. It’s OK. What is it, the Playboy Channel?”

“No, it’s not . . . There’s no third thing. It’s just two.”

“You said three before.”

“I misspoke.”

“I don’t think you *ever* misspeak.”

I tear myself away from her eyes and her hand, stepping back, looking down. Those hazel eyes. Can’t look in them and lie. It sucks.

I can’t tell her, though. Not the third thing. I’ll look too needy. It’ll become a self-fulfilling prophecy or something like that.

“I can’t tell anyone,” I tell her finally, after a painful silence. I meet her eyes again. I’m not lying now. Not at all. “I can’t tell.” That’s the truth. “If I do, I might never get it.”

I don’t think she realizes she’s doing it—she flicks her tongue out to lap at the ring in the corner of her mouth. I gulp. I think it’s just a reflex, but man!

“It’s OK,” she says after thinking about it. “Sometimes you need to hold on to one thing. You should never tell someone *everything,* after all.”

Moment over. Safety preserved.

“Thanks for under—”

“Shh!” She’s moved on already, now intent on the pages and settling into my chair. I hush, as directed, and sit on my bed, which isn’t exactly made but isn’t exactly unmade either. I vaguely remember yanking the covers up to the headboard this morning. So I sit there and after thirty seconds or thirty years (not sure which), I start to move, quietly gathering up copies of *Powers* and *Ultimate Fantastic Four* and some graphic novels from the floor, stacking them in a corner where Kyra won't see the capes and spandex suits on the covers.

"How long is it?" she asks, never looking up. Her legs are crossed, the dangling foot jittery and hopping like it's on caffeine all by itself, the rest of her almost preternaturally still, except when she turns a page.

"So far? I'm a hundred pages into it. It'll be longer. I don't know how long, really. I'm just gonna write until it's finished, and that's that. I figure I need twenty really good pages to take with me on Saturday. I'm happy with about ten right now, so I have a lot to do between now and then."

"How are you going to show them to him?"

She's thinking presentation. Most people don't even think like that. But comics are visual. You can't just bring a stack of pages up to someone like Brian Michael Bendis and dump them in front of him and expect him to be wowed.

"I'm going to go to the copy shop and get them printed on the big laser printer there, at eleven by seventeen," I tell her. "Then I'll put them in this." I reach under my bed and pull out my portfolio. I bought it six months ago, when I saw that Bendis would be in town, when I decided that this was My Time. It's a creamy maroon leather, crackled, with a built-in handle that slides down into a hidden slot. It unzips on three sides to open like a book. I unzip it now and show her the clear poly inserts for artwork. I've customized it, using paint pens to detail the edges of the inserts (where the art won't be obscured), etching my name, phone number, and e-mail address like frosting on glass. There are twelve inserts, enough to hold my twenty pages if I put two in each insert, faces out. That leaves two inserts empty; the last one I filled with a bunch of flyers and postcards that I designed featuring the characters from *Schemata* and my contact information. The first one is already filled, too: I designed a huge mockup of the *Schemata* cover, influenced by something my dad showed me once: Sam Kieth's ad for the *Sandman* series. Kyra sees it and gasps. Of course. *Sandman* was Gaiman's big book. She must have seen the image somewhere Morpheus, god of sleep, emerging from the dark, only his face and right hand visible as he cups a handful of sand, as if offering it to the reader.

My cover shows Courteney in a similar pose, her face gazing at her own palm, which contains dancing multitudes: the dreams, fears, and secrets she's externalized with her power. At the top of the image is a stylized "SCHEMATA." Beneath: "a very graphic novel" followed by "by" and my name.

"Nice," she murmurs. "This is gonna look great. I can't wait to see the look on his face."

It takes me a second to catch her meaning. "You're coming?"

She nods, ring-grinning at me. "Yeah. I'll come. I want to see you walk this bad boy up to Bendis. I want to see that."

Wow.

Before I can say anything, I hear the front door open, rattling in its frame like it always does. I find myself holding my breath as Kyra leans over to put my pages on the desk. I can tell from the footsteps if it's the step-fascist or . . .

Mom calls out my name in a tone that has anger leashed just out of sight.

"Down here, Mom!"

"Whose car is that?"

She's a step away from losing it, I can tell. I've broken the cardinal rule in more ways than one. Not only did I invite someone to the house, but I did so without asking first, without checking ahead . . . And by doing so, I put Mom in the position of either busting my chops and looking like a total bitch, or dealing with the stranger in her midst and hating every minute of it.

My name again. And: "I said, 'Whose car—?'"

I look at Kyra and consider trying to explain the car's provenance in shouts. Not worth it. "Kyra's," I shout back. Casually. Shouting casually. Tough to do.

Pause. I can *hear* Mom thinking from upstairs. *Is he screwing around under my roof, right under my* feet? *But wouldn't it be stupid to admit that it's her car in that case? And my son is many things, but not usually stupid.* That's what she's thinking.

"OK," she says, drawing it out into uncertainty, designed to make me think that she's *not* OK with it, that she'll be down soon enough.

"She's pregnant," I tell Kyra. "She doesn't like coming down the stairs so much."

"Whatever." She shrugs, bored now, and looks around. "So, where do you keep your ammo?"

"Shh!" I jump up and close the door to keep her big mouth from causing problems. "Jeez, what are you trying to do to me?"

"Just messing with you. It doesn't *look* like an armory in here."

"Right here," I tell her, taking the bullet from my pocket and slipping it into the old hard drive case. "God, you're the only person who knows about the, you know, about the bullet."

"OK, OK, don't get your jockstrap in a wad." She stands and stretches, going up on tiptoe like some inky ballerina. "What's this?" She grabs a pad of paper from my nightstand.

"My sketchpad. I just doodle and write down dialogue there sometimes."

She flips through the pages in her hands while I flip through them in my mind. Anything embarrassing? Anything stupid? I did some nudes once, just for the hell of it, just to see if I could. I think I threw that pad away, though.

"What's the deal with her name?"

"Huh?"

She turns the pad around to show me a pencil sketch of Courteney in three-quarter profile and repeats her question: "What's the deal with her name?"

"Courteney's name? I got it from Courteney Cox."

"No, I mean the whole . . . It's like, Courteney Abbott Pierce DelVecchio. That doesn't even sound real. It's this WASP name and middle names with DelVecchio just crammed onto the back. Who has a name like that?"

"It's intentional."

"Yeah?"

"Yeah. It's like . . ." It really *is* intentional. I've just never explained it before. "See, I'm trying to contrast upbringing and . . . When we studied immigrants in history, there was all of this stuff about the people who were already here and how they looked down on people based on their names. It's like an upper-crust thing." I'm not explaining it well, I know, but she's watching me, intent, wanting to understand. Which is cool. "I'm playing with stereotypes. The idea is that she sort of married beneath her station."

"Like your mom?"

I stare at her. I never thought of that. The step-fascist's last name is Marchetti. In his own words, he's "a fourth-generation wop." He said that to me. He honestly did. Mom's parents claim they can trace their bloodline back to the Civil War. So did Dad's, for that matter.

Kyra grins because she can read my mind. I guess I would grin, too. She flops onto the bed and starts flipping more pages when there's a knock at my door.

I freeze. Mom calls my name. Kyra's on the bed. I want to tell her to get off the bed, but Mom would hear that and assume the worst. OK, no need to panic. She's on the bed, but I'm standing near the door. Six feet between us, easy. Act fast, so she doesn't think you've jumped up.

"Come in."

Mom opens the door and almost hits me with it. See, Mom? Standing right here. More than an arm's length away from the girl on the bed. The *clothed* girl. You're seeing this, right, Mom?

Yeah, she sees it. Her eyes narrow. Kyra looks up at her like Mom's a waitress and Kyra hasn't decided on her appetizer yet.

"I need to speak to you for a moment," Mom says to me, smiling with nothing like mirth.

CHAPTER THIRTY-ONE

IN THE BASEMENT, NEAR THE STEP-FASCIST'S workbench, I inhale gun oil and grease while Mom gets started.

"I cannot *believe* you did this—"

"Mom, please. Shhh."

"Do *not* tell me to be quiet. *I* am the parent. Did you *forget* that?"

"No." I look toward my room. Can't tell if anything's going on in there, or if Kyra can hear. I assume she can't because if she *could* hear, I think I would die of embarrassment. "I didn't forget. I was wrong, OK? I know that. But please please please yell at me later."

"You brought someone into this house without asking first," she goes on, as if I hadn't said a word. "You *know* how I feel about that. You *know*."

Oh, yes, I know. "Mom, seriously. I am *way* sorry. And you can punish me or whatever, but please, just not now."

"And then you—" She stops, grimacing, clutching her belly. "Oh, God, that's a hard one. Ugh." She shakes her head. "Your sister thinks she's Mia Hamm."

Half sister, I think, but now's not the time. "Mom, I swear to God I didn't plan this. She drove me home because I wanted to show her *Schemata*. I'm really, really sorry."

Mom leans back against the workbench and blows a little through her mouth, rubbing her belly. I focus on her face. It creeps me out to see her belly jump when the baby kicks.

"You showed her your comic book?"

"Yeah, Mom."

"I thought you weren't showing it to anyone yet. Not even Cal."

"Mom . . ."

She reaches out and touches my cheek, stroking one finger down to my jaw, and for just a second I'm seven years old again. I'm in the basement at the old house and Mom isn't pregnant and there's no Kyra and there's no *Schemata,* but that's OK because Dad is upstairs.

"I just want you to be happy, honey," she tells me. "I'm glad you have a friend you can share things with. But you can't have a girl in your bedroom with the door closed. You know better than that."

Oh, God, *this* again? "Mom, seriously!" I keep my voice down. I would not only die if Kyra heard this stuff, but I'd also be spontaneously resurrected just so that I could die a second time. "Mom, there's nothing happening. *Nothing!*"

She winces again as the baby kicks. She pushes against the workbench and huffs and puffs back to standing straight. Before I stop her, she grabs my face with both hands and pulls my head toward her and plants a kiss on my forehead.

"Door *open,* got it?"

"Got it."

She nods and waddles off. I wait until I hear her clomping up the stairs before I go back into my room. Kyra's sitting at the desk, sorting through rough drafts and half-finished pages.

She's absorbed in concentration, her tongue jutting out, a little pink afterthought.

"Hey."

"Hey," she says back. "Busted?"

"I guess."

"Do I have to leave?"

"No, but—" No. I'm not going to tell her that we have to keep the door open. That's just ridiculous.

"But what?"

"Nothing."

"You know what I think?"

"What?" I'm not sure I like the sudden devious look on her face.

"I think I noticed something mighty weird." The look gets even more devious.

"What?" I'm a broken record.

She holds up two pages from *Schemata.* Courteney's on both of them. "Notice anything?"

"No."

"Come on."

"What?" There I go again.

"Look closer."

"I *drew* the damn thing!"

"Try."

I stare at the pages. "I don't know."

She puts them down and picks up two more. More prominent shots of Courteney. "See it?"

"No."

"She doesn't look familiar to you?"

"Jesus Christ, Kyra! I *drew* her!"

"Look!" She shoves a page closer to me. "Look at her! It's Dina Jurgens!"

"No, it's not!"

But it is. Holy crap, I never realized it before! Courteney's a dead ringer for Dina. Aged a little bit, wearing adult clothes, but still. It's Dina. I don't see how I could miss it. I don't see how *anyone* could miss it.

"Everyone is influenced by people around them," I say, somewhat lamely. Kyra's smirking. She's not buying it. "You draw things that you see. People you see."

"*Things* you see," Kyra taunts, tapping one black-nailed finger on Courteney's chest.

"People you see," I repeat. Man, this is the worst! Thank *God* I never showed this to anyone at school. "Artists use photo reference and models and—"

"Models? You had her model for you? Or do you just *want* her to?"

Whoa. That conjures all kinds of images I don't have time for right now. "I didn't say that."

Kyra sighs and drops the pages back into the stack. "What *is* it with you guys and Dina?"

"I don't know what you mean."

"Oh, please. You all act like she's sex personified or something."

"Jealous?" It comes out nastier and colder than I intended, but then again, I'm on the defensive and in hostile, unknown territory.

Kyra isn't fazed by nasty or cold. "As if! You think I want that kind of attention? You think I want brain-dead jocks following me around like horny puppy dogs?" She sniffs and raises her head high as if insulted by the very idea.

I can't help chuckling. "Not much chance of that, is there?"

Her eyes narrow. "What's that supposed to mean?"

"Hey, look, I didn't mean—"

"What *did* you mean?"

"I just meant that even if you *did* want guys following you around—"

"What? That they wouldn't? You follow me around fine, fanboy."

That *bitch!* "We're *friends*. That's different."

"So it's OK to say your friends are ugly?"

OK, I take back the whole bitch thing. Mental do-over. Jeez, I'm screwing up left and right. "I never said you're ugly. You're not ugly." Don't ask me if you're beautiful. Don't ask me if you're beautiful. Because you're not. You're not ugly, but you're not beautiful, and if I call you pretty or cute, I think you'll probably kill me.

She leans back in the chair, considering, watching. I know how gazelles feel on the Serengeti, how the adults felt when they encountered the lions in that Ray Bradbury movie they made us watch in English last year. "You don't think I'm ugly?"

"No. *I'm* ugly." It's pandering. It's changing the topic. It's also true.

It works. Her gaze softens. "Why do you say that?"

"Well, it's true. I know it's true." And I do. Let's get real: This isn't a new face for me. I've had it my whole life and I have to look at it at least a couple times a day. I see it. I know. No one besides my mom or my grandmother has ever called me handsome. No girl has ever looked at me like she was interested. I'm not stupid. I know what I look like. I try not to think about it, but I know.

"It's not a big deal," I tell her. "It's not like it's my fault or anything. I can't help the way I look."

"You really think you're ugly?"

"'Think' doesn't enter into it. I'm talking objective, empirical truth." I smile to show that it doesn't bother me, my most successful lie to her yet.

"You're not ugly." She says it softly. I can barely hear her, so I pretend that I didn't hear her at all. It's what I do when I don't want to continue the conversation. It's easier to pretend you didn't hear someone. I don't want to talk about it.

But she won't let me off the hook. "Did you hear me? Did you hear what I said?"

God damn it. God damn *her*. I want out of this conversation. I want it over. How did we get here? "Fine," I tell her. "Fine."

"No one else matters," she reminds me. "If they aren't helping, they're just in the way. You run over everyone else, right?"

"Sure."

"So what about me?"

"What do you mean?"

"Am I ugly?"

It's the closest thing to insecurity that she's shown me since I met her. I want more than anything to tell her that she's the most beautiful creature on the planet, the hottest girl in school. It would be nice to tell her that. But she can always tell when I'm lying.

"You're not ugly." Which is the truth. She's not. She's not Dina, but she's not ugly.

"Then why couldn't I have guys following me around?"

I let out a breath, exasperated. Back to this again? "Oh, come on, Kyra!"

"What?" Tension evaporates as she blesses me with the ring-grin. We're on an even keel again. "Come on, fanboy. Tell me. Tell me how to get my own pack of drooling idiot-boys."

"You know how."

"No, I don't."

"Sure you do."

"Humor me, fanboy. Pretend I've decided to dye my hair blond and wear pink skirts and—"

"It's not *that.*"

"Then what is it?"

I glare at her in frustration while she just smiles back at me. She loves making me uncomfortable. What am I supposed to tell her?

"Come on. You know. It's . . . It's . . ." I'm getting cold under her watch. She's torturing me. "Come on, Kyra. Guys are . . . You know. Guys like . . . Come on, Kyra." I'm perilously close to whining. Hell, if whining were a country, I'd be checking my passport right now, just to make sure my entry visa was in order.

She shakes her head in disappointment. "Yeah, I know all about guys. I know what guys like."

I shrug my shoulders triumphantly, if that's possible. "See? That's all." I catch myself before I say, "You just don't stack up in that department," because it's such a terrible, terrible pun. Instead, I say, "Some people are just born . . . You know, just born . . . fortunate, I guess. Like Cal is bigger than me and better-looking, and Dina just has—" I'm not going to say it. Forget it.

Kyra throws her hands up in the air as if I'm an eager, stupid dog that keeps peeing on the carpet. "Guys . . . You guys are stupid about it. I mean, they can be pushed up. Or padded. Or pushed together."

"I know."

"Or *fake.*"

"I know."

"So what *is* it about this?" She points at her chest.

I hold back a snicker. Does she really not get it? She's my friend. I can't tell her this, can I? How would I? I mean, do I write a compare-and-contrast essay? *Similarities and Differences Between Dina Jurgens and Kyra Sellers.* First paragraph: Size matters.

I didn't say a word, but she's looking at me like I did. "You weren't listening. Weren't you listening to me?" She sounds pissed off.

"I was listening."

"They can be—"

"Pushed together. Or up. Yadda, yadda. I know. I got it."

She shakes her head. "No. You don't get it. God. If you can make them look bigger, you can do the opposite, too."

"What? Come on. What the hell does that have to do with this? What are you talking about? Why—"

I break off because she's just shaking her head, not even looking at me, looking down, shaking her head, and I realize that she's unbuttoning her blouse.

Oh. My. God.

CHAPTER THIRTY-TWO

THE DOOR IS OPEN. That's all I can think: *The door is open.* Mom could come back down. She could see. The door is open.

The door is not the only thing open.

Kyra's shirt is open from neck to waist, black cloth parted over a smooth, dead white stretch of skin, interrupted only by the sterile white of her bra. There's almost no contrast: It's white on white. It's nothing like the Victoria's Secret catalog or the stuff on TV, but it's better somehow. Because she's only a couple steps away.

She's still looking down as she undoes the last button. She doesn't look up at me.

"What are you doing?" someone says. An unfamiliar voice. It's mine, I realize. I don't know why I asked. I don't know what answer I want.

She shrugs her shoulders as if to say, "Beats me," but she's really slipping her blouse down her arms, baring flawless, alabaster shoulders with almost painful bones described under the skin. Something's strange. Something's different. Something's not right. It's my artist's eye. Noticing something for the first time. Something . . .

She looks up at me, holds my gaze, stares unblinking at me. I can't look away from her eyes, but with my peripheral vision I catch her hands moving, then the bra falling away. I swallow hard, like something solid had been caught in my throat until now. I cannot tear my eyes away from her eyes.

Yes, I can. I'm a guy.

So there they are. And this is what was wrong: proportion. The baggy shirts and blouses, her thin frame . . . It's all wrong for *this*. I mean, it's just all wrong. She's . . . they're . . . Wow. The door's open, but who cares? I'm burning memories into my brain.

"Not everyone flaunts it," she says, as if she's teaching.

"I understand." But I don't know if I do. I find myself taking a step forward. My fingers itch.

She sighs, and the sigh . . . Good Lord, the sigh! Who would ever have thought that such a simple thing, a simple expulsion of air from the lungs, could be such a . . . such a *magic* thing?

I take it back. She's beautiful. She is.

I take a step closer and she blinks; the bra somehow has come back together, squeezing, compressing, concealing. "You don't get to touch," she says.

"I wasn't going to." Honestly, I don't know if that's a lie or not. She knows, but she's not telling.

Nimble fingers button up the blouse, hiding away her skin. I feel woozy all of a sudden, and I realize that I'm uncomfortable *down there* and I sit on the bed, leaning forward awkwardly, necessarily.

"So, uh, why do you, uh—"

"Cover up the goodies?" She's sarcastic, caustic as she turns to me, all buttoned up again. "Maybe I don't *like* guys who are drooling idiots. Maybe I don't *like* guys acting like I'm in heat or something."

"That's not fair. Not all guys are like that."

"Really? You're a pretty smart guy, right? And your IQ dropped about fifty points a minute ago."

"You surprised me." Lame excuse.

"How? Were you surprised that I have tits? I'm a *girl*, genius. They come with the ovaries and the monthly visits from Aunt Dot."

"No, I knew you had—" Oh, jeez, I almost said it! And "Aunt Dot"? Oh, man!

"Well, then what surprised you? That they're *biiiiiig?*" She draws it out like we're talking about King Kong or something. She strikes a pose and a part of me can't help noticing that nothing jiggles or moves, and I offer silent admiration to the bra designer who figured that out. "Oh my God!" she screams in a falsetto, pointing to an imaginary horizon. "Look! It's Kyra's tits! They're blocking out the *sun!*"

"Stop it."

"Now, I know they're not as big as Dina's, though, so I can just imagine what would happen if you saw *them*. You'd go into cardiac arrest right there."

"Why are you doing this?"

She ignores me, pacing, angry. "All the same. All the same. It's so stupid. They're *tits*. Don't tell me you've never seen them before. You've been to a goddamn rated R movie. They're all the same. Why is everyone so *obsessed?*"

"*You're* the one who's obsessed. God, you're the one who's all, 'Tits this! Tits that!'"

"You looked!"

"You took off your bra!" Jesus, what was I *supposed* to do! "I didn't ask you to. I don't care."

"Yeah?" She grabs a page of *Schemata*. "You sure got *Courteney* looking nice and healthy here."

"So what? It's just a drawing."

"It's not just a drawing!" She stops and comes closer. *Too* close. A few minutes ago I wanted to be this close, but now it's like I'm being stalked as prey. She leans in. "It's *Dina,* isn't it?" She's almost whispering now. "Dina, Dina, Dina."

"Shut up." My cheeks flame, burning up. So what? So what if I like Dina? So what?

"I don't take gym, but I still have to go into the locker room, you know." Whispering. Whispering, but *loud*. "I've *seen* them."

"Shut up."

"I've seen them, you know. I could *describe* them to you. Do you want that? Is that what you want?"

No. Yes. No.

"It's not the real thing, but you've got a good imagination, and then you could draw her, or maybe that's in a later scene, maybe that's on a page you haven't shown me yet?"

"No."

"Are you sure? Are you sure there isn't a shower scene in your little love letter to Dina?"

"It's not a love letter. It's a graphic novel. It's *literature*."

"I have my camera phone. I can do *better* than describe them. I can take pictures."

Why? Why is she doing this to me? "Stop it, OK? Just stop it."

"Does it hurt? Does it hurt to be the big bad artist up here"—she taps my head—"and just another one of Dina's lust-puppies down here?" She reaches for it, but I grab her wrist, grab it too hard. I'm a skinny little nothing, but I'm still a guy, and I have more strength than her. She yelps with pain, and I can't let go. My hand won't work. She tugs, grimacing, but I'm like a lobster or something.

"Let go of me!"

"Fine!" My hand springs open and she falls back, arms pinwheeling. She crashes into my bookcase.

"You're a goddamn freak!" she yells.

"*I'm* a freak? *I'm* a freak? You're the one who flashed me! You're the one who offered to take pictures in the locker room!"

"Oh, please! Don't be such a prude! You've been checking me out every chance you get. You like to pretend you're different, but you're just like the rest of them."

"I am *not!* I am not like those guys! I'm—"

"What, an *artist?*"

I'm stumbling over my own words. I'm incoherent with anger and confusion. I don't know how I got here. I don't think she knows, either. "At least I know what I am! At least I'm *doing* something!"

"Oh, yeah, you're doing something. Comic book wannabe."

"Ha! Wannabe? You want to talk about that? You're a freakin' Goth wannabe. You're a Neil Gaiman wannabe. You're a *suicide* wannabe."

She freezes. Freezes like death. But I can't stop. I just can't. It's like she stabbed me in the heart and instead of gushing blood, I'm gushing every awful thing I can imagine.

"You and your scars. Please! You don't kill yourself like this!" I gesture, holding a wrist turned up to the ceiling, then pretending to cut across it with my other hand. "That's just a cry for help. That's just attention. *Everybody* knows that.

Cutting across just gets you to the hospital. That's just from movies and TV shows and stuff like that. You didn't really try to kill yourself. You just wanted attention, but you screwed up. Try harder next time."

The room goes loud with silence. Neither of us talking. Our chests both heaving, but no sound of breath. Did I really just say that? Did I?

"Go to hell," she says. She doesn't say it loud. Or with anger. Or with venom. She says it with exhaustion. And she walks out of the room and up the stairs and out the front door.

A minute later, Mom's standing in my bedroom door, her hair wet. She must have been in the shower.

"What happened?" she asks. "I heard voices. Did you guys have a fight?"

I look around the room. Nothing's really changed, but somehow nothing's the same.

"What happened?" she asks again.

"I don't know," I tell her. And I don't. I really don't. "She got pi—uh, angry about something and left."

Mom fixes me with her tell-me-the-truth look, the one that hasn't worked since fifth grade. "Did you say something? Did you *do* something?"

"No, Mom! Jeez!" I drop onto the bed and stare at my feet. "Everything was going fine." Kyra's naked torso has burned itself into my brain—I think I can still see it, like an afterimage of a camera flash. "Everything was fine. I think she hates me now."

She joins me on the bed, *whuff!*-ing as the springs groan at the preggo-weight. She puts an arm around me and makes me lean my head on her shoulder, even though I don't really want to. Her boobs are too big because she's pregnant and it's *really* weird being close to them.

"I don't know what to tell you," she says, taking on that tone that proclaims her adulthood and her superior wisdom. "But, you know, someone told me once that the opposite of love isn't hate. It's indifference."

"I don't get it." Never mind that love isn't an issue here.

"It just means that if someone hates you, they still have feelings for you. If they really didn't care about you, they'd just forget about you. They wouldn't even waste the time hating you."

Sort of like Mom hating Dad? I think about that for a second—is there a chance? Does she even realize what she's saying?

"I don't know, Mom. Doesn't make much sense to me."

"Well, what can I tell you. Women are complicated."

"Yeah. Hormones." Heard it on a sitcom once.

It doesn't get me a laugh. She just sighs, hugs me tighter, and says, "No. Men."

CHAPTER THIRTY-THREE

ONCE THE STEP-FASCIST COMES HOME, Mom disappears upstairs, leaving me in my room, where I indulge in some shocked crying for a little while. Crying is fine, as long as you're alone. It's not a big deal. I do it all the time. Poor me.

I shake it off after a little while.

"Other people are just . . . there." That's what Kyra said before. *"If they aren't helping, they're just in the way. Weave around them, knock them over, do whatever you have to, but get past them."*

Good advice. Best advice I've ever heard. I figure it applies to her, too.

I work into what I once heard described as "the small hours," fixing pages, Photoshopping, counting away the moments of my life on computer progress bars that go way too slow. I don't even bother with the Internet, except for a quick log on to check that Bendis is still appearing in a couple of days. All's well on that front. I don't even know the guy, but he hasn't let me down yet.

After midnight, I remember my homework and spend a couple of hours on genotypes and phenotypes, the Middle East, and Poe. I occasionally tap my fingers on the hard drive case for good luck and comfort, but I don't open it. No need. It's right there.

Before my eyes blur to complete uselessness, just before I

shut down, I make myself send an e-mail to Kyra. I barely type "I'm sorry" before I have to crawl into bed. I'm not even sure what I'm sorry about. I'm not even sure if I *am* sorry. But I send the e-mail anyway.

Just to make things perfect, I get an e-mail from eBay, telling me I was outbid on the *Giant-Size X-Men* #1.

CHAPTER THIRTY-FOUR

I'M ALONE. NOT LITERALLY, in that there are people around me, but for all intents and purposes, I'm alone. Cal's nowhere to be found and when I see Kyra in the hall, she looks away.

Wednesday. The word comes from "Woden's day." A day to honor the Norse god of wisdom and battle and stuff like that. The Norse always managed to mix violence up with their wisdom. Gaiman's book *American Gods* is actually all about Woden, which makes me start thinking about Kyra, which just pisses me off all over again.

I thought life at South Brook High was hell before. I was wrong. *This* is hell. No one to talk to. No one to look at. No one at all. I don't even have my bullet with me. I was up so late that I only woke up when Mom pounded on the door with just minutes to spare until the bus arrived. I never had a chance to grab it from the hard drive case.

I sure could use it, though. In English, Lisa Carter is wearing a skirt, but she keeps her legs primly crossed, as if she knows. And maybe she does. My eyes dart to Cal, who's ignoring me, staring instead at his book. Maybe Lisa knows. Maybe *everyone* knows. Maybe they've known all along and the conspiracy of silence is just to make me complacent until they decide the time is ripe to really bust me open.

I find my Panty Algorithm notes. It's a code I invented; no one knows what it means. But looking at it now, it seems suddenly, hugely obvious. As if anyone looking at it could tell instantly that I've spent the better part of my sophomore year English class exploring Lisa Carter's inviting crotch with my eyes. I tear the sheet out and fold it up, then quietly tear it into strips.

"Why would he do that?" Mrs. Hanscomb asks as I come back to earth. "Does anyone know? Does anyone have any idea why he would destroy himself with drugs and alcohol?" No one says anything. "Come on, everyone. He was enormously talented, a brilliant, innovative writer and poet. Why would he—oh, good, yes?" This last because I've raised my hand before I even know what I'm going to say.

"The question isn't why he did it," I say. "The question is why *not* do it?" Every eye is focused on me. I look down at my desk and the pile of scraps on it, all that remains of the Panty Algorithm experiment. "He didn't really have any friends. He never had money. His own family couldn't stand him. He washed out of West Point, and he was a great writer, but in his own time no one appreciated it. No one would publish him. So it's a miracle he didn't die sooner. Face it: No one cared about him or his work until he was dead."

When class ends, Mrs. Hanscomb calls me over to her desk. "I just wanted to thank you for your comments," she says, smiling. "You always have something interesting to say. I love the way you play devil's advocate. You really get your classmates thinking."

This has got to be a joke.

I am truly, completely alone, a fact driven home to me in gym. Mitchell Frampton's lip has healed, but otherwise nothing else has changed, including the precise spot he's chosen to hit me. When I lift my eyes to the bleachers, there's no one there. Kyra's gone, and I know what hell really is. I guess I always knew.

Hell is being alone.

CHAPTER THIRTY-FIVE

TERRORISTS HAVE TAKEN OVER South Brook High School. They—

No. Screw it. Who am I kidding? Terrorists are *never* going to take over friggin' South Brook High School. More's the pity.

So it's me. It's just me.

And I walk through the front doors like Keanu, long black trench concealing a pistol and a shotgun that I filched from the step-fascist's collection. The List is rolling through my head like a credit reel, and I'm taking them all down, all of them, precise and perfect in my aim. I wheel around, exploding jocks and tormentors and I—

And I—

And I wake up on the bus. Someone's been flicking my earlobe and there's some paper in my hair, which I brush out, to titters and laughter from the anonymous masses. My hand goes to my pocket—nothing. I forgot. I left the bullet at home.

God, I'm exhausted. That dream . . . That dream was *way* out of line.

Schemata. It's my revenge. It's my way out. I'll start out with this one and move on, and I'll win awards and accolades, and I'll have the revenge of never having to think about these people ever again for the rest of my life.

At home, I blow through my homework first, then move

on to *Schemata*. I'm so close to having this ready for Bendis that it hurts.

Tap the hard drive case. Feel the comfort of the bullet leaking through.

But while I'm working on pages and adding in cool Photoshop effects, I find that my mind keeps drifting. Sometimes I can't use the computer to draw; it's just not organic enough for sketches and light work. It's something like automatic drawing, I suppose—where you just let the right brain take over entirely and let the pencil do what it wants.

I lie back on my bed with a sketchpad and a soft pencil. I start out with a thin parenthesis of a curve, growing slightly thicker at its terminus. Then some feathering along the length of the curve, giving it dimension and weight.

It's starting to look like someone's back, as seen in profile. I frown and shut down the analytical part of my brain and give my hand free rein. Shadows start to gather on the paper. Then a "C," heavier at the bottom. Almost graceful.

It's definitely someone's back. Definitely a profile. A woman. But not Courteney. My pencil strokes out the line of her shoulder, lengthens her arm out, bends her elbow so that it comes up to partly conceal, partly distort the visible breast. It's a study; I should be using charcoal.

But I'm not really thinking now. I'm an observer. When it's really coming—whether it's art or story or both—that's what it's like. It's like watching someone else do the creating, watching other hands and hearts at work. And it's *easy* that way. It feels *great*. It's not like work at all. It just *happens*, and I blink and it's been hours and it's done. And it's perfect.

Like this. Like this sketch.

Yeah, it's Kyra. No doubt about it. A profile, which is weird because I never saw her naked from the side, but I know—the way an artist knows—that I got it right. From the sweep of her neck to the arch of her back to the way her body goes slightly concave just under her ribs before swelling to rise. She holds her arms crossed in front of her, obscuring her breasts, making herself slightly folded.

Her neck is perfect, vanishing into a morass of sketch lines and vague forms. How much time have I spent gazing at her face, and I can't even draw it?

And then, as if I've successfully completed some bizarre, ancient summoning ritual, the phone rings.

"It doesn't work," Kyra says.

CHAPTER THIRTY-SIX

I'M TOO STUNNED BY THE SOUND of her voice to respond. Wasn't it just yesterday that we screamed at each other and she stormed out of here? I find myself looking down at the sketchpad. Kyra, naked. Kyra, on the phone. I shiver. Does she somehow know? I didn't mean anything by it. It's just a sketch. It's just art.

"I thought you were pissed at me."

"I am. Look, it doesn't work."

"What doesn't work?"

"I'm reading those script pages you gave me. It doesn't work. The scene where she uses her powers on her husband and sees his fantasies."

"OK." I try to remember the scene she's talking about. "Look, can we talk about *Schemata* later? I wanted to say I'm—"

"There's nothing else to talk about. I got your e-mail apology already. I don't give a shit if you're sorry. I'm trying to make this graphic novel better, do you understand? And I'm telling you that the scene doesn't work. You've got her seeing that her husband has these fantasies and she runs off crying, all horrified that he has these thoughts in his head, and it's just bullshit, man. It's complete bullshit."

On the sketchpad, the lines and scratches that should be Kyra's head start swimming.

"I don't understand what you're talking about."

"It's like you can't imagine that she could *deal* with it."

"So, what, she kicks him in the nads instead of crying?" In spite of myself, I'm getting into this.

"No, you idiot." *Not* said playfully. It's like she really thinks I'm an idiot. "She *deals* with it. Why the hell does her reaction have to be emotional? Why does she have to break down or bust his balls? Why can't she just figure it out? Why can't she realize she's turned on by it? Or realize that her fantasies would be just as tough for *him* to see?"

Courteney's fantasies? Courteney doesn't have fantasies. What's going on here?

"Kyra, help me out here." I turn the sketchpad over—it's too distracting to look at. "What happened yesterday? Why didn't you e-mail me back? You had me thinking you hated me."

"Stop talking about that!" she yells. "God, you're so wrapped up in your own pathetic little fantasies that you can't even see what's going on in front of your face! This is a terrific graphic novel, but it has a problem and I'm trying to help you fix it! Do you understand that?"

"No. Why are you helping me if you don't like me?"

"I'm *not* helping you! I'm helping the *story*. God! You get . . . You get, like, ninety-nine percent of it. I never knew a guy who . . . It just drives me friggin' crazy that you don't get that last one percent."

"So tell me."

"After you came so far on your own? Are you nuts? And besides—I hate you. Fix the scene."

She hangs up. I stare at the phone, trying to figure out what just happened with one part of my brain while the other part parses what Kyra said. She's right, I guess. It's such a cliché to have Courteney freak out. There's got to be something else she can do, something deeper and subtler.

I'm about to *69 Kyra when Mom shouts down from upstairs. I trudge on up out of the dungeon to find her and the step-fascist watching something romantic on TV—I can tell by the way the step-fascist is zoning out.

"When is this convention thing?" she asks.

"Saturday. Like I told you last month."

"I was afraid of that. Look, I can't take you."

What? Is this some kind of joke?

"It's this baby shower this weekend. That's all. I have to go to it."

This *is* a joke. Some bizarre, messed-up joke. I look over at the step-fascist, who's actually paying attention, watching to see if I blow up, no doubt.

"Mom . . ."

"I know. Look, I can take you next time."

"Next time doesn't matter." I say it through clenched teeth, using all my willpower to keep from shouting. This can't be happening to me. God, a day ago it wouldn't have mattered; Kyra could have taken me.

"I have to go to this shower."

"Mom . . ."

"Don't start, OK?" Her voice goes hard. I see how she's rehearsed this in her mind: She breaks the news with contrition in her voice, offers to make it up to me, and I'm just supposed to swallow it. I'm just supposed to swallow raw sewage and pretend it's Evian because she says so.

"Mom, I *have* to go. I *have* to."

"There will be other conventions."

Which is true, but what are the odds Bendis will be there? And there won't be another convention around here for a *year* at the earliest. "Mom, you promised. You said you'd take me."

"I didn't know they were going to throw this shower for me. Look, these are the people I work with. I didn't even think they liked me. This is important."

That's it. That is *it*. "So what?" My voice jumps up, cracks. "So what? This is just a small thing, Mom. You can take me down in the morning and pick me up–"

She crosses the line from I Am A Patient Mother to Why Did I Have This Kid? "I am *not* driving all the way down there, then back here, then down there again, and then back here."

"It's only, like, an *hour*, Mom!"

"Yes, which is four hours after all the up and back! And that's without traffic, *maybe*." She winces and holds her stomach tighter, and I wish it would just explode already. "I'm not even supposed to be driving that much."

"I can't believe this! I can't believe you're doing this to me!" Bendis is slipping away. He's going to be an hour away from me and I won't see him. All my work, all my efforts, for *nothing*.

"It's not about you," she says, tired.

"It isn't? You mean it's someone *else* you're not taking to the convention?"

"I don't like the tone in your voice."

Tough titty, Kyra's voice says, deep inside. "God, Mom! This is the *one* thing I need! I never ask you for *anything*. This is the most important thing in my *life*."

"You always exaggerate. Trust me, you'll be *lucky* if this ends up being the most important thing in your life."

It's not an exaggeration. I may lie, but I don't exaggerate.

She sighs and turns back to the TV. It's over because she's the adult and she *says* it's over. She has the power. Or so she thinks.

I go nuclear. Full-on ICBM assault. Every missile in my arsenal.

"I'll call Dad," I tell her, dumping every last ounce of spite I possess into my voice. "I'll call Dad and he'll come pick me up and take me to the show."

She spins around *much* faster than a pregnant woman should be able to, her eyes blazing, her face twisted into a mask of horror. "You will *not* call your father, do you understand me?"

"You can't stop me!"

"I do not want your father here. Do you understand me? I do *not* want your father in this house! I will not allow it!"

Mom's got a pathological thing about Dad even *looking* at the house. He's never even driven down this street before. When I visit him, we meet on "neutral ground" at a bank parking lot halfway between here and Dad's house. I think of it as "getting furloughed" when going to Dad's and "back to solitary" when coming back, but I don't tell Mom that.

"You can't stop me," I tell her. "I'll walk up to the intersection and he can pick me up there. You can't do anything about that." And I cross my arms over my chest, triumphant over the seething, hormonal she-creature in front of me. Trump *that,* Mom.

"Don't you *dare* call your father," she hisses.

I stare at her, then I turn on my heel and walk away.

"Don't walk away from me! Come back here!"

Yeah, right. Chase after me, fatso.

The gamble pays off. Her yells follow me down the stairs

and into my room, then are cut off when I close the door. She's not coming after me.

I sit at my desk for a while, staring at the telephone. I just need to pick it up and call Dad. That's all I need to do.

I reach out for it, but my hand is shaking. It's not the idea of defying my mother. That's not it.

It's just that . . . It's just that it's "out of sight, out of mind," like I told Kyra. It doesn't just apply to my friends from my old neighborhood. It used to be that when I saw Dad for my one weekend a month or over the summer, he'd set his time around me. I was the most important person in the world. When I first had to move to Brookdale, I used to call Dad all the time. Just to talk about . . . anything. Anything at all. It was an excuse to talk to him because I never saw him, and Mom was always either miserable or angry or off being a newlywed with the step-fascist.

I would tell him about school, or about comic books I'd read, or something I'd seen on the Internet. But after a little while, even though I was talking to him . . . It didn't seem like he was talking back much. He sounded distracted. Like someone clicking a remote while the TV's on "mute," which, now that I think about it, he may have been doing. A lot of "Mm-hmm" and "Uh-huh. Sure" from his end. And I can remember telling him about how I met Cal, how we were going to do a comic book website together (this was a while ago; never happened), and I finished and I waited for Dad's reaction, and there was silence until he said, "OK, well. All right. That all sounds good. Anything else?"

I stopped calling him after that. It just didn't make sense anymore.

And then my weekends and vacations became Xbox and fast food between his dates, and . . .

So I snatch my hand away from the phone. The joke's on me, Mom. You get your way. I won't call him. Not because you don't want it, but because I guess I'm afraid that . . .

"This weekend? Oh, I wish I could. Really. I have something I have to do. Some errands. I'm sorry."

"Saturday? I'd love to. Oh, no, wait. There's something else."

I hit *69 on the phone, but it's blocked. Right. Kyra's dad works for the phone company. And I never got her phone number.

I stare at the computer, but I don't know why. There's no point to working on *Schemata*. I can't go to the convention. I can't meet Bendis.

My official bedtime rolls around, and as if by instinct I put the plastic up over my door and return to the computer. Maybe . . . Maybe Bendis will be at another convention soon. Not one as close by, but one that I could get to somehow. I can look into that. That's an idea, right?

No e-mail from Cal or Kyra. No instant messages. No nothing. It's like I'm persona non grata on the Internet.

I lay my hand flat on the hard drive case. I imagine the bullet's cool, brassy comfort floating up from within.

There's a knock at my door that shocks me away from the hard drive. I say, "Come in" before I realize that it's past midnight, turning in my chair just as the door opens, tearing down my plastic sheet and wrecking any future hopes of staying up late. Mom will *not* take kindly to this deception.

But it isn't Mom who walks in. It's the step-fascist.

My jaw tightens as he enters. There's no reason for him to

be here. None. The basement is neutral ground, but this room and the shower are my sovereign territory. I'm angry and a little bit afraid, too. I don't want to hear him lecture me about how I shouldn't have mouthed off to Mom. It's none of his business. I'm not his kid. I want to tell him off and let loose all the venom in me, but he's bigger than I am. And he's not like my dad; I get the impression this guy wouldn't think twice about smacking around a kid who talked back to him.

He looks around my room for just a second, taking in the plastic sheet, which now clings to the door by scraps of tape. I think there's the hint of a grin. He's got a rolled-up paper in his hand.

"You left this upstairs," he says, holding it out to me. I grab it like a wary stray grabbing a snack from an untrustworthy hand.

He looks at the plastic again and shakes his head. "I don't get you," he says.

I don't care. I bite my tongue and unroll the paper. It's a *Schemata* page, of course, an older version of a page where Courteney (who really does look *way* too much like Dina) is sitting in her car in a parking lot, crying, the memory of a student's abuse still fresh in her mind. Damn, Kyra's right. She cries too much.

"I mean, me and your mom've been together for six years now and I still don't get you."

This doesn't bother me in the least. I stare at the page, waiting for him to go away.

"I never got into all this school stuff." I look up. He's leaning against the doorjamb, studying my room as if seeing it for the first time, as if it's some amazing, ancient archaeological site he's discovered. "Never seen *anyone* read as much as you.

Christ, it's like your goddamn nose is *attached* to a book or something. I don't get it. Makes no sense."

He sighs. "But I see you with these papers all over the place." He points to the one I'm holding. "You been leaving that stuff all over the house ever since I met you. I don't know anything about funny books, but I keep seein' this all around the place, so I look at it and like I said, I don't know anything, but to *me* it looks like you're getting better at it." He shrugs. "Maybe I'm wrong. I don't know. Not the smartest guy in the world and haven't read one of these things since I was a little kid. But it looks like you're getting better. I don't know why you'd bother with all this, but I know that you work your ass off at it. You saw something you wanted and you worked your ass off for it." He nods. "And I respect that."

"So I'll take you to this whatever-it-is on Saturday."

A bullet to my brain. Electricity through my scrotum. A knife between the ribs. A crazed dog gnawing off my arm. *None* of these could surprise me any more at this moment.

"What did you say?" I ask him.

"What time does it start?" He knows I heard him the first time and he can't be bothered repeating himself.

"Ten. Line for tickets starts earlier—"

"OK. I got nothing else to do. God knows I ain't goin' near that baby shower. Make sure you set an alarm and be ready to go at seven. Get you there in plenty of time to get your tickets."

I just stare at him. Every mean, nasty, cold thing I've ever thought about him or said to him—though at the time they didn't feel mean, nasty, or cold—collides in my brain, fighting for space, laughing at me.

I respect that. Respect. He said "respect."

"Thank you" is what you're supposed to say here. That much I know. But I can't make it come out. Because it's *him*. The guy who knocked up my mother. The guy who's so *wrong*. I can't make myself thank him.

Respect. *Respect.*

"That's . . ." I can't say "thanks." I can't make myself. "That's great."

He nods and turns to go, then stops to look back at me.

"Y'know, you could be a little nicer to your mother these days."

In the past, when I would get angry at Mom and yell at her, he would yell at me on her behalf, saying stuff like, "Don't back-talk your mother!" and generally getting in my face. But this time's different. It's like he's asking me a favor instead.

"I know."

"I mean, you want to talk shit to me, I don't care. But she's your mom. She counts. And I don't like seeing her upset." He shrugs his shoulders, as if to say, "Listen or don't, I don't care."

"I'll try."

"She's the best thing to ever happen to me," he tells me, which I know is true, but it's weird to hear him say it. "Hell, she's the *only* good thing to ever happen to me. I don't know why she's with me."

"Neither do I." I wince. It just slipped out before I could stop it.

But he's not offended. He just thinks it over and then nods in agreement. "Well, whoever figures it out first, tell the other one, OK?"

"Deal."

CHAPTER THIRTY-SEVEN

WHEN I'M NOT IN CLASS, school's just an exercise in muscle memory: Go here, go there, hit the locker, grab the books, go somewhere else. The hallways are places to be tormented by the thousand indignities that high school gleefully visits upon the skinny and the weak. I get shoved, pushed, jostled aside, knocked into the wall, slammed against lockers, and pressed between dullard giants on a regular basis. I give people the benefit of the doubt and assume that they're just in a hurry and/or utterly clueless. The first time, at least. After that, they go on The List. Where they belong.

Seeing Cal and hanging out with him is usually the high point of the average school day for me, but that hasn't been true since our argument about the lacrosse game. I see Kyra in the hall a bunch of times, but she doesn't look at me, instead keeping her eyes down, her books clutched tight to her chest, both arms folded across them. It's like she feels naked, and I flash back to my sketch. Was that a violation? *Is* it a violation? It's not like I, like I *drooled* over it all night or anything.

Classes whip by like movie montages. And then the film breaks and the theater goes dark because I see something I never thought I'd see.

Rounding a corner, hustling to Trig after lunch, I see Cal and Kyra standing together near one of the water fountains.

Cal isn't doing his usual school-time routine with the poses and the physical attitude. He's just leaning against the wall, his backpack dangling off one shoulder. He's staring at Kyra very intently, as if she's revealing some kind of incredible secret, something too serious to greet with shock. Something that requires contemplation.

And Kyra . . . She's still got her books pressed against her chest. She's got her hip cocked against the water fountain, but she's standing like a kid who's been caught joyriding in the family car. She doesn't even look at Cal—her eyes dart around, as if worried she'll be seen with him. I'm not close enough to hear them, but I can't help watching her lips move, trying to figure out what she's saying.

She doesn't see me. Neither of them sees me, which both surprises me and doesn't surprise me. I've always considered myself something of an invisible man at South Brook. Unless I do something to attract attention to myself, it's like I don't even exist for most of these people. But if any two people would notice me, it would be Kyra and Cal. *Especially* when they're together!

I hug the wall and let people pass by me, watching. A few seconds later, Cal nods, clearly says something like, "Thanks," and walks away, his hands jammed into his pockets.

Kyra fidgets.

I have to know what's going on. Her walkout. Her call last night. Now this.

I fight my way through the press of bodies to the water fountain. Kyra looks up, grimaces, and takes a step back, only to find herself trapped between me, the water fountain, and the endless tide of students.

"Move." Her eyes are hard.

"No. What's going on here? Why did you walk out the other day? And why did you call me if you say you don't like me anymore?"

"Did you fix that scene?"

"I don't want to talk about that right now."

"Tough shit. That's *all* I want to talk about with you." She looks around for an opening to leave, but there's still no way to get away. "So move your ass so I can go."

"No. Not until you tell me what's going on."

"You want me to tell you everything, huh? You want me to tell you all my secrets? Why should I be honest with you when you're not honest?"

"I don't know what you're talking about." But I do.

"Yeah?" She tugs gently at the ring in the corner of her mouth, as if reassuring herself that it's there and that it would still hurt if she yanked it out. "You won't tell me your magical third thing. You didn't even tell your best friend that you were working on a graphic novel. You're a real open and honest guy."

Oh my God. "What did you tell Cal? What did you say to him? Did you tell him about *Schemata*?" That would be the worst thing *ever*. I've been working on it for years and I never said anything because I always figured I'd wait until it's done. I didn't want to show it to him unfinished and have him think it's lame. God, why did I even show it to Kyra?

"No, I didn't tell him about *Schemata*. I told him the truth."

"What do you mean?"

She leans in close. "I told him you're gay. And you've got a thing for him."

I want to scream "What?" at the top of my lungs, but nothing will come out. She has to be joking, right? This has to be a joke. But she's dead serious. "Tell me you're kidding."

"I'm not. Now get! Out! Of! My! Way!" Pushing me with each word, finally knocking me aside long enough to slip by and get away.

She didn't. She couldn't have.

Why would she?

And besides—I hate you.

Does she really hate me?

Women are complicated, Mom said.

I feel like an invisible man no longer. I feel like the *extra*-visible man. Like everyone can't help but to look at me.

CHAPTER THIRTY-EIGHT

I REACH FOR MY BULLET AND REALIZE—in sick horror—that I don't have it with me. I forgot it. I *forgot* it. How could I *do* that? This isn't like yesterday, where I was rushing to get ready and just didn't have the time. This is *ridiculous*. How could I be so stupid? Especially now. Especially today, when I *need* it?

There's no Kyra, no Cal, no one. I'm alone. Alone in a school of two thousand people, but I have *Schemata* and Bendis in my brain, right? Isn't that what matters?

And then it happens. The world, the universe, everything, just slams into me.

Cal is in biology with me; he sits three rows up and a column over, so usually he'll toss a grin or an eye-roll my way every now and then. But throughout the entire class he hasn't so much as twisted his neck even slightly in my direction. I stare at the back of his head, willing him to turn to me, then realize that if he *did* turn, he'd see me mooning over him like a lovesick . . . person who's lovesick. And that would be as bad as not getting the chance to talk to him at all.

Gay. She told him I was gay. Would he even believe that? Does it matter? If I *were* gay, I wouldn't care who knew, but I'm not.

It's the middle of biology, and that's when it starts; I can't tell if I'm glad—because I'll miss gym and Frampton's punching routine—or terrified because of the entirely different pain I'm about to endure.

I look down at my notes for a moment to make sure that I've connected two molecules correctly, and then I lose my eyesight.

It's not like in a movie, where everything goes black. There's a sudden patch of fuzziness that settles over my notebook, blotting all but the edges. It's like TV static when the cable goes out, only threaded with gold and red, shaped like some amorphous amoeba. At first I think there's something on my desk, and I swipe my hand at it, but my hand disappears as it passes into the patch.

I tilt my head to one side. The patch moves, following my line of sight. I can barely make out things on the periphery of my vision. It's like the reverse of tunnel vision.

A migraine. A migraine's coming.

My stomach tightens. This is how it happens. I used to get these all the time, years ago, when my parents first got divorced. My doctor said they were stress and diet related. Mom wanted me to go into therapy, but they stopped coming as frequently and she forgot about them. Honestly, *I* forgot about them.

But now I remember. God, the pain. The pain comes later. First, the loss of vision. It's like a herald, like a vanguard, an advance scout. I lose my vision and my guts churn. Soon the patch of blindness will start to shrink, and even though I shouldn't I'll feel relief that I'm getting my sight back. But once the patch is gone—in the very instant that I can see again—that's when the pain will hit.

I breathe slowly, trying to forestall a panic attack. Looking down, I can see only the extreme edges of the pages of my notebook: a molecule of heme on one page, a molecule of chlorophyll on the other. Don't ask me why, but for some reason I notice that the only difference between them is that heme has iron in it, little "Fe" notations. So maybe that's why science-fiction aliens have green skin: They're missing iron in their blood, so they have chlorophyll instead, which means that Brainiac 5 and J'Onn J'Onzz can photosynthesize . . .

Oh, God, this is going to hurt so bad. Do I have any of my migraine medicine at home? I can't remember. It's probably expired by now anyway.

The patch of fuzzy light has contracted a bit. Just enough that I can see to stand and walk—carefully—to the front of the class, where Mrs. Reed is grading tests while we all copy molecular structures from the board. I avoid even glancing in Cal's general direction; my face is probably screwed up into something horrific.

"Is something wrong?" she asks.

"I think I need to go to the nurse's office," I tell her, keeping my voice low.

"What's wrong?"

I can't tell what she's thinking; I can't read the expression on her face because there's just a blotchy welt of static there.

"Please."

There are benefits to being a geek, a goody two-shoes, a guy who's never gotten in trouble: She lets me go without forcing me to launch into some sort of explanation. Halfway to the nurse's office, the patch shrinks further and I take advantage of my partially restored sight, almost breaking into a run.

I tell the nurse that I need to go home. Right now. She

starts to ask questions and I gnaw on my lip in frustration, glaring at the slightly vapid expression on her face, and I realize I can *see* her face, and it *hits,* the pain, oh *God,* my head explodes no I *wish* it would explode because then the pain would stop because I'd be dead which is fine being dead is fine better than this my teeth come together *hard* and I groan and she looks at me like I've pulled a gun terrified and I throw my head back and I want to scream I hear her picking up the phone I want to scream into the world vomit the pain out through my eyes and my mouth and my nose and my ears there are spikes driven through my skull spikes with more spikes growing out of them and more spikes growing out of *them* like fractals ever growing into infinities of agony phone dialing she's talking to someone and she comes to me and her hands are on me and she sits me down and she's holding my hand and she strokes my forehead and I'm getting aroused I can't believe it my skull is rupturing from within like Krypton and it's stupid old Mrs. Hennessey and I'm getting turned on even though I'm dying just because something female is touching me and now I'm embarrassed on top of everything else—

"I can't give you anything. There's nothing in your file for medicine."

I don't *care.* Give me *something.* Give me an aspirin or a Tylenol or a goddamn *Midol* just put something in my body that has a chance in hell of dimming the bright, hard light of the sun that has blossomed inside my brain.

"Your mother is coming to pick you up, OK?"

Do the math. Do the math. Mom's office is in Lake Eliot. Fifteen minutes from Dad's house. And Dad's house is an hour from here. Do the math.

I can't. I can't do the math. My brain won't work. All I can think of is pain and arousal and Dina (thank God, Dina, yes, think of Dina) and Courteney and how aliens could have photosynthesizing blood, it could really work, it really could, maybe you could genetically engineer humans that way, too, and we could process our own food from sunlight and you'd save the world that way and I'm the first one to think of it and we'd all be green, a green world, green people, that would work, that's a great idea that's a—

I should remember it to tell Bendis.

CHAPTER THIRTY-NINE

INFINITIES PASS. UNIVERSES EXPLODE from their Big Bangs, expand and cool over billions of years, contract into primal atoms, and explode again.

Mom picks me up. I'm on a cot in the nurse's office, curled into a fetal position on my side, rocking because movement seems to lessen the pain, though just a little bit.

In the passenger seat, I resist screaming when she starts the car, the rough growl of the engine like claws in my ears.

"This is just like you," she says. "I can't believe I had to drive all the way back here. You're getting back at me for not driving you on Saturday, aren't you? This is your way of getting back at me."

"I'm sorry, Mom, OK? I'm sorry?" I'm trying to talk through a brick that's been thrown through my head. My *teeth* hurt. I can't even think. I just keep playing back the bass line to an Eminem song in my head. I don't know. It just keeps thumping there. "I'm sorry. I'm sorry." I'm crying now because I *am* sorry and because it hurts so bad and crying should make her loosen up, right? But she just stares straight ahead and hits the gas and we go.

At home, when I miss the next-to-last stair on my way to the basement and stumble, fall, and slam into a wall, she decides this isn't pretend. I've got the Eminem song mixed up with something from Outkast and those green aliens seem pretty cool, and then a BIG wave of pain crashes over me and I whimper, whimper like a puppy that's been kicked over and over again and she helps me into my room and then my mother is taking off my belt and I don't want my mother to undress me and thank God she doesn't she just takes off my belt and my shoes and unsnaps my jeans then makes me lie back and pulls the covers over me and I curl up again like a baby and rock rock rock back and forth because it feels a little better that way and I want to cry some more so I do I let it go in big wracking sobs that jerk my body and that actually feels better, the pain is more manageable until I *stop* crying–it comes back bigger and worse and angry, like how dare I stave it off even for ten seconds? How dare I? I was going to call Cal, really, really I was going to call him and try to explain about the lacrosse team and make us be friends again, but now it's all ruined how can I call him now how can I–

Mom puts a cool, wet washcloth on my forehead, which feels great and I start to breathe calmly and my heart slows and my body rests until a bead of water starts to run down my temple and it seems magnified a million times, like a boulder rolling down and I move to brush it away and the movement wrecks the rhythm I had going and I'm in agony again and I can't stop it and I don't know what happens next because I open my eyes and shut them immediately against the light and there are voices.

"Can't you give him something?"

It sounds like my grandmother. When did my grandmother get here?

"He used to have medicine for these."

"Don't you have something over-the-counter?"

"I can't find my Excedrin. I had a whole bottle that I never opened because of the baby."

"I'll go out for you."

Wham! Bam! Another wave of pain, a fresh dose of it, just to remind me, and I thrash on the bed, crying out, and a new voice, my stepfather's: "That's it. Call the ambulance. Take him to the emergency room."

"No . . ." I make myself say it. I force myself to form the words through the pain. "No hospital. Don't want hospital." Hospitals mean tests and doctors and beds and overnights and I need to be free, free on Saturday.

Someone puts something against my temple, the only part of my head they can reach, as I've turned to my side again. I feel and hear the scrape of ice cubes in a towel. My temple starts to burn with the cold. I want to die.

The lights go out. The ice burns until my skin goes numb, and then turns into a sharp, shifting weight.

I force myself to breathe regularly. I think of Courteney. I think of Dina. I think of sex, which takes my mind off the migraine pain and brings a different, familiar, manageable pain.

I hear the casters on my chair squeak briefly, coming closer to me. In the darkness, someone takes my hand and strokes it, gently, in perfect repetitions. The exact same time span between each stroke. The exact same pressure each time. The exact same path of motion. The pattern-matching part of my brain takes note and obsesses, and my head goes numb, and someone holds my hand as I fall asleep.

CHAPTER FORTY

FRIDAY STARTS WEIRD. Even weirder than the sensation of being a marked man as I walk through the halls. Even weirder than the migraine yesterday. It's almost like I've never recovered from the migraine, like some wiring in my brain blew out yesterday and is sparking and sputtering, shooting facsimiles of reality through my cortex.

For one thing, I once again have ventured outdoors without my bullet. Yeah, I had the migraine without it, but I *survived.* If I could survive that without the bullet, maybe I don't need it anymore. Why not put that to the test? So I deliberately walked out of the house without it in my pocket this morning. I did spend a few seconds stroking the hard drive case, though, just for luck. I'm dedicated and courageous here, not stupid.

For another thing, Cal is nowhere to be seen.

And for *another* thing, Mom is acting weird, too.

When I woke up this morning, she wanted me to stay home. But she didn't seem to understand that I felt fine. How much more obvious could I make it? Yesterday: drooling moron moaning in pain. Today: regular guy sitting at the table, eating cinnamon toast. I can't believe I had to make the case for going to school. Wouldn't most parents be *thrilled* to have a kid who *wants* to go to school?

In school now, I glimpse Dina heading up the stairs, my eyes and brain and everything else arrested and at attention. A sudden fear thuds in my heart along with the usual useless lust: What if someone finds out how I feel about Dina? What if Kyra blabs or Cal says something? I see myself pounded by more than Frampton, or laughed at as I walk by, or . . . Dina herself watching me with pity and contempt . . .

It's a weird day, like I said. I see her a lot. It's like someone's guiding us through the halls, toward each other. She's wearing a short denim skirt that shows off flawless sculpted legs, and a sheer blouse that looks like it would melt under the heat of your hands. Rich blond hair swirls down to her shoulders. I file it all away, knowing full well I'm obsessed. She's made it into my unconscious world, where I invented Courteney.

Or . . . wait.

I stop dead in my tracks in the hallway as Dina approaches from the other direction. Someone jostles me, pushes me out of the way against the wall. She's closing in on me. *Is* it Dina? Or is it Courteney? Which one did I create? Every curve of her is in motion, and I can't stop my mind from capturing those motions like a camera, and what if she uses her powers? What if she looks into my mind and plucks out my lusts and fears and projects them for everyone to see?

She passes me in a whiff of perfume, my thoughts no more obvious than what I fear is a look of abject lust or maybe puppy-dog love on my face. But no one's looking at me, so it doesn't matter.

It takes me a class period to finish shaking off the strange sense of unreality that permeates the day. It wasn't Courteney—it was just Dina. I didn't create her. If anything, she created herself. She created Courteney, using me as her instrument and her medium. I actually like the way that sounds.

In my classes without Cal, I feel terrible. In the ones *with* Cal, I feel worse. I don't even bother looking at him or for him. I go through the motions, hand in papers, take notes, but I don't care, not really, and I keep my hand down even when I know the answers.

I want to go to Mrs. Sawyer and apologize for the Tortoise Blight. I don't know why.

Instead, I trudge through to the end of the day, glance around for a glimpse of Kyra and one of her cars, then get on the bus so that I can go home, wrap up my preparations for tomorrow . . .

But first, there's dinner.

Mom is in one of her "We're a family" moods when I get home. The house smells like a Taco Bell exploded, meaning that the promise implied by the chili ingredients I saw the other day has come to pass.

"We're all going to eat *together* tonight," Mom says, beaming as if all's right in the world. And maybe it is for her. She's got her shower tomorrow and I'm going to the convention still, so she doesn't have to worry about that.

I can think of ten million things I'd rather do than eat homemade chili with them; I can think of at least *five* things I actually *have* to do tonight, but my stepfather gives me this look and I remember my promise to be nicer to Mom. Besides, I need one of them to drive me to the copy shop later, so I guess I should butter them up.

More than anything else, I hate being wrong. So believe me, it sucks when I sit down and make myself eat a bowl of the lousy, smelly chili . . . and find myself liking it. I've been forced to eat this stuff on a semiregular basis for years now, but this is the first time I actually kinda like it. Before I realize it, I'm gobbling it down, scooping up the sauce with pita bread.

Across the table, my stepfather pauses long enough to say, "Best batch yet," his voice a bit gruff. I think he's happy.

Later, stuffed with chili and pita and cornbread (it's like I've become an entrée), I prepare to make my escape downstairs for an hour or so with the portfolio. But I see Mom struggling to get out of the chair, and I guess all that food and the late-night talk are having lingering effects because I hear myself saying, "I'll get the dishes, Mom."

Mom looks like someone slapped her, but in a good way. She eases back into her seat, and I take on the task of rebuilding what was once a kitchen. There are dirty dishes, utensils, and pots everywhere. Every surface is filthy. Cooking is not a clean operation, it seems.

I get everything into the dishwasher first, then start rearranging things and wiping up the messes—anthills of cinnamon, crushed cayenne pepper spills, bean detritus. My rag gets dirtier than what it's supposed to be cleaning, so I start to sweep off the counter with my hand. Mom gets up and goes to watch TV.

I keep at it, working out the final details of my presentation to Bendis in my head as I go. Finish up page 20. Rewrite some dialogue. Sweep up that pepper . . . Rinse that rag. Print out a new copy of page 13 . . .

Suddenly *he's* at my side, grabbing my wrist hard, *too* hard, and I want to scream. "Hey!" I settle for a sharp tone instead, praying that my voice won't choose now to crack. "Get off me!"

“Just trying to help. You don’t want that in your eye.”

I realize that I had been about to rub my eye with a finger that had just been close to the crushed cayenne. He’s still holding my wrist, not so tight now, and my finger is an inch or so from my eye, which is already starting to water.

“Oh. Oh.”

He releases my wrist and shrugs. He looks at me for a few seconds, then shrugs again and steps back.

I guess I should say “thanks.” That’s what I should do, really.

By the time I turn to apologize, though, he’s joined Mom in front of the TV. Just as well. I suck at apologizing.

CHAPTER FORTY-ONE

I HAVE A PORTFOLIO THAT I'VE CUSTOMIZED, filled with twenty pages of the best work I'm capable of producing right now. And that's all I need.

It's Saturday morning, seven o'clock. I'm not sure if I slept last night or not. I know I turned off the light; I know I crawled into bed. But I can't remember anything until the alarm went off a minute ago.

I shower and shave and generally primp as if I'm headed for a date with a Playmate. I don't know what people normally wear to a comic book convention, but I think of this as a job interview of sorts, so I put on decent slacks, my dress shoes, a white shirt, and a tie with Astro Boy on it, just to solidify my geek cred.

And the bullet? Well, other than some longing glances and the occasional reassuring tap of the fingers on the hard drive case last night, I've been bullet-free for a few days now. It's a good feeling; a *strong* feeling. I decide to leave it behind today. I have to be as cool as Bendis. You don't bring your baby blanket to a business meeting, right?

"What if something goes wrong?" Mom asks nervously. She would be pacing if she could, but her feet hurt all the time, so instead she's sitting on the sofa in the living room, tapping her fingernails against the arm.

"Like what?"

"Just *something*."

"Nothin' ain't gonna happen." My stepfather comes into the room, yawning, mangling the English language, buttoning up his shirt.

"Mom, I'll be fine."

Her eyes flicker to the coffee table and the cell phone cradle there. I can tell that she wants to give me one of the cell phones, but the two of *them* have to have them in case she goes into labor or something.

"Do you have money to make a phone call?"

"Yes, Mom."

She grunts as her stomach moves on its own—my half-sister-to-be, getting in her morning calisthenics. "How much money?"

"Oh, for God's sake, Mom!" I plunge my hand into my pocket and bring out a handful of change. "Look. Fifty, eighty . . . a buck twenty-seven. I can make four or five calls with that. And I have dollars I can break if I have to."

She finally relents, and I march off to grab my portfolio, check my tie, and head out into the big, bad world.

Or, at least the driveway.

"Get in." I need to find a new name for him. "Step-fascist" is so appropriate, but I just can't bring myself to use it anymore. "Dad" is obviously right out. Mom calls him "Tony," and I just don't see *that* happening, either. Fortunately, there's only three of us in the house at any given moment, so it's not like we need signs or nametags.

He gestures to the passenger side of his battered premillennium Ford pickup, built in 1993, I've been told; "the last year Ford made a truck worth a shit," as I've heard over and over again. It smells like black licorice inside. I hate getting into the truck because I'm short for my age and the thing sits up so high that it's like rock-climbing. I struggle with my portfolio, wary of dirt and road scum that might mess up my clothes, and try to find handholds all at the same time. Eventually, I manage to fling myself into the seat.

Tony (I guess that'll be it, for now at least) fires up the engine before I even have the door shut and my seat belt on. I notice he doesn't bother with his seat belt. With a roar, we're down the driveway, onto the road, into the future.

My glee abates quickly—within five minutes, he's pulled into the local Stop-n-Go to gas up and get a cup of coffee. "You want anything?" he asks. I think about it. Does he expect me to pay?

Better safe than sorry. "No, that's OK. I'm not hungry." But now that I think about it, I *am* hungry.

He shrugs. He's not going to push it. He gets his coffee and we're off again, and I realize that I've got an hour ahead of me with absolutely nothing to do except sit in uncomfortable silence. I'm a little terrified that he'll turn on the radio and play some of that terrible grunge crap he listens to, the stuff that's as old as the truck.

I spend the silence planning my angle of attack. Bendis will be signing copies of his comics. There will be a long line, with lots of fans and poseurs and annoying people clustered around, competing for his attention. He'll be easily distracted and he won't really have time to talk. So I need to think of something that will make him sit up and take notice immediately. Something that will forge an instant connection between us and communicate to him that I'm not Just Another Fan. I'm a

Kindred Spirit. Something that will get him to spend the time to look at *Schemata.*

Along with the *Schemata* pages, I've got some of Bendis's books in my portfolio: a copy of the first volume of *Ultimate Spider-Man* and a copy of *Fortune & Glory*. Each is radically different from the other, yet each shows off Bendis's talent in no uncertain fashion. Which is the best one to have him sign? Which one will make me stand out from the crowd?

I unzip the portfolio. Tony is tapping his fingers on the steering wheel, keeping the beat to some song in his head. Traffic's light. I stare at the two books, wondering.

Then I see it. The *third* book. I'd almost forgotten it was in there. Of course.

Of course.

CHAPTER FORTY-TWO

THE CONVENTION IS BEING HELD in a hotel near the business district, a couple of blocks from the baseball stadium. I can see a line from two blocks away as Tony inches through traffic. I check my watch. I have plenty of time, fortunately.

I chew on my bottom lip, wondering how best to phrase "Just let me out here." I don't mind the walk, and I would drop dead of embarrassment to be seen rappelling down out of this piece of junk.

The truck shudders and squeals as it sidles up to the curb. "OK to let you off here?" Tony asks.

I blink. I open my mouth to speak.

"Just easier to make a left at the next block. If I go all the way down to the hotel, I gotta go around another block and up a bunch of one-ways to get back to the highway. You mind?"

"No. That's cool." I fumble with the door, opening out to city air, now mingling with the black licorice.

"When should I pick you up?" he asks.

I'm halfway out the door, my feet about to hit the sidewalk, when I realize: He's going home. He spent an hour on the road to get me here, then he'll spend an hour getting home, just so that he can spend yet *another* hour to pick me up, and *another* hour getting me home . . .

The convention closes today at five-thirty. Figure I spend an hour or so talking to Bendis afterward . . . "Seven," I tell him, hopping down and landing neatly. I half expect him to snort and tell me he'll be back at noon, he's got better things to do than haul his ass up and back and up and back all day.

Instead he grunts an "OK," and I swing the door, which won't shut because he's leaned over to hold it open. "Hey. You OK for food?"

I didn't bring anything to eat because I didn't want to carry anything other than the portfolio. A backpack or something like that just doesn't scream professional artist and writer, you know? And the idea of putting food into my portfolio, where a single accident could ruin my work, or end up leaving some kind of smell . . . No way.

"I've got a couple of bucks."

"That don't buy you nothing down here." He sighs and cocks his hip, lifting his butt so that he can get to the wallet in his rear pocket. Before I can say no, no, don't, please don't, he's handing me a twenty.

"Pick you up right here at seven." And then he's gone, merging with traffic, leaving me on the sidewalk with a crumpled twenty in my hand.

I feel vulnerable in the middle of the city with my tie and my leather portfolio and money visible in my hand. I don't want to take my wallet out, so I stuff the bill into my pocket and head for the hotel.

Walking those two blocks is like walking through the crowded hallways of South Brook High, only with greater ethnic diversity, strange smells belching from the subway system, and loud, raucous laughter that seems aggressive somehow. It's like there's a thousand anthems competing with a thousand dirges on the street.

But once I start to walk, it all falls away. The pulsating life of the streets, the fear, the aggression . . . It becomes background noise. It's not personal. It's not directed at me. It just *is*. And that's OK. I don't feel threatened because no one knows me here. No one cares.

I see kids my age and some even younger, threading through the adults on the sidewalk, dodging cars, hopping buses, and I think of how great it would be to live here, where you can take a bus or the subway somewhere instead of needing someone to drive you.

The line of people waiting to get into the convention is like a homecoming. I stand there, quiet, listening. I hear debates about the pre- and post-Crisis versions of Krypton, Joss Whedon's *Astonishing X-Men*, the way Grant Morrison redefined the meaning of "mutant" in the Marvel Universe before Bendis re-redefined it. And more. It's like being at the comic book store, only better: more people, different people, *new* people. I can't help smiling.

At last, I buy my badge and ticket and march through the hotel lobby. A hand-lettered sign points me to "The Banneker Ballroom," where the convention is roomed.

It's like hell and heaven combined. It's like a food fight without food. It's like home. *Real* home.

Thousands of bodies are packed into the ballroom, spilling into the hallways and jostling for position. There are two guys walking the perimeter of the room dressed as stormtroopers from *Star Wars,* and it's amazing how good they look. As they walk past me, blaster rifles resting on their shoulders,

I want to say, "These aren't the droids you're looking for," but they're gone.

My dad would love it. *Cal* would love it.

Kyra would . . . Who knows?

I just stand against the wall, taking it all in. There's an overweight guy sitting in the middle of the floor, thumbing through a comic book while people walk around him. I see a guy who looks like Neo, a girl who looks like Ranma's girl-type, a man dressed in a disconcertingly accurate Wonder Woman costume. But there's also a pack of kids who could have stepped off any elementary school bus, a man carrying a baby and a bag of comics, a guy in a suit. It's like the real world and geek world have collided. *Crisis on Disparate Earths.*

They gave me a program along with my badge, so I sidle up to a potted plant for company and flip through. Even though everything looks chaotic, there's a plan underlying it all. According to the map in the program, the ballroom is divided into two zones. In one zone you've got the booths from the publishers, where the creators sit and marketing guys give away crappy buttons and stuff. The other zone is where comic book dealers are set up, hawking their wares.

There's a list of guests—it's like seeing the credits from a lifetime's worth of comics all coalesced in one place. There are some names I recognize only from websites and interviews, names that Kyra chattered about incessantly. I look around for her, but that's stupid. She's not here.

I do some quick flipping. Bendis's bio has a booth number with it. Back to the map. I locate him, rotate the map to match my vantage point, and do some quick figuring. Then I plunge into the crowd, pushed and shoved and cursed and generally abused. Fortunately, two years at South Brook High and three years at South Brook Middle prior to that have prepared me well for such treatment.

Bendis's table is empty. There's a sign that says "Brian Michael Bendis," but nothing else. My heart slams against my ribs, hard. I check the program again. There's a note: "Brian Michael Bendis will sign at his booth from one to closing on Saturday." I check the program again; he's on some kind of panel in the morning, then lunch I guess. I should have thought of that.

It's not quite eleven yet. Should I go get something to eat? I'm hungry, but I don't want to leave the hotel, and the food here is probably expensive. And what if I spill something on my clothes? I don't want to meet Bendis while wearing my lunch. Or breathing it on him.

So I tell my stomach to stop complaining and I go to the dealers' area. Again: Heaven meets Hell. Too many people clogging the aisles, but the booths that line those aisles are like Mecca to a pilgrim. Endless lines of long white storage boxes brimming with poly-bagged comics, tote boards, and custom shelving and wire racks loaded down with comics and graphic novels. I see porn magazines displayed out in the open, old French science-fiction journals, pulp mags, battered paperbacks. Hunched over the white boxes, fans rifle through the stacks at blinding speed, pausing only to compare the issue numbers with the want-lists they've brought on laptops, PDAs, old notepads.

I kill time going through the long boxes like everyone else, almost gagging on the musty smells that rise up from the depths of old plastic-sealed comics. I can't believe the sheer amount of *stuff* there is!

Cal would go crazy here. The thought of it makes me sad, then angry. He'd be in his glory among all these old relics, these historical documents from the ancient 1980s and even older. But no. He had to engage in the rigorous, vastly more important activity of throwing a ball using a net strapped to the end of a stick. What a waste.

At the end of an aisle I stop at one booth long enough to switch my portfolio from one hand to another. My shoulders hurt and my feet are killing me. I should have worn kicks. I'm hugely overdressed.

"See anything you like?" the guy behind the table asks me.

I'm not buying, but to be polite I look around. He's got the usual long white boxes of comics, three of which are labeled "50¢ each," a real temptation to a guy with twenty dollars in his pocket. That's forty comics if you don't include sales tax.

Behind him, on a board that's high up to prevent theft, are the *really* valuable comics, pinned there through the archival Mylar bags that protect them. I scan them quickly, covers I've only seen in price guides and websites: a Superman comic where there are two Supermen, one red and one blue; something called *Showcase;* an old Spider-Man comic with a blond girl—not the redheaded Mary Jane—kissing Spider-Man.

And in the second row from the top, third book in from the left, there it is. Just sitting there like it's any other comic book.

Giant-Size X-Men #1.

I try not to stare, but I can't help it. It looks like it's in terrific condition. The background is a very bright white. The blues on Cyclops's costume are deep and rich. It's gorgeous.

I shouldn't even ask. I really shouldn't.

"How much for the *Giant-Size X-Men*?"

The dealer smirks. "Out of your league, kid." He's not nasty about it. He just makes it plain that he doesn't want to waste the energy taking the book down when there's no chance of a sale.

"Come on. Please?"

He yawns and plucks it down, flipping it to look at the backing board, but there's no price there. The comic is maybe three feet from me. Some part of me wants to lunge at him, grab it, and run like hell. Disappear into the crowd, then vanish out into the street, like Gollum grabbing the One Ring.

"Eight hundred," he says after a few seconds.

"Eight hundred? Are you nuts? *Overstreet* says—"

"Don't talk to me about *Overstreet,* kid."

"It's nice, but it's not Mint. Come on. It's not worth eight hundred." Man, this is crazy! Five hundred, tops. That's a fair price.

"It's worth whatever someone pays for it. And I'm asking eight hundred."

"I wouldn't buy it for that."

"What *would* you buy it for?" He's holding it right in front of me. I can almost taste it.

"Five hundred," I tell him, making myself sound as confident as possible.

"OK. Sold." He grins.

I freeze. I don't have five hundred dollars on me. I don't have five hundred dollars, *period.*

"Four hundred," I say, weakly. I don't know *what* I'm doing now.

He shrugs. "OK. Four hundred."

From eight hundred down to four? My head's spinning.

Can I call someone and get money somehow?

"Come on, kid. Four hundred." He holds the book out to me and gestures for money with his other hand.

Grab it. Just grab it. Disappear. Would anyone really be able to find me?

Of course, I'd have to escape through a crowd like packed tuna. While carrying my portfolio. Not a chance.

"I don't have four hundred on me." It's tough to admit it.

"Yeah, I know." He leans back, pulling the book away. "I was just messing with you. I really want eight hundred."

Great. So now I know what Pete Vesentine would look like if he were twenty years older and sold comics. "Can I at least flip through it?"

"Are you nuts? If you tear it or smudge it, I can't get squat for it." He carefully pins the comic up on the board by its bag. "Now, you see anything you can *afford?*"

I pretend to consider the box of fifty-cent comics, then slip away when he turns to talk to someone else. It's almost one.

My heart kicks into overdrive. Why did I waste time drooling over something I can't have when I've got a mission?

I head for Bendis's table. Just my luck—in the time since I've been gone, trolling through back-issue bins, a line has already started at his table, snaking around a partition, into the aisle, behind the booth, and into the next aisle. I resign myself to another wait and get in line. I should have just waited here. I could have been first in line.

Pretty soon some other people get in line behind me and I'm not the last person in line anymore, so I don't feel as stupid.

I've got the perfect book to have him sign. But I still need a hook. Something to say. Something that is quick, but immediately communicates to him that I matter, that I'm not just another fan.

As the line inches forward and around and forward some more, I think and think and think. What should I say? Should I just pull open the portfolio and go into my pitch? No. That'll take him off-guard. I need to make a connection first.

As I get closer, I hear someone talking loudly at the front of the line, then another voice in response: Bendis. I'm too short and there are too many people; I can't see him, but I can hear him. Someone is complaining, loud and abrasive. Then Bendis. I know it's his voice. It has to be:

"Yeah, man, OK, but that was *years* ago. Can we stop calling it the monkey sex issue? Please? Can we get past that?"

The fan says something pretty rude, but I expect Bendis to laugh because he always lets fans insult him and fires right back in his editorials. Instead, he just sighs.

The monkey sex issue. Yeah, the first chapter of *Forever*, the big story that revealed the truth behind the *Powers* characters. There was something about these prehuman superheroes having sex. I don't know why this fan is so pissed off about it. But that's my in. That's it.

"I thought that the prehistoric chapter of Forever *was an intricate and powerful examination of sociocultural sexual mores, with its subtle message disguised effectively by apparent crudity."* Yeah, that's it. How can he *not* respond to that? How can he not smile and shake my hand and say, "*Finally*. Someone who under*stands* what I'm getting at."

I roll it through my head again. Working on inflections. And wording. And tone. I get one shot. One chance.

I'm so lost in my thoughts that I don't realize why someone

behind me is saying, angry, "Move it, kid!" until I look up and see that there's no one else standing in front of me. I'm the next person in line. The only things in front of me are a table with a white tablecloth, and Brian Michael Bendis.

Meeting Bendis

So here I am. It's just me and Bendis and the rest of the world.

He's shorter than I thought he would be. Not like a runt or a shrimp or anything, but just a little shorter than I figured. Stocky, too. It's tough to tell that from pictures on a website, where they show one of those "author's photos" from the shoulders up in black-and-white. He's wearing a plain blue T-shirt and jeans. He looks a little tired, but he smiles when he sees me, perking up.

He's bald, which I've known since before I ever saw a picture of him—he makes fun of his premature baldness in his comics, and he drew himself hairless in *Fortune & Glory*. But it's weird to see a bald person up close—I never realized that there was stubble around the temples.

His smile starts to dip a little. I've been staring. I have a moment where I realize that my mouth no longer works and I can't speak and I'll have to use sign language or notes.

But then: "Hello, Mr. Bendis." Whew! My voice hits the right tone. I don't quaver or crack. "It's a pleasure to meet you." I shift my portfolio to my left hand so I can shake hands with my right.

His lips quirk as he shakes my hand. "I don't think 'Mr.

Bendis' is necessary, do you?" His first words to me. Do I call him Brian? I've never seen him called anything but "Bendis" (sometimes "BENDIS!" or just "B!") online or in print. I'll just avoid names.

But first I tell him mine and I realize I should stop shaking hands, which I do.

"Well, nice to meet you," he says. "Thanks for coming down."

"You're welcome." This is going great!

He taps a pen against the table. It's one of those silver paint pens, the same sort I used to embellish the portfolio. He's also got a black Sharpie. "So, what would you like me to sign?"

Sign. Right. The perfect book.

I open my portfolio, making a show of letting it fall open so that he can tell that I have artwork inside. I have *Ultimate Spider-Man* and *Fortune & Glory,* both of which I'd love to have signed, but no. It's the *third* book that makes this perfect. I didn't even bring it to have it signed—I just thought I might need something to read if I had to wait around or got bored.

I hand over my copy of *The Powers Scriptbook.*

Years ago, Bendis compiled the scripts to the first eleven chapters of his *Powers* epic, had his cohort Mike Oeming do some spot illustrations, and published *The Powers Scriptbook.* It's like a bible for me, an opportunity to see the inner workings of the mind of the master. I've spent hours with the *Scriptbook* and a *Powers* book side by side, comparing Bendis's instructions and panel breakdowns and dialogue with the final, finished product. It's how I learned to write a comic book. It's how I learned to improvise and to be flexible and to think visually so that the art carries the story.

My copy is dog-eared and damaged, the finish on the cover

cracked, the spine worn. I have notes scribbled to myself throughout. This isn't a collectible, like *Giant-Size X-Men*. It's a *tool.* An important weapon in my arsenal.

Bendis chuckles as he takes it. "This looks like it's been read a couple of times."

Laugh or don't laugh? I decide not to laugh; it's more professional. "I use it almost every day, when I'm working on my own comic." Wait! "Graphic novel. I meant graphic novel."

"Oh?" Something in his eyes shifts. I press on.

"I, uh, I thought that the first chapter of . . ." First chapter of what? My mind's gone blank. "The monkey sex issue . . ." Oh, crap! He *hates* when it's called that. "I thought it was a sexual commentary—I mean, a sociocultural—"

"Wait a second. Wait a second." He holds up a hand to stop me. "The *monkey sex* issue? You *read* that?"

"Not when it first came out. I read the *Forever* trade paperback." *Forever!* That's the story! *Now* I remember.

"Wait. How *old* are you?"

What does that have to do with anything? "Fifteen." He looks at me skeptically, and I guess I don't blame him. I'm small for my age, and skinny, and if I've shaved I guess I look a lot younger. "No, really."

"Do your *parents* know you read this?" He waves the *Scriptbook* at me.

"I don't know." It's the truth. I have no idea. My parents don't care *what* I read. I read all *kinds* of stuff.

"Because this is . . ." He stops, as if unsure how to go on. "Look, I mean, I appreciate that you like my stuff—"

"It's more than *like*. You're my inspiration." That sounded gay.

"OK. But look, *Powers* is really written for adults. I mean, you could read *Ultimate Spidey* or—"

"I read that, too." Should I show him the one in my portfolio to prove it? "I read *everything* you write."

"That's great. I appreciate it. I mean that. But I don't want you to get in trouble with your parents for reading something that's—"

"My parents are cool with it."

"But you just said—"

"No, really, they let me read whatever I want."

We both stop. I feel like I've been arm-wrestling. This whole thing has gotten off-track.

My portfolio is resting on the table, partly unzipped. I tug the zippers down the rest of the way. "I'd really like to show you something," I tell him, forcing my voice not to tremble. Best to cut right to the chase.

Holding my *Scriptbook,* Bendis watches with a helpless expression on his face as I flatten the portfolio to reveal the first page, the cover mockup for *Schemata.*

"What's this?" he asks. And before I can answer, he says, "I'm sorry, man. I really am. But I'm not doing portfolio reviews."

"I don't want you to review my portfolio. This isn't even my portfolio." Which we both recognize is sort of ridiculous because it's clearly *a* portfolio. "I mean, it's *in* a portfolio, obviously, but it's . . . Let me show you." I flip the page, a little aggravated because I wanted him to be impressed by the cover, but maybe I was a little too slavish in my Sam Kieth impression. He'll like the interior pages better; they show my individual style.

"Seriously," he says. "I can't do a review. I mean, there's a line like you wouldn't be*lieve* . . ."

"I know. I stood in it."

"Well, then you understand. I have to get to everyone, you know? I have to be fair. A lot of these people traveled really far."

"But I just want you to look at my graphic novel."

He looks at me sadly. "I understand. I do. I wish I could spend more time with my fans, but—"

"I'm not a fan!" Ugh. That was wrong. "I mean, I'm not *just* a fan. I'm a creator. I'm a writer/artist. Like you. See?" I flip another page. Courteney shrinks from a student as the kid's overwhelming fear of Grandma dying of cancer comes alive in three dimensions, threatening the entire page, shaking the panel borders. It's a really great page.

"I get you, man. Look, you obviously put a lot of work into this stuff, OK?" He's barely looked at it. How can he tell? "I really don't want to rain on your parade, but I gotta be fair to *everyone* in the line. If I looked at this now, I wouldn't be able to spend any real time on it. I wouldn't be giving it the attention it deserves, you understand?"

Despite myself, I find my head nodding up and down. Yes. That makes sense. The solution is easy: I want him to be unfair and screw everyone else in the line.

"Your best bet—seriously, I'm not BS-ing you here—is to find one of the editors at one of the publishers' booths and see if he'll do a portfolio review."

"But it's not a—"

He holds up a hand again. "I know. That's just what it's called, OK?" He grins at me. "That make sense to you? That sound cool?"

No. No, it doesn't. He's supposed to read it. He's at least supposed to *read* it!

He opens my *Scriptbook.* "I'm really flattered that my stuff has influenced you. I remember being fourteen, man. Frank Miller's *Daredevil.* God, I thought that was part of my *blood.* I would see it in my *sleep.*" He scribbles with the Sharpie, pauses, then scribbles again.

"I'm fifteen," I remind him.

"Right. I'm sorry. Did I say fourteen? It was still Miller's *Daredevil* for me." He hands over the *Scriptbook.* "It takes a few minutes for the ink to dry, so hold the book open like this until then, OK?"

What can I do? He's holding the book out to me. I take it.

"Don't forget your . . . this." He points to the portfolio, still open to Courteney's moment of terror, on the table.

Is this it? Is it over? All my work, all my time, for *this?* What did I do wrong? I don't understand what I did wrong.

I gather up the portfolio.

"It was really nice to meet you," he says, and he seems serious and sincere. I want to shake his hand again, but both of my hands are filled.

Say something! It sounds like Kyra's voice in my head. But I can't think of anything to say. And he's already looking over my shoulder, making eye contact with the person behind me.

I step out of line.

I've met Bendis.

CHAPTER FORTY-THREE

I'M CONFUSED. MY HEAD'S BUZZING with crowd noise and befuddlement. What happened? How did I botch it so badly? It was so simple: Shake his hand, introduce myself, make a connection, show him *Schemata*. And bang, that's it! Simple.

I don't get it. I'm the smartest kid in my school. How did I mess this up?

I'm numb as I head to the bathroom. I feel like something's going to happen and I don't want to be in public when it does. I struggle with the door, my hands occupied with the portfolio and the book. I shove the book into the portfolio, zip it up, and go into the bathroom, which is, thankfully, unoccupied.

I'm trembling as my stupid, ugly face floats into view in the mirror.

"What did you do?" I whisper. I'm snarling at myself. "What did you *do*? You didn't do anything right. Not a single thing. You messed up your one chance. You dumb, ugly piece of crap. No wonder no one wants to be your friend. No wonder everyone hates you." I'm starting to tear up. I wipe my eyes so hard that it hurts. "Don't cry. You little baby. Little momma's boy. Don't cry. It's your fault. It's your fault and no one else's."

The door opens and two guys walk in, punching each other in the shoulder and talking about some girl in an Elektra costume. Heading straight for the urinals, they don't even look at me, but I feel like I've been caught red-handed. I've been found out as a crying loser, hiding in the bathroom. I wipe my face with some paper towels, then wash my hands in scalding hot water because public bathrooms are just about the grossest places you can imagine.

I check my watch as I leave the bathroom—after spending an hour in line and then talking to Bendis, it's close to three. I have *hours* to wait for Tony.

Bendis said to go to an editor. I kill another hour or so wandering the convention floor, but every publisher booth I walk by is packed, busy, and I can't tell who's an editor and who isn't. And they all look like they have too much to do. Why would they want to look at my pages, anyway? Why should they be different from anyone else?

"Hey."

I look around. Me?

"Hey, when do you see him?"

Still looking around. It's packed in here. I can't even—

God.

Kyra.

CHAPTER FORTY-FOUR

My heart doesn't exactly soar at the sight of her, but *something* happens in my chest, some kind of strange, electric hiccup, like when I suddenly remember good news.

Surprise, surprise, she's all in black. Not so much *wearing* black as swaddled in it—a black poncho that looks like you could make a parachute out of it, along with black leggings and the ever-present black boots. Her arms are bare, poking out at angles from under the poncho as she plants her fists on her hips.

"Well?" she asks again. "When do you see him?"

I can't focus on anything but the way her lips—curves of coal—move as she speaks. The photo-negative smiley face hangs on a thread around her neck. "See who?"

"Bendis, you moron."

"He's—I—" How do I tell her this? And why? What the hell is she even doing here? "I can't hear you," I lie, stalling for time. We're in the middle of an aisle, with people shoving and pushing and shouting all around us, so she rolls her eyes and grabs my wrist hard enough to hurt, then drags me off to a quiet spot near the bathroom.

"When do you see Bendis?" Her voice and her eyes tell me that she's tired of asking.

"Why are you here? I thought you were pissed at me."

"What makes you think I'm here for you?" She runs a hand through her hair, which is brushed entirely to the left, so that it falls over one eye and half her face. "Maybe I'm here to see someone."

I run through the list of creators in my head. "Nah. There's no one here you want to see that badly."

"You're right. And I'm *more* than pissed at you." She pokes me in the chest. "But I *love* your graphic novel and I want to be here when history happens. So when do you see him? He's got a long line. I saw it already."

"Yeah. I know. I saw him already."

"You did?" Her eyes shine and she leans toward me, and suddenly all I can think about is the other night, in my room, when she took off her bra. I don't know how to think or talk anymore. What's wrong with me?

"I saw him," I hear myself say. "He turned it down." And now we can talk, she and I. We can work out whatever's going on—

"He *what?*" She jumps back from me, her face twisted in anger. "He *rejected* it?"

"Hold on. He didn't really reject it. He didn't even see it."

She shakes her head; she looks like someone just slapped her across the face for no reason. "Didn't *see* it? He didn't even *look* at it?"

"He said he—"

"What kind of dickhead *is* he?"

"He's not a—"

"I mean, what kind of a complete idiotic *dickhead* is he? Not to even look at it? What a dick!"

Now, here's the weird part: All of a sudden, I don't *care* about *Schemata*. I don't care about Bendis. All I care about is the utterly stricken look on Kyra's face, the way she's flushing just slightly pink (I don't think even a full rage could color her cheeks much more than that), the way her eyes dart around like she's looking for an enemy. I just want her to calm down, to breathe regularly again, to stop saying "murder" with her body language.

I reach out for her hand. "Kyra, let's go to—"

"Back off!" she hisses, smacking my hand away. "Don't touch me, you freak."

"I thought—"

"You still don't get it. Fine. I don't give a shit. I'm not here for *you,* dumb-ass. I'm here for *that.*" She points at the portfolio. "I'm here because it's *better* than you. And I can't believe that asshole doesn't get it."

She spins on a heel and takes off. I don't even stop to think about it—I follow right after her. "Kyra! Hey, Kyra! Come on!"

She ignores me, but the older teens and adults in the crowd find it funny. I hear a couple of *How cute*s and some *Lookit 'er go!*s and one guy nudges me as I push past him and says, "Are ya *sure* you wanna catch her, kid?" to the laughter of those around him. Me, I just keep my focus on Kyra. The black clothes makes it easy—just follow the dark bead shoving its way through a sea of comic-book-fan-flesh.

After a minute I notice that she's headed out of the dealer zone and into the publisher zone. She weaves past a small press table, ignoring the guy who tries to hand her a mini-comic. I'm on her tail; I know where she's headed.

"Hey, Bendis!" she shouts, and the noise level is too high for him to hear her, thank God.

"Kyra!" I'm closer to her than she is to Bendis. I know she

can hear me, but she's ignoring me like she ignored Mini-Comic Man. "Kyra!"

"Bendis!" she shouts again, this time closer to him. People start to turn her way, some jumping out of the way of the ghostly girl in black who moves with fury.

"Dickhead!" she bellows. "You stupid dickhead!"

"Kyra! Oh my God!" I scream. I can't believe it. I can't believe it!

Bendis looks up, turning from the comic he's signing. Kyra hurls a battery of expletives at him—in the aisles, some of the fanboys laugh, some turn away, and parents clap hands over their kids' ears.

"Kyra, don't do this!" I beg her. If I could get to her, I'd put my hand over her mouth.

"You stupid piece of shit!" Kyra rants, and Bendis, who at first was grinning like he thought this was some kind of prank, is now changing his tune. Kyra's facing away from me, so I don't know what her expression is, but something on it has told Bendis that this isn't a joke.

"Look, can you keep it down?" He starts off calm, smiling comfortingly. But he doesn't know Kyra.

"Keep what down, asshole?" She's at the table now, and I'm almost there with her. Just a few more seconds. "Keep what down? I'm supposed to just let you be a dick? You don't know genius when you see it? You don't know quality when you see it?"

The crowd at Bendis's table can't decide which way to move: get in closer to see the action, or back the hell away from the lunatic chick in black? The subsequent shoving and foot-shuffling keeps me away from Kyra for a few more precious seconds.

"I don't know what you're talking about," Bendis says, still sitting, trying to keep things calm.

But it's like Kyra can't hear him. "What does it take to get your attention? What does someone have to do? What does it take?"

I break through the crowd and make eye contact with Bendis for just a second as I reach out to grab Kyra's arm, but it's too late.

"What does it take?" she screams. "Does it take this?" And she grabs the hem of her poncho and hikes it up over her head, and even from behind I can tell that she's not wearing anything underneath.

So, yeah, that's it. My life's over.

CHAPTER FORTY-FIVE

THERE'S A HEARTBEAT'S WORTH OF SILENCE from the crowd, and then a chaos of reactions—laughter, applause, some whistles, some cheers. Bendis is up and out of his chair in a half-second, holding his hands out like someone trying to ward off a monster in a horror movie.

"Yeah, that's it!" he says. "That's it! I'm outta here!" And he backs up, almost falls over his chair, then turns and darts away through the booths.

Kyra drops the poncho back into place. "Yeah, you saw *that,* didn't you?" Her voice cracks as she screams after him. "You got a good goddamn look at *that,* didn't you? Got an eyeful, right? Right?"

Me? I'm just standing there. It's like the world's a blur of color and motion, just spinning and churning around me. The line for signatures at Bendis's booth starts to grumble as one. Someone says, "Dude, I don't think he's coming back."

The chunk of Kyra's naked back that I saw tunnels through my brain. Smooth and sleek and colorless. Taut skin over bone. I saw the bumps of her spine at the small of her back. They're sketched in my mind now.

"It was her!" someone says. "That girl."

I realize that I'm standing next to Kyra and people are

pointing at us as a big black guy wearing a blue jacket with a walkie-talkie presses through the crowd. He's wearing a badge that says "Security" and a mean, mean look on his face.

I can't believe it. I'm going to get arrested. She got me *arrested!*

Kyra grabs my hand and pulls. Next thing I know, we're squirting through the crowd, ducking under people's arms, squeezing between bodies. I'm damp with sweat—my own and some sponged off smelly fans. My portfolio keeps getting caught in the crowd and I pull at it, tugging, worrying about damaging the pages inside, but they're copies and I can always make more.

My wrist slips free from Kyra, but I keep pushing onward, following the outrage she leaves in her wake. She's stomping on feet, shoving grown men—at one point, I hear her shout, "Hands off, you goddamn mutant!"

I keep up a steady stream of *excuse me*s and *I'm sorry*s as I cut through after her. I lose sight of her, then emerge from the crowd near the door to the lobby.

Kyra's walking through the lobby. Her convention badge is on the floor near me. I pick it up and run after her. "Kyra! Hey! Wait!"

She doesn't slow down at all. I chase her outside, where she's stopped by a trash can. Her hands are shaking as she tries to light a cigarette.

"What the hell was that all about? What were you *thinking?*"

"Leave me alone." She can't get the lighter and the end of the cigarette to meet up.

"You can't—"

"Get out of my face." Her voice is rising. People start to look in our direction.

"Not so loud," I tell her.

"Don't tell me what to do!" her voice goes higher and louder.

"Please, not in public. Don't make a s—"

"Don't tell me what to do! You stay the hell away from me!" She clenches her hands into fists, crushing the cigarette. "Get off my back!"

"Please, please, not so loud. Let's go inside and—"

"Shut up!" she shrieks, her face a screwed-up, twisted mass of rage, and then *my* face hurts suddenly, and I realize that she hit me. Not a slap, not really—she whaled at me. I felt the knuckles and everything. It almost knocked me over.

"What the hell are you *doing?*"

But she's gone, a whirl of black fabric vanishing up the street.

A guy in his twenties, walking by with a woman the same age, says, "Nice technique, kid," and laughs. I force myself to stand my ground, tamping down the anger burning in my gut. Because otherwise I'd launch myself at the guy and he'd kill me. But if sheer anger could kill on its own, he would have exploded, and there'd be nothing left of him but blood and memories.

The show is still going on. I go back into the hotel, but I can't bring myself to go back inside the convention room. Everyone saw me with Kyra. They know who I am. They know I chased Bendis away.

I can't go home without my ride, and I don't want to call Tony for a favor, so I sit in the lobby, away from the smells and the heat and the noise and the possibility of arrest. Bendis signed the inside front cover of my *Scriptbook:* "Keep at it, you'll make it!" with a little cartoony doodle of himself giving a thumbs-up.

Unreal. Unbelievable. Is that supposed to make me *feel* better? I don't want a pat on the back—I want to publish my graphic novel! I'm not some little kid who's drawn the family dog with crayons. I've spent every waking moment on this thing. I've done *research.*

An hour later, the show closes for the day. Everyone filters out, and soon I'm one of the only people in the lobby. I'm ready to walk up a couple of blocks and wait for Tony when I see Bendis out of the corner of my eye. He's pacing, jittery, like he's filled with nervous energy.

From nowhere, four other people approach him. He laughs and shakes some hands, gives a couple of them hugs. I recognize the guy who writes *Flash,* the artist who draws *Ultimate Iron Man,* the writer who brought back Phoenix after Grant Morrison killed her. They all stand around laughing.

It's like in school. It's just like school.

"—won't believe what happened today—" Bendis says.

"The girl?" someone else says. "I heard about that."

"Crazy. Crazy shit."

"Like one of your books."

"Like one of *your* books, maybe!" And they all laugh.

"—grab something to eat?" Bendis again.

"Not the same place as last night," someone answers.

"God, no. That place was—"

"—good *seafood—*"

"Sure, but what about a steak or—"

"—don't care as long as it's not *here!*"

They all laugh.

They laugh.

Friends, standing together in the lobby. Friends who get to do whatever they want.

I hate them.

That's it; I hate them all.

Bendis is on The List.

CHAPTER FORTY-SIX

TONY DOESN'T SAY ANYTHING the whole way home, which is good because I think I'd probably jump out of the truck into traffic if I had to talk. I stare straight ahead through the windshield, trying to decide if it's me or him. Me or Bendis. I don't know. I can't figure it out. Maybe *Schemata*'s no good. Maybe it sucks and he just didn't want to tell me.

But Kyra liked it. Kyra liked it enough to go ballistic and flash Bendis.

But Kyra doesn't like *me*.

But . . .

I don't know. I don't know.

We get home and I charge into the house and downstairs. I don't know and I don't *care* anymore. I was supposed to *win* today. I was supposed to have my way for once, just for once in my life. I did everything right. I did a great story and I brought it to the perfect person and I got *nothing* for it. And now I have to go back to school and look at everyone and be a failure and stay that way.

I throw the portfolio across the room.

I want to kill them all. No, better yet, I want to die. No, even better than that: I want to kill them and *then* die. I thought high school was the end of it, the end of the bullshit cliques and the groups and kewl kids. But it's not. It's just the beginning. It's just the beginning and it only gets worse from here. College won't be any better and *after* college won't be any better and I might as well finish it. Finish it *now*. There's no point. I'll always be a loser. I'll never have friends, *real* friends, friends I can keep. No one will ever care. My mother will have her baby and my father will get married someday and it'll be like I was never here, and that's better for them all, it's better for them that I go now, that I leave now, it's easier that way because I'll never be *anything* and I'll never be *anyone* and I'll always be a virgin and I'll never kiss a girl even and who can blame them, I'm just a skinny, ugly freak and I don't blame them, I don't blame a single one of them.

I'm crying by now, not little tears that make quiet trails—big, angry tears, sobs that other people could hear if anyone else were downstairs.

I need my bullet.

I need it.

I look for it. Where did I leave it? On the desk. Hard drive case. That's right. But it's not in there. I toss aside the keyboard, scrounge around behind the monitor. I move the printer, look inside it. Nothing. Down on my hands and knees, snorting down tears and snot, too occupied to cry now, looking under the desk, back where it meets the wall, did it fall behind . . . ?

No. It's gone. Where the hell is my bullet?

When was the last time I saw it? Jeez, it's been . . . Yesterday I was busy all day at school and I was so stressed about getting ready for the conference I didn't even take it anywhere with me. Which is weird because normally when I'm stressed I need it, but I've needed it less since I met—

And wait a sec. Thursday . . . Thursday I had the migraine, but I didn't have it on me then, either.

Wednesday was so busy and I was trying to figure out—

So, where

—what was going on with Kyra—

So, where do you

What?

So, where do you keep

What? Where do I keep . . . Where do I keep my bullet?

The phone rings.

In the hard drive case, but it's not—

My mom yells for me.

I'm sitting on the floor, half under my desk, trying to remember what I did with it, trying to remember—

She yells again.

"What?" I scream it. I'm humming with adrenaline. A half-second ago, I was ready to . . . I don't know what. Kill someone? Would I have done that? Where would I have gotten a gun, even if I could find the bullet?

"Telephone!" my mom bellows back.

You're kidding. I grab the phone. "Hello?"

From the other end: "Guess who?"

CHAPTER FORTY-SEVEN

I SWALLOW HARD. My heart's pounding and my breath is coming too fast. I lean against my desk as my body slowly comes down from whatever pumped-up high it was on. Mom hangs up the extension.

"Hey," I say. "Hey. How, uh, how are you?" Casual and cool, that's me.

"I had a *really* lousy day."

I can't help it—I laugh. Not too loud and not too long, but I laugh anyway.

"You think that's *funny?*"

"No! No, not at all. It's just that my day sucked, too."

"Want to talk about it?" Cal asks.

And I *do*. But not with him. Not now. I've never told him about *Schemata,* never revealed that part of myself. I *will,* but I'm not ready just yet.

"No. Not now. What happened to you?"

He sighs, heavy and sad through the phone line. "It's about the playoffs."

Right. Lacrosse playoffs. Who cares? I remind myself: Cal does, for some reason. "I guess you guys lost?"

"Not exactly."

"I don't get it."

"Neither do I."

It turns out that a few of the guys on the lacrosse team were—big surprise—not exactly academic geniuses. No shock there, but apparently they were failing a couple of classes each. Normally, this would disqualify them from the team. It's automatic—when the grades go into the computer, it spits out a report of who's eligible and who isn't.

But someone—probably not the flunkers in question, who would lack the smarts—changed the grades in the computer. This was discovered late Friday night, probably as I was helping to clean up the chili dishes. Dr. Goethe, the principal, happened to be talking to a teacher who had flunked one of the players. The teacher didn't realize that the student had failed another class, too, but Dr. Goethe seemed to remember *another* teacher complaining about the same student. So he went back to the paper records and found some F's, and then he compared them to the computer and saw D's, and then he got *really* ambitious and checked the whole team, staying up late in the night, alone in the darkness of his office, painstakingly double-checking the grades of every player on the team. (OK, I added the details about late in the night and all that—it sounds better that way.)

The next morning, he reported his results to the people who run these things (like I know) and the rest is history.

"The whole team's on probation," Cal says, his depression like a liquid, moving *thing* that can crawl through the phone line. "They revoked every single win we had back to the beginning of the season and we had to forfeit today's game and every game through the end of the year."

I try to care, but it's tough. A bunch of Jock Jerks finally sowed what they'd reaped (or reaped what they'd sown, whichever). I have difficulty summoning pity. I feel something like glee instead. Behold the awesome power of The List!

But Cal cares. It's tough to be too gleeful at the downfall of the South Brook High Lacrosse Team when it means Cal's miserable.

"I'm sorry," I tell him, and I do my best to mean it.

"Yeah. It sucks."

Silence. We just sit on the phone, breathing together. I feel warm and whole. I had forgotten how much our friendship meant to me. With all the craziness of getting ready for the convention and dealing with Kyra, I hadn't had a chance to miss Cal. And now it's like all that *missing* has been dammed up somewhere, and the dam's broken loose, and I'm feeling the effects even though he's back.

"Hey, Cal?"

"Yeah?"

"Look, I know it's been a little weird lately, and . . ." I don't know how to fix this, how to talk about it without actually saying it.

"I know."

"You do?" Oh, God. He "knows" I'm gay.

"Yeah, and it's cool."

It is? Oh my God! What if *Cal* is gay? No way! "Are you sure? Because—"

"This is stupid," he says. "We're talking around this and we shouldn't have to. We're better than this. I know all about this graphic novel you're working on."

He what? "Um, what did you say?"

"At first I thought that you were overreacting to the lacrosse thing. I mean, you didn't talk to me for the rest of the day and it was like I just didn't exist to you anymore."

He knows about *Schemata*? Huh?

"But I kept thinking about it and thinking about it and it just didn't make any sense. I couldn't see you staying that way for so long. Not even if you were really, really pissed at me."

"I wasn't pissed at you."

"Yes, you were."

"Cal . . ."

"Do you think I'm stupid?"

I wait. He asks again, and I realize it's not a rhetorical question.

"No, Cal."

"Good. I know you hate all of those guys. I know that. I know you wanted us to hang at the comic book convention. And I wanted to go, too."

"Then why didn't you?"

"Because we had a *game,*" he says, like I'm a slow learner. "Dude, I made a commitment to my team, OK? That means something to me."

What about your commitment to me? I want to ask.

"And you'd been so distant for a while. I mean, I'd see you hanging out with that goth chick in the halls and stuff. I figured you wouldn't get all bent out of shape about the convention."

He *saw* me with Kyra? He *saw?* The idea that Cal—superstud, star athlete, ladies' man—would even be *looking* for me in the halls is like cold fusion: impossible, but exciting. I had no idea.

"And then she came up to me the other day and she told me that you were stressing hard-core on this graphic novel that you wanted to show to Brian Michael Bendis. I couldn't believe it! I told her she was nuts because you would have told me about that."

"I'm sorry," I tell him.

"Man, don't worry about it. It just caught me by surprise is all. She told me to stay away for a little while, not to bug you, because you needed to focus. And I'm cool with that. So I left you alone."

I can't believe it. Kyra was *helping* me. Just like she said all along. "Man, Cal, I don't know what . . . I'm just really sorry, man. I'm really sorry this happened."

He laughs. "Don't worry about it. Jeez, it's not the end of the world. Really. It's nothing. It's—It was just a fluke. We weren't on the same page is all. And you have such a chip on your shoulder about anyone who even goes *near* a sports team—"

"Hey!" *I* have a chip on my shoulder? I'm the victim here, not them.

"You do. I'm being honest with you. I think I get it, but you just reek of attitude, man."

"It's mutual. They hate me."

"Not really. Maybe once. But I defend you to those guys." He says it like it makes him a hero, like I've been waiting my whole life for SuperCal to step in and save me from the big, bad Jock Jerks.

"That's not what I want."

"What *do* you want?"

I want you not to be their friends at all, I think but don't say. This is starting to sound like the teary scene in a bad romance movie.

I sigh and stretch out my legs. My feet, still in my dress shoes, feel like they've been pounded with a meat tenderizer.

"Look, this doesn't . . . It doesn't matter, man. It's all over, OK? But why . . ." I drift off. Don't ruin it. Don't.

"Why what?"

"Nothing."

"Come on."

"*Nothing.*"

"Come *on.*"

"Why did you call *me* about this?"

"What do you mean?"

"This lacrosse thing. You know I don't like those guys. Why did you call me?"

He pauses, and there are infinities in the pause before he says:

"Because you're my *friend.*"

"Cal, can you hang on a second?"

"Sure."

I put the phone down and walk to the other side of the room, where I indulge myself in some quiet tears.

CHAPTER FORTY-EIGHT

HERE'S THE THING: The rest of the lacrosse team is pissed that the guy who hacked the computer or faked the records got caught, forcing them to forfeit. But Cal is pissed that it happened at all. He doesn't understand why his teammates aren't angry about it, that no one acknowledges that it's wrong. It's a pretty cool scenario to use for *Schemata,* actually. As long as I change the names and the sport to keep from getting beat up.

"It's like a criminal saying he should go free because no one should have caught him in the first place," Cal says. "It's just *wrong*. You get that."

"Uh-huh."

"So, tell me about the convention."

No. Not yet. Just not yet. In person, maybe.

"Nah. Nothing happened."

"*Something* had to happen."

Yeah, Kyra flashed Bendis. Much to my surprise, I giggle at this.

"See? Something happened."

"Well, this guy was selling *Giant-Size X-Men* #1."

"Yeah?" He sounds excited. "How much?"

"*Too* much. But I got to hold it. That was cool."

"You know, they've reprinted that all over the place—"

"I know. But I want the original of this one. I guess . . ."

"Because it's the one that your dad doesn't have."

I think about that for a minute. "Yeah, maybe."

"So, we both had bad days."

He doesn't know the half of it. Not yet. "Yep."

"I have an idea to make it better."

"Yeah?"

"Yeah. It means you'll have to do something you've never done before."

That doesn't necessarily narrow it down. There are entire encyclopedias of things I've never done. "Like what?"

"Do you trust me?"

"Yeah."

"Good. Tell your mom you're staying at my house tonight."

CHAPTER FORTY-NINE

MY BEST INSTINCTS TO THE CONTRARY, I'm going to a party tonight. How do I get into these things?

Forty-five minutes after I hang up the phone with Cal, I'm changing into jeans and a golf shirt and—thank *God*—a pair of sneaks. I ask Mom if I can spend the night at Cal's and she's all good with that. Her phobia about people visiting our house doesn't make her at all sensitive about me staying elsewhere, and she thinks Cal is a good influence on me, which is a joke considering he's smoked (hated it), drunk (got sick), and had sex (lucky bastard), while I'm as pure as the driven snow.

"There's a party at Ves's," Cal told me over the phone before. "Everyone's getting together to shake off the lacrosse thing and have some fun."

"You've *got* to be kidding me! I'm not going to Pete Vesentine's house!"

"There's gonna be a *million* people there."

"Forget it. I'm not going someplace where everyone hates me."

"Did you not hear the 'million' part? There's going to be people from West Brook and some of the guys from last year's team . . ."

"I won't know anyone."

"Oh, for God's sake!" He was exasperated with me. "Which is it: Everyone there hates you or no one knows you? It can't be both."

True.

"I don't know."

"Look, we won't stay long. We'll go, mingle a little bit, relax, try to forget about our crappy days, then go back to my house and chill out and you can tell me all about the show and this graphic novel, OK?"

So, I gave in. Packed a bag, talked to Mom, and now I'm standing outside, waiting to be picked up, feeling—oddly—like I should be looking for one of Kyra's cars.

Instead, a gray sedan pulls up. I hesitate, not sure if I should approach, thinking of scenes in movies where a guy is on stakeout or something and he goes up to a car with mysterious people in it and BANG! He's gunned down before the opening credits start.

Cal rolls down a window. "Come on!"

He opens the door for me and I hear him tell someone to "shove the hell over!" I get in. Even though I'm skinny, it's a tight fit as I close the door—how many of us are in the back seat, anyway?

"Go," says Cal, and we're off.

As my eyes adjust to the dark, I realize that I'm sitting behind Ronnie Warshaw, who's riding shotgun. Mike Lorenz is driving and Jason Benatovech is sitting on the other side of Cal.

Oh, God. This is hell. It's like my own personal Rogues Gallery. It's like Batman going into Arkham Asylum alone, unarmed, and needing to pee really bad.

"What's the *bag* for?" Warshaw asks, tittering as he twists to look at me from the front seat. I feel like a little old lady with my overnight bag perched on my lap, my shoulder crushed against the door.

I don't know what to say, so I go into ignore mode, as always. Just ignore him. He'll go away. Only he won't because we're in a car. Kyra would know what to do. She'd zing him. Or light his pants on fire. Something.

"Shut up, Warshaw," Cal says. "He's staying at my house tonight."

I wait for a gay joke, something about Cal and me sleeping together, but it doesn't come. Of course not. They wouldn't say that about Cal.

"He needs a *bag* for that?" Warshaw sneers, as if an overnight bag is some sort of sign of weakness.

"Yeah, because he actually changes his underwear, Ronnie."

Lorenz and Benatovech both howl with laughter. Warshaw shrugs and turns to face front again, mumbling, "Whatever," but now the others won't let it go. Lorenz chimes in with, "Yeah, Ronnie, at least *he* swaps out his skivvies. How long you been wearing those briefs?"

"How long?" Benatovech asks, laughing. "They started out as *boxers!*"

I can't believe it. I just sit there, silent, as three of my tormentors gang up on a fourth. It's like I'm a diver who's been saved from a shark by other sharks.

"—smells so bad," Lorenz is saying, "that his zipper has a hazard alarm hooked up to it!"

More howls. Wow. The pecking order doesn't just peck *me*. Cool.

CHAPTER FIFTY

PETE VESENTINE'S HOUSE IS LIKE something out of an old sitcom, if you imagine the sitcom colliding with a vice raid. Picture-perfect furniture, walls that aren't painted the white that came with the house, wallpaper borders, molding. All the stuff Mom keeps threatening to do but never does.

If I didn't know better, I'd say every student at South Brook is here, crammed into the living room, mostly. The lights are down so low that you almost have to feel your way around. Maybe that's the point. There's an array of gyrating bodies, moving as if in spasm. This is supposed to be fun?

I waste a moment scanning the crowd for Kyra. The idea that she would be at a party like this is such a ridiculous notion that I feel like an imbecile for even considering it. Then again, *I* shouldn't be here, either, so there's precedent.

But she's not here. Not in the living room, at least.

I wish I'd brought along a notepad or a sketchbook or a camera. This is great research for *Schemata*. I can see a whole scene like this, a party, maybe Courteney comes to find one of her students . . . I don't know. But this is what kids my age do, apparently, so if nothing else it's good to be exposed to it. It'll add some good details to the story.

The stereo is cranked up so loud that you don't hear the

music so much as feel it through the soles of your feet, an endless repeating bass line. Vesentine himself cruises the house, jerking his head like a turkey, allegedly in time with the music, but as near as I can tell he's not keeping any kind of rhythm.

"White man's dance," Cal says, smirking, and I feel like an honorary black kid for a minute.

The place reeks of beer—it's like ten thousand Tonys decided to crack open brewskis all at once. Someone shoves a bottle into my hand and I stare at it in revulsion. I had beer once, a few years ago, on New Year's. My dad let me try some. I puked.

But I figure if I hold the beer bottle, I'll look like I fit in and no one will pressure me about drinking.

Cal's got a bottle, too, and I feel a flare of disappointment until I see that the liquid level in his hasn't budged either. He leans over to me. "If you really want to fool people, spill a little into the ficus over there every now and then."

A horrifying thought occurs to me. "Is Frampton here?"

Cal gives me the look he usually saves for when I try to do my bad 50 Cent impersonation. "Who?"

"Mitchell Frampton?"

"Oh, that burnout? Big blond doofus?"

"Yeah."

"No way, are you kidding? Ves can't stand him. No one can stand him. He's a total loser."

No argument there.

Someone shouts out, and then the music dips low, almost to silence, becoming a backbeat. Vesentine jumps up onto a table, pinwheels for balance, and then raises his beer bottle to hoots and hollers from the crowd. He launches into a long, slurred, invective-filled rant against the school system, the county, the head of the lacrosse program, and pretty much the rest of the planet. One word figures into his monologue repeatedly, used as noun, verb, adjective, and adverb, often in the same sentence.

The crowd receives him like he's Caesar. Let me clarify: like he's Caesar at the *beginning* of the play.

I look around for Cal to see his reaction to all this, but he's nowhere to be found. I'm alone in a sea of faces, some familiar, some unknown. Even the familiar ones are strange to me, remembered from hallway glimpses and not much else. There's almost no one from the sophomore class who isn't on the lacrosse team, but there's entire packs of juniors and seniors, roaming like confident soldiers, safe in numbers and age.

No Kyra. I don't even realize that I'm looking for her again until the depression that she's not around hits me. I don't understand what happened at the convention. I don't understand why she even showed or why she did what she did. Was that supposed to help? Jeez, every time she shows off her breasts, bad things happen to me.

"Yo!" A hand claps my shoulder and I almost collapse. "Need a beer?"

I turn to the face of a stranger. He's grinning widely, his eyes slightly unfocused, his breath a tidal wave of alcohol.

"Dude!" he says. "Dude, do you need a beer?"

I have no idea who this guy is. I raise my beer bottle and he goggles at it as if discovering Troy. "*Ex*cellent!" He hugs me and staggers off. I am officially weirded out.

Definitely using this in *Schemata*.

I push through the crowd a little bit, finding the going

tough in the dim light. Vesentine's monologue is over, having ended in a flourish of profanities linked by the occasional preposition, then a defiant roar from the crowd. The music comes back up and the walls start to vibrate. I try to figure out how to get through the crowd without rubbing against anyone the wrong way. In the end, I think it's probably impossible.

I don't want to drink. I don't want to be here. I don't do stuff like this, stuff that's wrong. It's illegal to drink at my age. I shouldn't even be holding this beer. It's like I told Kyra: There's right and there's wrong. That's it.

I manage to make my way through to a hallway, which is just as crowded as the living room. Girls are clustered with guys in couples up and down the corridor, kissing, grinding against each other. Like a porno with clothes on. I creep through. I just want some fresh air.

I make it to Vesentine's kitchen, which is a riot of ice cubes, beer bottles, smashed bags of chips, and something greenish gray smeared down a cabinet. I don't want to know.

I open the back door and go out onto a deck, into the cool night and blessed fresh air. At last! I breathe in deep, sigh in satisfaction, then lean against the railing and—after checking below—let my beer start to trickle out down to the ground.

"What a waste."

Kyra! I turn around, my beer all but gone now. There's a table with an umbrella sticking up from the center and it catches the light from near the door, throwing shadows into the corners, especially right up against the house. That's where she's sitting, in a deck chair, right where my blind spot would have been when I came outside.

My throat locks up.

"But it's pretty lousy beer, isn't it?" Dina asks. "No sin tossing it out."

Like I said: My throat locks up. I just stand there like an idiot.

Not Kyra; Dina. I could have sworn . . . Just like in those dreams; getting them confused. I don't understand.

She's wearing a sleeveless blouse that's unbuttoned about halfway, enough that there's what appears to be endless acres of visible cleavage. I remember Kyra's lecture about the wizardry and illusion possible as regards the female breast, but that just leads me to Kyra's *next* move, which is a bad thing to think about right now. I don't need any more stimulation.

Dina's also wearing shorts, the kind with cuffs at about mid-thigh. They fit snugly, sleek against her hips. She has one foot on an ottoman, the other crossed over it, a sandal dangling from that foot as she jiggles it in unconscious accompaniment to the music in the house. Even unaware, she has better timing than Vesentine. She's not drinking beer. It's something else. Something with berries on the label. Wine cooler?

It clicks that I'm staring at her, which I shouldn't do, but it's so weird. Just a minute ago I was thinking of a scene in *Schemata* where Courteney has to come to a party like this, and now here's Dina.

"I didn't know someone was out here," I tell her. "I'm sorry." I head for the door.

"Just don't tell anyone you saw me."

"I won't." Yes, the sophomore slug will obey the commands of the Senior Goddess. For a split second I fantasize that I might actually talk to her, but then I remember the one time on the bus. When I accidentally touched her and she looked at me like I was a bug. A big, disgusting bug with too many tentacles.

As I open the door, I hear a familiar sound. Dina has knocked a cigarette out of the pack and is getting ready to light up.

"Please don't do that," someone tells her.

"What did you say?" she asks. And yes, she's talking to me.

"Please don't . . ." I should shut up. But I think of Kyra's mother and I just . . . "Please don't do that," I say again. "Don't smoke that."

She arches an eyebrow at me. It's a Kyra-ism, something that until recently I never would have thought was at all sexy. Such a fool.

"I have a friend whose mother died of lung cancer. It's a really bad way to go. And . . ."

The eyebrow is still arched. I'm fixated on it.

She sighs, which does simply amazing things to the body under the blouse. She breaks the cigarette in half and makes a show of tossing each half over the deck railing. "There. Happy?"

"Ecstatic." Does my mental control go beyond making her stop smoking? Dare I command her to dance for my pleasure? Sh-yeah.

"Do I *know* you?"

"Uh-uh." I shake my head vigorously, which is a mistake. I feel nauseated from the sudden motion and the reek of beer, which seems to have taken up permanent residence in my nostrils. I pull up a chair and sit down before I embarrass myself by falling down at her feet.

"You OK?"

"Yeah."

"You *are* a little young to be drinking." She favors me with a mock-severe look that I'm sure she intends to be maternal but

I find nothing short of full-on erotic. That's it; I'm staying seated for the time being.

"So are you," I tell her. Which is true. *No* one here is twenty-one.

"What are you, an undercover cop or something?" She regards me with amusement in her eyes. So much better than contempt.

"I'm . . ." I had a pretty decent comeback on the tip of my tongue, but she tilts her bottle to her mouth and drinks. Her lips on the bottle. Her *lips*. On the *bottle*. God, I will never be able to stand again.

She finishes her swig. "Well? Are you?"

Only undercover with you, baby.

You seem to be thinking about getting under the covers with me, Miss Jurgens.

I do all *my work undercover.*

God. Where is *that* crap coming from?

"No, I'm the guest of honor. I'm the guy who hacked the school's grade computer." It comes out quick and easy and effortless, like all good lies.

She bolts upright in her chair. "Really? Are you serious?"

"No! No. It was just a joke."

"God, if you *were* the guy . . . Half of them"—she jerks her head toward the house—"would want to kill you, and the other half would want to blow y—" She breaks off. "How old are you?"

Old enough, toots.

Mature in mind, young in stamina.

Ugh! Stop it!

"I'm a sophomore." Sounds better than "fifteen," for some reason.

"Oh. Oh, wait a sec. I *do* know you. You ride the bus with me, right?"

Ah, busted. "You don't ride the bus."

She nods, takes another sip. Oh, Lord above. Her lips on the bottle. The working of her throat . . .

"Someone told me you were some kind of genius. Is that true?"

Huh? For once, I'm well and truly flabbergasted. Who's talking about me? Especially to Dina Jurgens? How does my name get brought up to her? Have I crossed over into an alternate universe or something?

"A genius? Not really. I mean, a genius is someone with an IQ over one-forty." I'm still holding the beer bottle, and my grip is precarious as my palms begin to sweat. I lean over to put it on the table, and I get an eyeful of long, smooth, tanned leg.

"Someone told me," she goes on, oblivious to my drooling, "that you messed with Sawyer's head. I had a friend in her class last year, and she told me that this freshman just shut down the whole class one day."

"Oh. The Tortoise Blight thing. Yeah. That was me."

Something amazing happens. Something so magical and mystical that it makes me reconsider the existence of not just God but also any of the usual subdivine helping spirits, such as Cupid and Uriel and the Silver Surfer: Dina Jurgens laughs. She laughs full and loud and honestly, her head thrown back, gracing me with the sweep of her throat. I flash briefly into fantasyland, my lips tracing a route down the smooth skin of her neck, into the hollow of her throat, then further, and I think I'll have to sit here until sunup.

"Oh, that was priceless!" She wipes tears from her eyes. "I

couldn't believe it when she told me about it. She said it was like you had the whole class in the palm of your hand. Like you were running the show."

"Really?" I was *there* and I don't remember it being like that.

"And I'll never forget: She said to me, 'This kid, he must be the smartest kid in the freakin' school. He's smarter than the teachers. He had everyone in the class agreeing with him, and we didn't even know what he was talking about.'"

She puts down her empty bottle and reaches into the shadows, from which she conjures another. She twists off the lid, raises it to her lips, then stops, smirking as she gazes at me. "Or are you going to tell me not to do this, either?"

Not a chance in any hell dreamed of in any theology. I shake my head.

"Want one?" she asks.

Again, a head shake.

She drinks. I watch. Seems like a fair deal to me.

CHAPTER FIFTY-ONE

I'd like to say that I talk with her, but the truth of the matter is that *she* talks. I just listen and watch.

She talks about people as if I should know who they are, and I guess I probably should. Just from context, I can tell that these are the crème de la crème of the school, the masters of the top clique of the senior class. In my usual willful ignorance of all things social, I have no idea who they are. If I did, I'd be getting a lot of prime gossip material right now. As it is, I know who's doing whom, who's pretending to do whom, and who swears she never, ever did *that* with *him,* but it's useless information to me. I don't have any faces to put to the names or actions.

But it'll be useful information for *Schemata*. Change the names, tweak the truth, and it's good background for the kids in Courteney's class, a way to make them more rounded, more three-dimensional. I file it away, hoping I'll remember all of it later.

"What about you?" she asks finally. "Who're you here with?"

"Cal."

"Cal?" She gets an expression on her face like I've just offered to dip her hair in pig sweat.

"Yeah. Cal Willingham."

"Oh. Oh. *Him*. Yeah, he's a lacrosse guy, right? Wrestler?"

"Yes." Wow. *Me* she knows as a genius. *Cal* she has to think about.

"You came with him? Are you guys . . . you know?" She waggles her hand, wrist limp.

"What? No. Jeez."

Dina shrugs. "OK. Whatever. Just wondering why you didn't come with your girlfriend."

"I don't have a girlfriend."

"Really?"

Now this is just getting stupid. This is starting to edge into unreal territory. I'm discussing my lack of a love life with Dina Jurgens? Stuff like this does *not* happen to guys like me.

More to the point, why does she sound so surprised that I don't have a girlfriend? I mean, even my *mother* doesn't act surprised. Sorry, yes. Surprised, no.

"Why don't you? Have a girlfriend, I mean."

I'm saving myself for you. I stifle a giggle. Sad, funny, and true all at once.

"Is there a law that I *have* to have one?"

"Well, excuse me for taking an interest." She swigs from the bottle. "Just wondering. I mean, high school is such a bullshit place. It's a little more tolerable with someone else, though."

I goggle at her. Did Dina Jurgens—Senior Goddess, Homecoming Queen, Lady of My Dreams, etc.—just say that high school was a bullshit place? That's like *Kyra* talking. Not someone who has every conceivable advantage. "I guess you're right." I don't know what else to say to that.

"Well, then go get yourself a girlfriend!" She says it sternly, again with the maternal thing. She's just *not* good at it, though. Her version of maternal is the antithesis of motherly. Unless you're Oedipus. But let's not go there.

"It's not that easy."

"Oh, right. The mystery of women." She chuckles. "Just find someone who's cute and you like and tell her she's cute and you like her. It's not brain surgery. You can handle it."

"It's really not that easy." I say it more quietly. I'm starting to get uncomfortable, but not for the same reason that I don't want to stand up.

"It's *exactly* that easy. I'm not saying find someone and propose to her. Just find someone who's cool and funny and likes you and you can have a lot more fun."

"I can't do that." Now I'm mumbling. It's only because we're sitting pretty close to each other that she can hear me.

"Why not?"

I don't say anything. I won't. This has gone far enough already.

"Come on, why not? I'm a girl and I'm *telling* you—"

"No one wants to be my girlfriend, OK?" I say it too loud, loud enough to shock her, really shock her, to the point that she looks a little scared for a second. Scared of skinny little me.

"I just told you to ask—" she starts, calmly.

"It doesn't matter. I'm . . ." Ah, damn. Don't do this. I sigh and wipe my palms on my jeans. How did I get to this? I'm alone on a gorgeous night with the most beautiful girl in the world, talking about *sex,* and I get to this point. Is this my hidden mutant power—the ability to screw up absolutely any decent situation?

"You're what?"

I shake my head.

"Come on."

"I'm not . . . like *them.*"

"Like who?"

I wave in the direction of the house. "Them. The guys that . . ." *The guys that you hang out with,* I almost say. "The guys that girls like."

"Which guys are those?" Her voice, soft.

"The big guys. The athletes. The good-looking guys. I'm skinny and I'm . . . not like them."

"What, you think you're ugly or something?"

She says it innocently. So innocently that I want to smack her, which surprises me, a rage that boils up and then vanishes so quickly that all that's left is rage-residue, like the stuff left in a pot after the water has boiled out.

"I *do* own a mirror," I tell her with all the sarcasm I can muster.

She shakes her head. "Girls are such dopes sometimes. We mature faster, but we can be just as stupid. You know what you are?" I know I'm a bunch of things, but I don't know which one she's going for, so I shake my head. "You're like a . . . what do you call it—the thing a caterpillar goes into."

"A chrysalis?"

"Yeah." She leans forward, the blouse spreading open a little bit, glory hallelujah. "I know how it is. You get these shallow chicks, and they see that you're not all pumped up and buff like some of those morons in there. Or your skin's not clear. Or whatever. But they don't get it. That's all like the chrysalis. That's what you go through before you become the butterfly. Guys like you are the ones to watch for."

She's leaning very close to me. I think about her advice. I want to tell her that *she's* the one. *She's* the girl I want for my girlfriend. But that would be stupid. She has a boyfriend. He's in college. That much even *I* know.

She pats my knee. I flinch, overpowered by the sudden, massive wave of arousal. I had thought I was as aroused as I could be. Wrong.

"Don't let 'em get you down," she says, unaware of my flinch. "Someone's gonna understand and appreciate you. It'll happen. Trust me."

You're the most beautiful creature on this planet or any other, I want to say to her but don't.

And why? Why don't I say it? I think back to all the things in my life I've wanted to say but didn't. Things I wanted to say to the Jock Jerks who torment me, to Cal, to my mother and my father, to Kyra, and to Bendis. And why didn't I say them? Because I was afraid? Because I thought they would make my life worse? How much worse can it get?

Kyra would say it. Kyra would say anything because she's fearless. But I'm no noble Indian warrior. I'm not—

You have no guts.

No kidding.

Dina grins at me. Kyra . . . She's inside my thoughts, where I really don't want her to be right now. Because here I am with Dina, with *Dina,* for God's sake! Why can't I get Kyra out of my head?

"You're . . ." I say, but then lose my nerve. I can't do it. *No guts.* Only now she's looking at me, curiosity and expectation in her eyes. I ransack my cache of lies, stories, and obscure facts, looking for something I can use to end the sentence gracefully, safely, neutrally. *No kidding.*

"What?" she asks, tilting her head so that a perfect cascade of pure *blond* washes down into my field of vision.

"You're the . . ." My throat closes. My hands twitch. Her eyes widen, and now I can't stop myself. ". . . most beautiful . . . most beautiful creature on this planet or any other."

She stares at me, and I try to figure out how to extricate myself from this particular predicament. I need to get up and get away *fast,* before she laughs at me or calls out for a muscle-bound moron to stuff me into a trash can somewhere. I can't get out of here on my own. I'll have to call home, wake up Mom, get her to pick me up. Oh, God, I'll be the lovesick pussy momma's boy who had to have his mommy pick him up from the party . . .

"That's very sweet," she says. She's being polite. Polite to the screwy, geeky sophomore.

My throat opens up again. I can breathe. "I'm . . . I'm sorry," I tell her. "I shouldn't have said that."

"Why not?"

"You probably hear stuff like that all the time."

"You think so?"

"You've got, like, a million friends," I blurt out. Might as well go for broke. "You're the most popular person in school."

And she laughs. But not *at* me. Not even at *me*. She's just laughing a sad little laugh, a knowing little laugh. "You know what people tell me? Do you want to know?" I bob my head. "The girls I hang out with . . . They tell me I'm pretty and I'm so lucky to be a natural blonde and they wish they had my body. And at first it sounded great, but after a while you hear the jealousy in it, as if it's my fault somehow that I have blond hair or good boobs. And the *guys* . . . I like to look in people's eyes, and guys just stare at my chest and I know they're watching when I walk away. And they're *always* trying to get into your pants, and even a compliment . . . I mean, they're just looking to get some, looking to score."

Then why dress like that? Why make it so we can't *help* looking at you? I don't get it. I don't understand.

Maybe I don't like guys who are drooling idiots. Kyra's voice, in my head, so strong and real that I can't hear anything but. What's happening to me?

"I'm sorry." I'm mumbling now, ashamed, but I make myself look into Dina's eyes. "I didn't mean—"

She's confused, and then she realizes what I mean. "I didn't mean *you*. Your compliment was so sweet and so real. I can tell you're not like the others." She reaches out and takes my hand to reassure me.

But I am! I want to scream but don't, and this time I will *not* say it. But I know that I *am* just like the others, that I want her so badly I would reach into my chest and pull out my own heart for her, that I've stroked her with my eyes more times than I can count, caressed her in fantasies without number. I meant everything I said to her, but I meant everything I *didn't* say, too. And if she didn't look like this, if she didn't *dress* like this, it might be a different world and a different story. If she didn't look so perfect, maybe . . .

I'm caught in a crossroads. I'm paralyzed. Her hands, holding mine, burn and burn and burn. I'm helpless and lost and I don't know what to do or say. My brain's too full and my body's off on its own. I just can't handle this.

And then it happens.

She leans in more and there's a little tilt to her lips, a little smile, almost like Kyra's magic grin, only without a piercing. But almost the same.

But no ring. No ring. It's missing.

She kisses me. Her lips on mine. I freeze solid, but I thaw *fast*. It's just a chaste little kiss, a favor, a boon from a Senior Goddess, lips on lips, but nothing more, and then it becomes something more, and I think of coal smudges on my lips, black lipstick pressed between us, but this is Dina, right, not Kyra, why Kyra, stop Kyra, and then somehow Dina's got my mouth open using *her* mouth, which is soft, the lips firm and moist, but red, not jet black. She tastes sweet. Like sugar and something else. Alcohol, I guess. Beer. Wine. Can I get drunk from kissing someone who's drunk? I *feel* drunk. My head's spinning, but in a good way. She's still holding my hand, and now she moves it, and now I'm doing more than just kissing a Senior Goddess. It's a little bigger than my hand, and full, and heavy, and somehow strong. Is this . . . ? Is this how *hers* would—

Stop it. Stop it. Don't think of that, don't think of her that way. It's wrong. She's a friend. It's wrong to think of touching and kissing a friend, but why is it all right to think of that with strangers? And she's not my friend anymore, is she? I don't— God. Oh, God.

Don't ask me how long it lasts. I don't know. I haven't the slightest idea. But she breaks contact and puts my hand into my lap, where it blessedly covers up the all-too-evident proof of my arousal. She leans back, wipes her lips, looks at me.

"You OK?"

"Yeah."

"Because," she says, grinning, "you look like you're gonna faint or swoon or something."

Which is true. "I'm fine," I lie.

"See, it's not a big deal," she says. "The earth didn't stop turning. It was just fun, right?"

And it's weird, but I can barely remember it. All I remember is being transported, going away somewhere else, kissing someone else, feeling someone else. Right or wrong, that's what I felt.

"You've got some lipstick," she says, miming a swipe at her mouth.

I rub my lips, which feel puffy and too moist. My first kiss.

The tips of my fingers come away with a red cloud imprinted on them. Kyra wore red lipstick once, one time that I can remember. My first kiss, and it's all wrong.

Before I can say anything else, the door swings open. A huge, hulking form looms there, a shadowy threat against the backlight from the kitchen. I'm deader than dead.

"Hey!" Cal says. "There you are!"

"Oh. Hi, Cal."

Cal steps out onto the porch and lets the door swing shut. "I called my dad to come pick us—" He breaks off, noticing that I'm not alone. "Hey. Dina, hi."

"Have we met?" Dina asks, frosty. I think she's doing this for my benefit.

"I'm, uh, Cal Willingham. I'm friends with Steve's brother? We went to soccer camp last—"

"Hmm. That's nice." Dina settles back into her chair. Cal shrugs. He's better at dealing with this sort of thing.

"My dad's on his way," he tells me.

"Do we have to leave?" says the alien that has possessed my body.

Cal does a double-take. "Uh . . ." He has no idea how to handle this. He probably figured I'd be *begging* him to get out of there.

"No, no, it's OK." I've come back down to earth. I think I get it. "I'm ready."

We head for the door together. Dina calls out before I go inside. I turn back to her.

"Remember what I told you before," she says. "It's all about confidence. Do you understand that?"

I nod at her. She smiles at me, then sighs and settles back in the chair, sipping her wine cooler.

Cal pulls me along with him. He's fed up with his buddies complaining about being punished for, well, doing something wrong.

"You ready to tell me about your comic book yet?"

"Graphic novel."

"Graphic novel. You ready?"

"Not yet."

He stews for a little while as we wait for his dad, then finally turns to me and bursts out with what's clearly bothering him even more now: "Dude, what *happened* out there with Dina?"

But I'm not telling.

CHAPTER FIFTY-TWO

OH, WHO AM I KIDDING? Of course I'm going to tell him. I've always told him *everything*. I'll even tell him about *Schemata,* probably when we get to school on Monday and I can show him the artwork.

But I'm not going to tell him about my kiss. Not yet. I want to keep it to myself for a little while. Nothing wrong with that.

At Cal's house, I yawn as I crawl into a sleeping bag on the floor next to his bed. We're both dead tired. We mumble a little bit, talking across and past each other. I think he's saying something about Vesentine's sister. I'm not sure what I'm saying, but I think it's about my aliens-with-green-skin theory.

In the middle of it, I think of *Schemata*. It's OK. I have some great new ideas, ideas that will make it even better than it was before. Maybe it's good that Bendis didn't look at it today; it'll be so much more powerful the next time I get to show it to him. There are other conventions. Other opportunities.

It's all about confidence. Dina.

If you've got something you want, you have to go for it, you know? Kyra.

"Hey, Cal?" I cut through the fog to make a connection.

"Yeah?"

"I'm gonna do something. Something momentous."

"Bathroom's down the hall."

"No, you idiot. I'm taking Bendis off The List. I've never taken anyone off before. And I'm—"

"What list? What are you talking about?"

"Never mind. It doesn't matter."

And then I sleep. For endless hours. If I dream, I don't remember it when I waken. They must have been really good dreams, or really bad ones.

CHAPTER FIFTY-THREE

IS THIS HOW IT'S GOING TO BE, THEN? I get back Cal only to lose Kyra? That doesn't make sense. That doesn't seem right. Why should I be doomed to having a single friend?

Home from Cal's on Sunday, I start to panic. I honestly figured that I would hear from Kyra after the convention. As pissed as she was at me, I figured she'd calm down at some point. Or want details about my meeting with Bendis.

But nothing. No messages. Nothing.

I send IMs and e-mails into cyberspace, but nothing comes back.

You're a suicide wannabe. I see myself pretending to slash my wrist. Taunting her.

You're a suicide wannabe. That's just a cry for help. Everybody knows that.

What if Kyra didn't, though? What if she really didn't know that?

Try harder next time.

What if she did try harder next time?

No. I'm not going to let myself believe that. I won't. I did not push her to really kill herself.

I hope.

I go through all of the logs of our IM sessions, all of her

e-mails to me, looking for clues to . . . anything. Anything at all. But nothing's changed. All I turn up are the JPEGs she sent me: Frampton hitting me. The Phys Ed teachers ignoring the whole thing. Etc.

Last night's sleep was great. Tonight's is a mess. Half-remembered nightmares and dreams that seem to be more like badly edited highlight reels from hell.

I wake up Monday to a realization. I've made a decision.

If he hits me in gym today, it will be the last time Mitchell Frampton hits me. Ever.

CHAPTER FIFTY-FOUR

IS IT WRONG FOR ME TO WANT THE PAIN?

I can't help it. I suddenly *want* Frampton to hit me in gym. I'm looking forward to it. I'm praying that he does it. How messed up is that?

As soon as dodge ball starts, I purposely step in front of the ball and get sent off to the Dead Zone. I scan the gym quickly. As usual, Mr. Burger and Mr. Kaltenbach are off in a corner, blissfully ignorant. Kyra is nowhere to be seen.

Mitchell Frampton lopes over to me, grinning, his blond hair hanging into his stupid face. I try to look scared. I try to contain my glee. The only thing that makes this less than perfect is Kyra's absence. She would *love* to see this. She would want to record it for posterity on her cell phone.

I've rolled up my sleeve just slightly, just enough to show the lightening bruise there. A nice little target for him. How could he possibly resist?

The first blow is almost familiar. I wince with pain as the tender, bruised flesh reacts. But it's OK. This time, it's OK.

I turn toward him, bringing up my left hand. I have to do this perfectly. If I screw this up—

I don't want to think of that. I bring up my left hand.

And then Frampton steps back, surprised, shocked that

I moved, his face contorting in anger, in something like betrayal . . .

And then he squints . . .

And then he screams.

It's a short scream at first, not loud enough to be heard over the thudding feet of the dodge ball game. He looks almost ashamed of himself for screaming and he stops, blinking at me in confusion.

Big mistake, that blink.

He steps toward me and screams again, and this time the scream doesn't stop. It gets louder and higher and more primal. He cries out, tears streaming down his face. I step back, brushing my hands together as if to dust them off. Which, actually, is sort of what I'm doing.

Frampton bellows with pain. The squeak of sneakers stops and the dodge ball bounces off into a corner. Everyone's staring. I hear Mr. Kaltenbach say, "What in the *hell*—" and then he breaks into a run, heading our way.

Frampton keeps screaming, clawing at his eyes, which is the wrong thing to do, but I'm not about to tell him that. I imagine this is what Oedipus must have looked like.

Revenge is a dish best served cold, someone once said. And I agree. I just happen to like it with a little cayenne pepper.

Frampton keeps wailing and starts stomping his feet. The whole time, he's rubbing his eyes, rubbing that ground pepper deeper and deeper into his mucus membranes. What an idiot.

Mr. Kaltenbach huffs and puffs to a halt. Mr. Burger is close behind him. "What did you do to him?" Burger yells, pointing at me. "Talk to me! What did you do?"

I just shrug my shoulders, as if to say, "Search me." Which

they could do and all they'd find is a slight odor of chili, really.

I grin as Mr. Burger fumes and Mr. Kaltenbach tries, fruitlessly, to calm Frampton down. The pepper won't blind him—I don't think—but I bet he'll think very carefully before he decides to use me as target practice again.

Everyone's watching. Everyone's staring. And they're not staring at Frampton. They're staring at me.

So I cross my arms over my chest and strike as tough and defiant a pose as I can.

Mr. Burger's lips form a tight line. "Fine. Principal's office."

CHAPTER FIFTY-FIVE

IT'S A FIRST FOR ME. I've never been dragged to the office by a teacher. Not once. Not in elementary school or middle school. Never.

The secretary, Miss Channing, smiles at me as I come in. Sometimes I come down to photocopy stuff for teachers, so she knows me and likes me. But when she sees Mr. Burger behind me, clearly pissed off, her smile dissolves into confusion.

"Who's in?" Burger barks in that annoying jock tone of someone who's used to being listened to.

Miss Channing doesn't want to take crap from this guy. She pretends not to hear, making him ask again before she says, "Mr. Sperling."

Burger sighs. "What about—"

"Dr. Goethe is at the school board. Discussing the *lacrosse* incident." A smile tugs at Miss Channing's lips. Mr. Burger is the JV lacrosse coach, and while he's not implicated in what happened to the varsity team, the stink still rubbed off on him a little bit.

"OK, OK. Fine." Mr. Burger directs me to a chair. "Watch this one," he intones, pointing me out for Miss Channing as if I'm on a lineup of the world's most-wanted terrorists.

Mr. Burger stomps off into Mr. Sperling's office and closes

the door. Miss Channing looks at me, uncomfortable. I guess she's used to the burnouts and the head-cases sitting here, not the honor roll students.

"Hi, Miss Channing," I say.

She smiles at me, then loses the smile and looks at me like I'm a purebred racehorse that just fell flat on its face out of the starting gate.

A few minutes go by and then Burger emerges, throwing me a dirty look before informing Miss Channing that he'll be in the nurse's suite with Frampton if he's needed, and could she get someone to cover his next class? Miss Channing, forgetting that I'm right here, mumbles something fairly unprofessional under her breath as she picks up the phone. I never realized that adults could be so petty and hate each other, too. I thought that was the exclusive province of kids. I don't know whether this news is heartwarming or depressing.

I also don't know what happens next. Miss Channing gets off the phone and tells me to go wait in the chair outside Mr. Sperling's office. So I pick up, shuffle ten feet to the left, and sit down again. I sniff my left hand. A little peppery, but no big deal. I thought this through: I brought leftover chili for lunch as my alibi.

I wait and wait and wait. Kyra's right. Mr. Sperling is passive-aggressive. What's the point of making me wait out here all this time?

Finally, the door opens and Mr. Sperling fills it like a titan. He's big and fat, with a tie that hits only about midbelly, leaving a tract of uncovered shirt to bend around to the belt. He always looks like he's been running, no matter what he's doing. I've seen him a couple of times in the halls, at assemblies. And when I won a Math Team event last year, he shook my hand. But that's about the extent of my involvement with him.

"Come on in," he rumbles. And instead of going back to his desk, he turns to his side so that I have to squeeze by him in order to get into his office.

He shuts the door, then grunts as he makes his way back to his chair, which—I notice—has no arms. He sits down and the chair protests. "Have a seat."

I sit.

He picks up some papers on his desk and scrutinizes them, furrowing his brow and *hmph*ing to himself every now and then. I'm sitting here in my gym shorts and a T-shirt and he's doing paperwork?

. . . making me sit there while he's on the phone pretending to be important. Like he'd be a friggin' assistant principal in the middle of nowhere if he mattered at all.

I want to get this show on the road. I didn't do anything wrong. I defended myself. And no one even saw what happened anyway, except for Frampton, and who's going to believe him over me? For one thing, I'm an honor student. I've never been in trouble. And I'm a hell of a liar.

Plus, they've got no evidence. Nothing.

This is ridiculous. He's shuffling papers, glancing at his computer screen. Is this supposed to unnerve me? Instead, it just makes me imagine what he would look like as a giant sperm, his head and body this gigantic, bulbous mass of DNA, his legs tapering into a whipping tail. The Spermling. Yeah, it fits.

The Spermling finally looks up at me. He tosses something to me across his desk. It's the student handbook for South Brook High.

"I want you to turn to page three," he says without preamble.

I turn to page 3.

"You see the section on Zero Tolerance?"

"Yes." This is stupid. I get one of these at the beginning of every year and sign it to show that I understand the school policies.

"You see where it says that fighting of any kind is not acceptable in this facility? You see that?"

Who does he think he's talking to? "Mr. Sperling, I read and signed this handbook—"

"I asked you a *question!*" he thunders. "Do you *see* in that *handbook* where it says *fighting* of *any kind* is not acceptable in this facility? Answer the question!"

Holy crap! His head's going to explode.

After a second, I guess his head *isn't* going to explode. "Yes, I see it. I also saw it in September—"

"And do you see where it says that *weapons* of any kind, including pepper spray, cannot be brought into this facility for any reason?"

"Yes. But Mr. Sperling—"

"Do *not* interrupt me." He glares at me until I offer a facial expression that indicates that I'll shut up. "Further down, do you see the section that explains that you can be expelled from this school for violating these policies?"

Expelled? Is he *joking?* For defending myself? God, getting expelled—Mom would lose it. Where would I go to school? I'd have to start all over somewhere else. And what would colleges think? What—

"Do you see it?" he insists.

"Yes."

"Like the school, I have absolutely no tolerance for students who fight, for students who bring weapons into this building. Do you understand me? Do you understand that you're in serious trouble?"

And I realize: He doesn't care. He doesn't care about the truth or about what's fair. I'm just a problem to him, a problem to be dismissed and dealt with.

Adults are idiots. They think they're in charge and they think they have some kind of authority, but you know what? They're idiots. That's what Kyra said.

I have to appeal to his sense of reason. "Mr. Sperling, I've never been in trouble before and I didn't bring a weapon—"

"You used pepper spray on this other boy. This . . ." He shuffles some papers. "Mitchell Frampton."

"No. I didn't."

"Don't *lie* to me." He stands up, looming over me. "I already know *everything* that happened. So don't think you can *lie* to me!"

They're just grown-up kids with more money who listen to shitty music and hate everyone younger than them, Kyra says in the echo chamber of my memory. *But kids think that adults are in charge, too, so they get away with all kinds of crap.*

"Oh?" I'm shaking, on the verge of tears, but I'm not going to let this happen. This is *wrong*. I didn't do anything I shouldn't have done. "You know everything? Then where's the pepper spray?"

He glowers at me as he sinks back into his poor abused chair.

"Where is it?" I ask again. "You just accused me of bringing a weapon into school. Where's the weapon?"

He narrows his eyes. "You seem to be laboring under a misapprehension, young man. I don't have to answer your questions, but you *do* have to answer mine."

"Where's the pepper spray?" I ask. "You can't just accuse someone without proof."

"This is not a courtroom. This is my office, and what I say goes—do you understand? We have a *zero tolerance* policy for fighting—"

"Your policy sucks!" I shout. It's louder in the small office than I thought it would be, and for a moment I want to take it back, but the expression on his face changes my mind. He's shocked. Shocked into silence.

"Your policy is a *joke,*" I tell him. "There's no zero tolerance for fighting. Where was your policy when I was getting punched every day in gym? Huh?"

I roll up my sleeve to show my bruise. If this was a week ago, it would look more impressive, but it's still pretty nasty. "This is your useless policy! And I have pictures, too. I have *pictures* of Frampton hitting me and your useless, stupid teachers standing around *laughing* and not doing anything!"

He clears his throat and picks up a pen from his desk. Starts tapping it against the phone, which is *really* annoying.

"I never said that Frampton wouldn't be punished." He sounds a little calmer. Maybe he wasn't expecting me to fight back. Good guess, since I wouldn't have expected it, either. "But both parties in any fighting must be—"

"You know, if this had happened *anywhere else,* we wouldn't even be *having* this discussion." He keeps tapping the pen. "But it's ridiculous that I can be pounded on for *days* by someone larger than I am while I'm under the care of your teachers, yet when I defend myself, *I* get in trouble."

His eyes light up. The pen stops. "So you *did* pepper-spray him."

I grit my teeth and glare at the Spermling. "Prove it. Show me the canister of pepper spray."

He leans forward, eager, his face flush with excitement. "I don't *have* to prove it. We're not in court. I sign my name to a piece of paper, and you're expelled."

"Fine." I stare back at him. The truth is a great thing, but sometimes only a lie will do, so I pull out a big one. "Fine. Do it. And then be prepared to have to prove I had pepper spray because my dad's a lawyer and I *will* take you to court. And I *will* show the pictures of how your teachers stood around. And if you think this lacrosse team stuff is a headache, wait until I put you on the stand." He starts to deflate. He's not sure if he believes me, but he's like everyone else in the world: absolutely terrified of being sued. "Wait until you have to testify about how you put me into a violent situation through your own reckless endangerment. Wait until my lawyers get to subpoena everything in your world, including your office."

Kyra pops up again. Oh, yes.

"Just wait until they take your stuff," I say. I lean forward now, meeting him over the desk. "Wait until they find the child pornography on that computer."

It's like I've dropped the F-bomb in the middle of church. His florid face goes completely pale. It's a beautiful thing to behold.

He pushes back from the desk, away from me. His eyes dance over to the computer.

"I don't—" He can't get the words out. "I don't know why you would say that! There's no child pornography on that computer!"

"Oh, so just regular adult pornography?"

His eyebrows shoot up like in a cartoon. I love it. "No! No, there's nothing bad. Nothing bad at all!" Not sure if he's trying to convince me or himself. But I don't really care.

Silence. I wait. I stare. This has to be perfect.

"There's no child pornography on there," he insists. He wants me to believe.

I give it a second. This has to be better than the Great Ecuadorian Tortoise Blight.

"There *will* be."

His face twists to genuine horror. "You—you—"

It's amazing. Suddenly I know what it would be like to have ESP. Because I can read his mind. He's thinking of the lacrosse team. Of compromised security. Of my grades. My report card. He's thinking of the semesters I have of computer science, and a row of straight A's.

I've turned the Spermling into a thousand pounds of quivering, terrified blubber. I'm Batman and Wolverine rolled into one.

"You—you—"

"I'm leaving," I tell him calmly. "Because I'm running late for Trig and I've got a perfect score in there. So I'm going, because you wouldn't want to hinder my education, would you?"

"You can't do this!" he says. "You can't threaten me!"

I pause at the door. "I didn't. We just had a nice chat, that's all. Something bad happened to a bad kid and you asked me what I saw and I told you. End of story."

And before he can say anything else, I'm out the door, smiling at Miss Channing as I walk past her desk. I did it. And I didn't even need my bullet as a safety blanket.

If you have the balls to tell them to shove it, they crumble. Just like Kyra said. *Easy.*

Kyra.

I stop just outside the office. She walked past Miss Channing's desk, she told me, crying, with her shirt untucked.

Kyra.

You're a suicide wannabe.

So, where do you keep your ammo?

Kyra. It was *Kyra* who said—

Try harder next time.

Kyra who—

Can you get one of your stepfather's guns?

Oh, God.

CHAPTER FIFTY-SIX

"IS SOMETHING WRONG?" Miss Channing asks from behind me.

Can you get one of your stepfather's guns?

"Is something wrong?" she asks again. I'm frozen, standing like a statue, half in the office, half out.

My vision fades. I see Instant Messages in front of me.

XianWalker76: *You planning on shooting someone? :)*

Promethea387: *I didn't ask for bullets, fanboy.*

XianWalker76: *Bullets are easy to get.*

Promethea387: *I would only need one anyway.*

Oh my God. I told her . . . I told her how. And I . . .

So, where do you keep your ammo?

That's just attention. Everybody knows that. Cutting across just gets you to the hospital. That's just from movies and TV shows and stuff like that. You didn't really try to kill yourself. You just wanted attention, but you screwed up. Try harder next time.

I take off like a shot. It's Monday. Fourth period. Kyra has geometry. I haul ass upstairs and down the empty hall. Someone pokes a head from a door and shouts, "Hey! No running!" Like I'm gonna listen.

I find her class and burst in. Thirty or so heads swivel in the direction of the panting, red-faced moron at the door. A woman at the blackboard—a teacher I don't know—starts to come toward me.

"Where's Kyra?" I ask between gulps of air. I scan the room. I don't see her.

"What's this about?" the teacher asks. Some part of me notes the geometry proof on the board. It's *really* easy. "Let me see your pass."

"I need Kyra," I growl with as much testosterone and anger as I can muster.

"Went home sick," someone says from the back of the room.

"That's *enough!*" the teacher snaps before turning her attention back to me. "Who *are* you? Give me your name."

As if. I turn and bolt.

CHAPTER FIFTY-SEVEN

WENT HOME SICK. OK. SURE.

Back down to the office. I practically fling myself at Miss Channing's desk. "Do you have Kyra's home phone number?"

It's like I'm a wild lion that jumped out of hiding to attack her. She shrinks back. "What? What are you talking about?"

"Kyra. Kyra Sellers. I need to know her phone number."

"I can't give you that. You know that."

"*Please,* Miss Channing. Please! It's an emergency."

She looks at me helplessly. Poor woman. A star student dragged into the Spermling's office, then running all over, helter-skelter. Must look pretty crazy to her. I'd sympathize if I had the time.

"I can't help you," she says.

Fine. I wheel around and race out into the hallway. Fortunately, I'm dressed for all this running. I don't think my gym clothes have ever gotten such a workout before.

What do I do? How do I get in touch with her? She won't answer my e-mails or IMs. She never gave me her cell number or her home number. I don't even know where she *lives.*

God. I don't know *anything.*

If I were Courteney, if I had had Courteney's powers, I would know everything. I'd be able to see Kyra's thoughts and dreams and I'd know for sure. But I'm not Courteney, so I just have to go with my gut.

I stop in the middle of the hall. There's fifteen minutes left in fourth period, so the corridors are like tombs. I'm all alone. I'm the only person in the world. And I don't know anything.

So where do I go when I don't know anything?

CHAPTER FIFTY-EIGHT

LESS THAN A MINUTE LATER, I throw open the door to the media center. Mrs. Grant looks up from the circulation desk in surprise and calls out my name.

"This is very important!" I yell as I head for the computers. "Very important!"

I waste half a second of fantasy time imagining that I can hack into the school database and get Kyra's address and phone number, but after the lacrosse team fiasco they've probably got that sucker sealed off like a contaminated ward. Instead, I pull up an Internet phone directory and punch in "Sellers" for Brookdale. The hard drive cranks and churns. Mrs. Grant comes up behind me.

I don't even look up at her as the screen starts to fill in. "Mrs. Grant, I'm really sorry, but this is really important."

"What class are you supposed to be in? Why are you wearing your gym clothes?"

I like Mrs. Grant a lot. She's in charge of the books and computers, and those are in my Top Five Reasons Why I Go to School. But I just don't have time for this.

"It's a family emergency," I tell her, the lie sliding easily off my tongue as I scan the listings. "My mom's going into labor and I have to find my stepdad's work number."

"Oh. Oh!" She steps away, then comes back. "Isn't that on file at the office?"

May God forever *damn* librarians and their need to help! I'm trying to work here! "No," I tell her. "They never added it." I'm multi-tasking like I'm a dual-processor computer. I'm looking up the information, stacking lies for Mrs. Grant, and imagining Kyra calmly getting it right this time, spilling liquid garnets down that perfectly white skin. It would almost be art.

Mrs. Grant goes away, but I'm not sure how long she'll stay away. I've got twenty Sellerses on my screen, and a depressing "1, 2, 3" at the bottom of the page, indicating more pages with the same name. I don't know what her father's name is. How am I supposed to do this?

I stare at the screen. I need more information. I need an address or a first name. I have to do *something*. She could be lying dead somewhere, and it would be all my fault because maybe she found a gun after all and used my bullet . . .

An address. I need an address.

Wait a minute. I close my eyes. I remember last week, when Kyra and I drove around town. Just north of Brookdale . . . to that new development, with the swampy pond that she hated so much.

How did she know about that place? How did she know the details?

"That's where she *lives*," I murmur.

Mrs. Grant hates it when people touch the screens, but I can't help it—I put my index finger on the monitor and drag down, checking the street names. Halfway down the second page, I find "Sellers, R." on the same street that Kyra and I visited. I scribble down the phone number and then I'm off to the circulation desk.

"Mrs. Grant. Can I use your phone?"

She looks at me suspiciously, but not *too* suspiciously. As far as she knows, I'm a good kid. I like books and computers. And besides, I'm throwing out my most earnest and innocent face.

"Use the one in there," she says, pointing toward her office. "It's private. You have to push nine first."

"Thanks!" I dash into the office and tap out the number. Four rings later, a man's voice says, "Hello. You've reached the Sellers house. If you'd like to leave a message for Roger or Kyra, wait for the beep."

I wait for the beep and then I record some silence onto his answering machine. If someone's home, I could shout into the machine and maybe they'd hear me, but if *Kyra*'s home, she might just accelerate her plans.

I hang up. This isn't working. I need to talk to Roger Sellers and I need to do it now.

OK, so what do I know? Dad's name is Roger. I've got an address. Roger. And he . . . he . . .

My computer. Kyra thought my computer was ancient. And my Internet connection was dial-up, which she thought was bad because . . . because . . .

Her dad works for the phone company. Bingo.

I call the phone company and get lost in a maze of phone trees and voice mailboxes. I stab the 0 button, which kicks me to a receptionist.

"I need to speak with Roger Sellers." God, what if he works in the field or something?

"Who's calling, please?"

"I need to talk to him. Now. Please."

"I'm sorry, but Mr. Sellers is in the conference room, miss."

Ugh. My voice is cracking. She thinks I'm a girl. "I can put you into his voice mail."

"No! This is important. I have to talk to him right now. It's about his daughter." I can almost hear her thinking from the other end. "His *younger* daughter."

There's nothing and then: "His what?"

"His younger daughter. Kyra. Not Katherine. Kyra."

"Hold on a second."

There's a click and then a voice tries to sell me DSL and call forwarding. I wait.

Another click, and a masculine voice: "Who is this?"

"Mr. Sellers? Mr. Roger Sellers?"

"Yes. Who the hell is this and what's wrong with my daughter?"

I don't know what to say. I've been so worried about calling him and finding him that I never thought of what to tell him. How do you tell someone that you think their kid might be trying to kill herself . . . or might have done it already?

"I'm a friend of Kyra's. And I think she's in trouble."

"Kyra's *always* in trouble. If you're one of her friends, you're probably in trouble, too. Did she put you up to this? Did she tell you to prank me at work?"

"Mr. Sellers, please. I swear to God, I'm worried about her." I didn't realize *how* worried until just now, as tears start to flow. "Please. I think she's going to try to hurt herself." I bite my lip. "Again."

His voice goes angry and concerned at the same time. "Who *is* this? What do you know?"

"I just think she needs some help. She was at my house one day and I think she stole a bullet—"

"What?" He explodes. I don't blame him. "You gave my daughter a gun?"

"No! Not a gun! I didn't give her anything. She took it. A bullet. It was just a bullet that I carried around, and I think she took it." I take a deep breath. "But she asked me how to get a gun and I didn't tell her, but I think she took the bullet because she *wants* a gun. I don't know. I'm just really worried, Mr. Sellers. I'm just worried and I think that you or maybe your other daughter should be with her right now—"

"Wait a minute. Wait a minute." I can almost picture him holding his hands up to stop me. "Wait. What did you just say?"

I don't even know. I'm babbling, rambling. I scroll back the conversation. "Maybe you should be with her. Or if you can't, maybe you could call her sister to—"

"Her sister."

"Yes. Her older sister. Katherine."

The line is silent. Have we been disconnected? My hand goes for the button pad to redial.

"Her sister," he says again.

"Yes."

"Kyra doesn't *have* a sister. Who is this?"

She doesn't—? What? *What?*

"Her . . ." I'm stumbling over my words now. I'm lost in language. "Her *sister*." As if saying it again can make it real. "The one who was pregnant. The one with the cars." And before he can even reply, I make the connections and I feel like an idiot. How could I not have known? How could I have fallen for all that crap about her sister's car and her mother's car? I'm a moron.

From the other end of the phone comes anger and confusion: "What are you *talking* about? Look, I can see on my

Caller ID that you're calling from Kyra's school, and I want to know who this is *right now*—"

I hang up in the middle of his threat. I'm shaking with adrenaline. I'm completely spastic, my teeth chattering as if in fear or cold.

When I finally calm myself down and leave the small office, Mrs. Grant looks up from the circulation desk. "Do you have to leave?"

It's like she's someone from a thousand years ago, asking me a question about ploughshares. "What?"

"Did you get in touch with your stepfather? Is your mother OK?"

Oh. Right. That's the problem with lies. Tell enough of them and you can get screwed if you lose track.

"It wasn't labor," I tell her after thinking about it. "False alarm."

"Oh. Is everything all right, though?"

I stand there and stare at her. I don't know. I really don't. So I shrug my shoulders and leave.

CHAPTER FIFTY-NINE

I GO BACK TO GYM TO CHANGE into my regular clothes. Burger and Kaltenbach seem very solicitous and interested in my welfare. I wonder if the Spermling told them I have pictures of them yukking it up while I was being hit by Frampton.

I can't bear the thought of sitting through my last two classes, but I don't have any way to get home, either. I feel like I should go tell someone else about Kyra, but . . . what would be the point? I talked to her dad. What else can I do? I'm fifteen, for God's sake. What else am I supposed to do?

Cut class, I guess.

After all, it's been a day of firsts for me: first fight in school, first time sent to the office, first time threatening a school official. Why not compound it?

The day I met Kyra I wondered how she managed to sneak out of school. Well, mystery solved, and it's not exactly a Sherlock Holmes moment. You just leave, that's all.

I sling my backpack over my shoulder and walk like I've got purpose and a place to go (which, I guess, I do). No one even looks at me as I head down the hall and out the door. Just walk like you're supposed to be doing what you're doing and people's minds fill in the blanks for you. Lying without saying a word. A new high for me.

It'll take me a while to walk home, but I don't mind. I stand out in the parking lot for a moment, trying to figure out the right direction—I'm used to being in a bus or car, not hoofing it.

A car. Kyra's car. *Cars,* actually.

The first time I met her . . .

Home can wait. I'm going back to elementary school.

I cut around the high school, cross the access road, and head down the hill. It's too late in the afternoon for recess—the elementary school kids are all inside, but there's someone on the swing, drifting back and forth. From here, she's the same as the first time I saw her, a solid black figure with a white thumbprint for a face.

The swing squeaks. Her black boots have gone gray and brown with dust and dirt kicked up as she drags her feet to the rhythm of the swing.

I glide down the hill like I'm in a dream. I want to run to her, to scream her name as I go. She's not dead. She's not doing anything stupid. She's just here, just being Kyra.

But I make myself play it cool. I stroll when I don't feel like strolling, taking my time. By the time I get to her, she's got to know I'm there, but she doesn't even look up. She just keeps drifting back and forth, her eyes down, watching the furrows her boots have carved into the dirt under the swings.

I sit in the swing next to her. She's rubbing her hands together, and every now and then I catch a brassy glimpse of a shell casing reflecting the sunlight.

We're quiet for a few moments, as I start to match her pace and rhythm. My heart is throbbing.

"Kyra?"

"Shut up." It's not a snarl. Not a growl. It's a plea. It's the closest thing to "please" I've ever heard from her.

"I know you stole my bullet." Stupid. Stupid way to start. I need to tell her . . . I need to tell her . . . I'm not even *sure* what I need to tell her! It's all messed up. I want to do stupid, tender things. I want to get off the swing and put my arms around her and make her stop moving, just make her stop, make her rest.

"It's OK that you took it. As long as you—" As long as you don't use it. But I can't say that. I don't want to put the thought in her head. The thought *or* the bullet. "As long as you really need it. I mean, I know how it can help. It's like a security blanket, I guess. And I know you need that. I think you need help—"

"Oh, yeah?" she stops swinging, and I plant my feet, shocking myself to a halt in order to make eye contact with her as she looks over at me. "Yeah? When did you become the goddamn expert? Did the Fantastic Four explain it you? Did Spider-Man help you come to that conclusion?"

She's back to a growl again. Old Kyra. Classic Kyra. My usual defenses rise up like a force field and I'm ready to bash back, but I stamp them down with mental boots the size of clown shoes. This isn't the time for it. This isn't like a comic book crossover, *Fanboy vs. Goth Girl*. This is real life. This is . . . this is *Schemata*. This is defining and organizing experiences.

"No one told me anything, Kyra. I figured this one out on my own. Well, almost. I had a little help from you. From the things you've said to me. And a lot of it's true, and a lot of it's bull, but it's all there, and it's all important, even the bull. You made some things possible for me, so I want to make some things possible for you. But you need help, Kyra. You really do. You need—"

She jumps out of the swing and throws her arms out, one still tightly clenching the bullet. "What I *really* need is for people to stop telling me what I need! OK? Do you get that? Ever since my stupid mother went off and *died,* all I've gotten is people telling me what I need. You and my dad and my grandparents and my stupid goddamn therapist. And I'm sick of it, OK? I'm sick of it!"

Before I can say anything, before I can move or think, she collapses to the ground, as if someone underground grabbed her by the ankles and pulled her down. I jump from my swing, miraculously *not* getting caught up in the chains, and drop to my knees next to her. I'm thinking overdose. I'm thinking stroke. I'm thinking heart attack.

But it's nothing so dramatic. It's just tears.

She's weeping, and her eyes have gone red, and for the first time I get a hint of the true color of her face as tracks of tears bleed through the white makeup she wears. She's so pale underneath that it's almost like she doesn't even need the makeup at all.

In movies and books, the hero takes the woman in his arms. He holds her and comforts her. He says the right thing and he makes it all work out.

But this isn't a movie or a book. And worst of all, I'm not a hero. So I just kneel next to her on the ground as her body shakes and jerks, as the tears run down her cheeks. I don't know what to say or do. I just want to touch her, to feel her, to know that she's real, that I'm real. To find the exact, precise *right* things to say that will make it all stop and make it all go forward.

I want to tell her what happened the other night. How I lived the geek dream and made out with Dina Jurgens, but the whole time I could only think of her. And I don't even know what that means, but I know it has to mean *something,* and isn't that a good enough place to start?

"Kyra . . ."

"What?" She looks at me and her eyes widen, and I wonder why, until I realize that I'm crying, too. Crying in front of someone else. A tear dangles from my jaw, and I swipe at it.

"Kyra, I don't know what to . . . Look, the other night, something happened. I went to a party and Dina was there, and it's gonna sound crazy, but I ended up sorta kissing her, but the whole time I was thinking about you. And I know that you told me not to fall in love with you and I honestly don't think I am, but don't you think that—"

She groans and leans away from me. "God, what is *with* you?" She sniffs and wipes at her face, smearing her makeup and the tear lines. "Can't you get it? I thought you were different, but you're not."

"I am. I swear."

"No." She reaches out as if to touch me, and my skin burns where I anticipate her, but then she pulls back. "No. You've got this great story, this terrific story, but it's not enough."

"Then tell me what is enough."

"What the hell is it? What do you want from me? You want me to stop hiding my tits? You want me to wear tight sweaters so you can check 'em out? You want me to be *normal?* Is that what you want?"

I have trouble swallowing. Trouble forming words with my lips. "No. I want—"

"You want me to jerk you off so you can think of *Dina* while I do it?"

"No!" It's like being slapped. It's *worse* than being slapped. "No. I wouldn't do that."

"Yes, you would. You would. Because she's perfect. She's

perfect and I'm broken. Just a broken piece of–" Her body hitches as she suppresses a sob, and she looks down at the leather bands on her wrists. "Broken . . ." It's a whisper.

"Everything's broken, Kyra. Everything." I lean in close.

She looks up, looks right at me, our faces inches apart. "You want to kiss me, don't you? I can tell. You want to kiss me, but you're not allowed."

Black-smudged lips. Lips kissed by ink.

"Go away," she whispers, and stands up.

"I'm trying to help you." I scramble to my feet, the moment lost. So close. "I'm just trying to help."

"I don't need your help, fanboy."

"You need *someone's* help, and I'm the only one around you haven't managed to scare off."

"Bite me. Here." She flips the bullet into the air and I reach out for it as my lower gut explodes in pain and a familiar agony. I swallow the air, claw for breath, and collapse to the ground. She got me right between the legs while I was distracted by the bullet. I'm down to my knees again, ready to throw up.

"You think crying solves anything?" Kyra hisses, leaning over me. "I cried and my dad cried and we all cried when my mom died, and you think it solved anything at all?"

Her dad . . . I need to tell her that I called him . . . But my mouth only makes croaking sounds.

"You think Tinkerbell comes back? You think Jean Grey comes back as Phoenix? You think any of that stupid shit they've been cramming in your head since you could sit up straight is true? Do you?

"Welcome to the *real* world, fanboy."

And she's gone.

CHAPTER SIXTY

AFTER A LONG, LONG TIME, I feel like I can stand up again. My crotch is on fire and my gut is filled with lead, but I can move. Walking helps a little bit, and I'm a bit peeved to find that the insipid mantra of gym teachers everywhere—"Walk it off!"—actually seems to be good advice.

Back up the hill, the buses are just arriving. Perfect timing. I look around for Kyra and one of her cars, but of course that's a pipe dream.

As I get on the bus, someone nudges me from behind and I feel the rage flare and my fists tighten. I start to talk myself down as I slide into my seat. The guy who pushed me sees my face and the sneering expression he's wearing melts away. I sorta, kinda recognize him. From gym class.

"Oh, sorry, man," he says. "Sorry. Didn't know it was . . . Didn't mean to push you."

I don't say anything in reply, and he hurries past like I'm exhaling anthrax.

At home, I drop my books on my bedroom floor. This whole place is alien to me. It's like an environment from a special effects movie. Nothing's real. Not the computer, where I "met" Kyra. Not the bed, where she lay and read parts of *Schemata*. Not the chair she sat in. Not the hard drive case that she ransacked . . .

I put the bullet back in its hiding place, then wallow in the sense of unreality for a while. I imagine this is what it feels like to be high. You can see the world, but it's like you're not a part of it. I guess I see the attraction for some people.

The problem, of course, is that you can't sustain it forever. You have to come back down at some point. You have to come back down and deal with it.

I turn on the computer. From upstairs, the front door opens and Mom comes in, shouts "Hi!" to me, and lumbers her pregnant self across the floor.

I'm not supposed to use the Internet that much until everyone's gone to bed. We just have the one phone line, and I'm not supposed to hog it. But I have to know. I just have to send her an e-mail and see if she's OK.

Turns out, it's not necessary. As soon as I log on, my e-mail icon pops up. My inbox has one message. From Promethea387.

I hate you. You told my dad everything. I hate you and I never want to see you again.

Attached is a crappy JPEG from her cell phone—Kyra flipping me off.

Which, I guess as I slump in my chair, is better than the alternative. Better than no message at all and a headline buried in the paper tomorrow, right?

Right?

I look at the JPEG again, ignoring the finger thrust into the foreground. I can make out her lips, twisted into a grimace, in the background.

If she really hated me, if she never wanted to see me again, would she have even bothered to send an e-mail? Somehow I doubt it.

Whether she wants to think so or not, she's in my life now. And someday—not today, but someday soon—she'll even be ready to hear from me again. She went away once before—or tried to, at least. She marched out of here, angry and yelling, and I thought that was it, but she popped up again and again. She went; she came back.

Like Cal.

Like my dad, maybe?

I don't know. But I know I'm starting up a new List. The old one's still active, still tallying up the people who need a good smack. But the new one is for the people like me. The people who need help.

After a while, I make my way upstairs to make something for dinner. Mom's sitting at the kitchen table, looking over bills. I make a sandwich and contemplate swiping some of Tony's chips. To my surprise, though, there aren't any of his preferred ruffle-cuts in there. Just a bag of BBQ flavor, my favorite.

"Whose chips?" I ask.

Mom looks up wearily. "Sweetie, I don't know. Tony bought all of that. You'll have to ask him." She says it in the tone of someone who figures I won't bother.

I take out my wallet and look inside. I forgot: I tucked Tony's twenty in there after meeting Bendis. I felt so lousy that I never ate anything that day.

I put the twenty in the pantry next to the chips and sit down at the table. Mom makes a weird hiccuping sound and clutches her belly. Fetal Mia Hamm in action again.

"How was school today?" Mom asks, studying the bills.

"Fine."

"Anything exciting?"

"Not really."

"Well, they can't all be exciting, can they?"

"Guess not."

So, here's the thing: It looks like I'm back to square one, back to the status quo ante. But I'm not. There's Cal again, and Kyra, whether she likes it or not. And Tony. Who would have thought? And Dina, to some degree. And even Bendis. Everything seems like same old, same old, but there are new parameters now. They're all caught up and I'm caught up, all of us connected, drawn together, connected, even though the connections are tenuous and almost invisible. They're still there. They're still there.

I don't get it. Not yet. But jeez, I'm a kid. Give me some time.

What I do know for sure, though, is that everything that's happened—for good and for bad—will inform *Schemata*. That's what art is about, reflecting the world, reflecting experiences. I've been to a party. I've kissed a girl. I've been rejected. I've been kicked in the balls. There are new kinds of people for Courteney to meet. New fears to see. New dreams.

I can't wait to make them all come alive.

I finish my sandwich, get up, and put my dish in the sink. "Keep at it, you'll make it!" Bendis wrote in my book. And you know what? He's right. Time to go back downstairs and work on *Schemata*. I think I'll e-mail some of it to Cal tonight, get his opinion.

Mom groans as I walk past her.

"Baby really kicking a lot?" I ask.

She gives me a rueful smile as she nods. *That's* the look. That's the one Dina couldn't do.

"Hey, Mom?"

She's back to the bills. "Hmm?"

"Can I feel?"

There are three things in this world that I want more than anything. I've told you the first two, but I'll never tell you the third.

Acknowledgments

So, let's try to be efficient about this . . .

In roughly chronological order, thanks to

- Paul Levitz, whose writing I devoured at an early age and who was the first writer I associated with a specific style and quality;

- Tom Perrotta, who sat me down in his office at Yale and told me to embrace my reading of comic books, as they made my writing stand out;

- Sandra McDonald and Maria V. Snyder, fellow trench warriors who were always ready to listen to my woes;

- Jeff Dillon, for inspiring Fanboy's drawing methods and style;

- the original readers of the first draft, who made me understand I was onto something: Valery Brown, Penny Foster, Cheryl Guy, Bonnie Kreamer, Pam Lichty, Blair Reid, Louise Robinson, Laurie Walters, and Tim Whitney;

- Kuo-Yu Liang, for helping me to understand the publishing world from the inside out, and always offering the kind of tough advice writers need;

- my agent, Kathy Anderson, who loved the original manuscript enough to tell me everything that was wrong with it . . . and then let me fix it on my own;

- my editor, Margaret Raymo, who made this whole process go more smoothly than I'd ever dared dream;

- the entire team at Houghton Mifflin Children's Books—including Kim Biggs, Lisa DiSarro, Linda Magram, Alan Smagler, Sheila Smallwood, Alison Kerr Miller, and Karen Walsh—for their enthusiasm, generosity, and time; and . . .

- last, but certainly not least (and out of chronological order), a big, huge thanks to Robin Rand, who read the manuscript at every stage of its development (sometimes page by page as I finished them) and responded with helpful advice, endless energy, and boundless optimism. This book absolutely would not exist if she hadn't chained me to my computer and forced me to finish it by dint of her sheer willpower and stubbornness. Thanks, Robin.